Shadow of the Rainbow

Randa Lynne Zollinger

ISBN: 1470148072
ISBN-13: 9781470148072

Dedication

This book is dedicated to my mother, Helen Zollinger, (05/02/1920-08/11/2012), who inspired me throughout my entire life. She was my Sunday school teacher, my sports coach, my cheerleader, my mentor, and my best friend. She was open and loving to all people and taught me acceptance and tolerance by example.

I wish to thank the special people in my life, Anita Williams, Susan Datson, Leah Mason, and Bonnie Watkins for helping me edit the book. Thanks to Carolyn Scelza for helping with format and Darla Todd and Audreonna Blount for helping with the cover.

Prologue

With lights flashing and sirens screaming, the ambulance made its way through traffic, heading to Regional Hospital. As it passed Lake Griffin High School, the occupant on the stretcher was totally unaware. It had only vaguely registered when someone had shaken him, trying to bring him into consciousness, and had then loaded him onto the stretcher. It was Saturday, so there was no school traffic, but an event at the community center was just letting out, so the ambulance changed its course somewhat to avoid a jam. When it finally arrived at the hospital, attendants raced out to help, asking if the victim had been identified yet.

"We found his school ID in his pocket. His name is Jaden Hansen, age fourteen, with undetermined cause of collapse," said the EMT pushing the stretcher.

"Do you think it's a drug overdose?" asked one of the attendants.

"We just can't tell at this point," the EMT replied.

When the stretcher was settled in the ER and the EMT was filling in the doctor, a nurse began to draw blood for a toxicology screen. After nodding at the EMT, the doctor was all business.

"Get him set up for a head CT! Has anyone located the parents?"

The CT scan came back normal, but the blood test was positive for high steroid levels. He was immediately treated for a drug overdose and put on suicide watch in the ICU.

Getting a call from the hospital on her cell phone, Jaden's mother, Alice, immediately started to panic and shouted for her husband.

"Donnie, come here quick! Talk to the hospital. It's about Jaden."

Listening, then hanging up abruptly, Donnie said, "Let's get down there now! They're treating him for a drug overdose, but he's still unconscious."

"Drug overdose?" Alice couldn't believe it. "Not Jaden. He would never do drugs. He's a good boy. They must be mistaken." Her heart was pounding, and she was glad Donnie was driving, because she felt as if her arms and legs wouldn't cooperate. She wasn't even sure she could walk into the hospital. Thank goodness her daughter, Jenny, was spending the weekend with her friend, Sarah.

When they arrived at the hospital, they went right to the ER information desk and gave their names. Their anxiety heightened with every passing second.

The woman at the desk shuffled through some papers, and finally said, "Yes, here it is. Your son is in the ER annex." Heading down the hall where the volunteer had pointed, Donnie tried to ease Alice's panic, but he was nearly frantic himself. He hadn't always been the best dad in the world to Jaden, but he did really love him. He knew he had constantly been on him about his activities and his friends, but he had felt that he had known what was best for his son.

"Oh, please," he thought, talking to some greater being. "Please let him be all right."

As they hurried into the annex, they saw a boy heavily bandaged around the head and face, with his arm in a sling, bound to his body. Even in the dim light, they could see there was no shock of pale, blonde hair. It was not Jaden. Feeling very relieved, they turned away to continue looking for their son.

"Dad? Mom? How did you know I was here?" The bandaged figure spoke softly. Their relief turned to bewilderment, then alarm, as they got closer and saw the boy on the bed was Brandon, their other son. Confused conversation ensued until Alice's cell phone rang again. When she noticed the caller ID was Regional Hospital, she gave it to Donnie with a terrified look. Then she kissed her older son on one of the few places on his head where there was no bandage. Listening to the phone, Donnie's face changed from consternation to fear.

"Alice, it was the ICU nurse. They're wondering when we expect to get there to see Jaden. And," he said flatly, "she said they think it was a suicide attempt."

Chapter 1

Miss Bonnie

I live on a shady street in a quiet neighborhood. It's located in a small, southern town situated next to a beautiful lake that families love to frequent in the summer and where teenagers gather at night to find the perfect hidden spot for a special date. The large oak trees on my street create a canopy where cats are free to roam. In the spring the flowering trees display a rainbow of stunning colors.

For the most part, my neighbors all live in similar homes and work nine-to-five type jobs. We have a couple of teachers, a construction worker, a pharmacist, and a lady who works in the DMV, among others. Seldom does anyone visit another's house, but many walk their dogs or ride their bikes, allowing for more than chance meetings and providing a certain familiarity with each other. We don't all know each other's names, but we certainly know each other's faces. There are a couple of neighbors that we all agree are odd. Someone who lives in the south and doesn't smile or wave when passing is certainly odd. Someone who avoids eye contact is considered downright un-friendly. But, still, we all share camaraderie.

I have lived here better than twenty years, ever since I retired. I was here way before the kids across the street were even born. Long enough that another neighbor's kids have grown up and moved out. Long enough that several families had lived in the blue rental house down the street before it finally sold to a permanent resident.

Up the street in the other direction, there used to be a wild strawberry patch that I frequented early on. The subdivision was laid out in the sixties, but never completely developed. There have been a few homes built since I moved here, but the neighborhood has stayed pretty much the same for years. There are people living here that moved in when the development first opened, and a handful of vintage residents who have died. There is a sense of continuity and community here. If someone's kid goes off to college, we hear it through the grapevine. When people are out of town, their houses are unof-ficially watched. We sign for each other's packages.

Like I said, I am retired and have no family living close by. I suppose some could call me nosy. I prefer, interested. It's only natural that I have been watching the *family across the street raise their kids since they were born. It's about this family I wish to tell you.*

There is a mother, Alice, a father, Donnie, and three children, two boys and a girl. Donnie was a great athlete in high school and still has the body to prove it. People in his hometown of Center City still occasionally talk of his exploits on the football field. He was the homecoming king, and his wife, Alice, was queen. Somehow, he has never been able to move past those days of glory, and it seems he must re-live them through his children. The older boy, Brandon, is sixteen now and a junior in high school. The other two are twins, in eighth grade, Jaden and Jenny. Brandon is dark-haired like his mom, and Jaden and Jenny are as blond as their father. Brandon, being three years older than the twins, was out in the neighborhood playing, long before his brother and sister could go out on their own. He was active, riding his bike, building forts out of palmetto leaves, and playing catch with his dad. Even as a little kid, his athletic abilities were obvious, and I knew early on he would be a star athlete. He was the apple of his dad's eye. Donnie began coaching him in baseball when he was just a little guy, and before he was ten years old, he had his picture in the paper as an All-Star. Every Saturday in baseball season the family would load up in the car to go watch Brandon play.

Chapter 2

"**B**randon, grab your ball stuff and get on out here. We don't want you putting your cleats on when everyone else is already warming up!" Donnie said excitedly. Brandon was seven, and this was the final game of the season. "Come on, Alice. Get the twins ready and loaded in the car. We need to go!"

The Tigers had nearly completed a successful season, losing only one game. Tonight they were again playing the only team to have beaten them, the Giants. Brandon, being only seven years old on an eight- to ten-year-old team, had started the season sitting the bench. But as the games progressed, he had gotten more playing time. He had practiced hard and had a good glove, but hitting was his weakness. His dad had been working with him on his hitting the previous two weeks, in preparation for this big game.

Alice and the little ones got situated in the bleachers, while Donnie went to stand at the fence. Brandon didn't get to start in the game, so Jaden and Jenny got bored quickly. Before long, they were running in the grass chasing a few other small children.

As the baseball game went on, it soon became obvious that it was a defensive battle. One to nothing, Giants. No one on either team seemed to be able to hit to an open field. It wasn't that they were striking out so much, just hard shots right at the defense. For mostly ten-year-old players, both teams were doing a great job. You could feel the tension mounting. Games in this age group only play five innings, and it was top of the fifth, Giants up. The first batter walked, and the second batter was hit by a pitch. Runners on first and second! The next batter hit a fairly long fly ball to right field which was caught, but the runner on second tagged up and was heading like a freight train to third. Joey, in right field, threw as hard as he could to third, but the ball bounced on the way in. Blake, the third baseman, stretched out for the ball at the same time the runner was barreling in. The collision that ensued was hard to sort out at first, but when the dust settled, the runner was out. But, so was Blake. His ankle had twisted, and his face was contorted in pain, a knot the size of a golf ball already forming. The coach only hesitated for a moment.

"Brandon! Go in for Blake." That got the attention of everyone in the stands. How was a seven-year-old going to handle a hot spot like third base in the last inning with a runner on second?

"Okay, Coach. I'm ready." The little guy trotted out there like he had done it every day of the season. The next batter hit a grounder to Brandon, who scooped it up, made the throw to first, and ran off the field with everyone cheering. His face was one huge grin. Brandon scooted over to the scorekeeper where he found he was in line to bat sixth. With a sigh of relief, he figured he had nothing to worry about. No way they would get that far down the lineup.

This was the do-or-die time at bat, and the players on the bench were yelling.

"Come on, Bobby. Get a hit."

"You can do it, Bob!"

"Make him pitch to you."

Bobby did his part. He broke the ice by getting a single. Trey was up next. He swung at the first pitch and hit it into right center, allowing Bobby to get to third, while he stopped on first. Curtis, always a hard hitter, hit right to short, but the shortstop fumbled it just long enough for Curtis to make first. Bobby was still stuck at third, and now the bases were loaded. The whole team was up on their feet yelling, as was the crowd in the stands behind them. The next hitter was the first baseman, who could hit a wallop, but he tried to swing too hard and struck out.

At this point Brandon realized that he probably was going to have to take his turn at bat and was struggling to stay calm and positive.

"That's okay, guys, just one out!" said Coach. "Come on, Jason, be a stick up there." Jason grounded to the pitcher, who threw home for the force out. Two outs, but bases still loaded. The roar became a crescendo. Then Brandon walked toward the plate. The whooping and hollering suddenly died down. Everyone was looking at Coach to see if he was really going to leave Brandon in.

Donnie yelled out, "Let him stay, Coach. I've been working with him on his hitting. He can do it. You can do it, Brandon!" Coach made no move to stop him, so Brandon took a couple of shaky breaths and stepped up to the plate.

"Strike one," called the umpire.

"You're the one, Brandon. Get a hit!" Everyone was yelling encouragement.

"Strike two!" Brandon stepped out of the box and looked pleadingly at Coach. His eyes were saying to let someone else do it. Coach just clapped his hands forcefully. The next pitch was a fastball down the middle, and Brandon shut his eyes and swung. Crack! The ball soared out of the infield, going, going. Was it going to fall in? Suddenly, the right fielder came out of nowhere, running hard, and caught the ball just before it hit the ground near the fence. The inning was over, and the Tigers had been beaten by the Giants again. Brandon stood near first base with tears in his eyes. His slumping body was a picture of abysmal failure.

"I let everybody down," he kept saying. Donnie was first to get to him, trying to console him.

"You did great, son! You hit a great shot. You got robbed by the right fielder." By then everyone was crowding around him telling him what a great job he had done.

"Good effort!"

"We could tell your dad's been working with you. You hit the ball great."

"You were robbed, Brandon."

"I couldn't have done better, Brandon."

As they were getting in the car to go home, little four-year-old Jaden hugged him, and said, "Don't cry, Brandon, I love you." By the time they got home he felt better, but he was determined to practice enough so that scenario would never happen again.

———————

Jaden

By the time Jenny and I were four, Mom thought we were old enough to play outside in the yard alone. We lived at the end of the street, so there wasn't any traffic, and Mom knew the neighborhood was safe. We loved to put on Mom's high heels and parade down the driveway pretending to be models on a runway, and once, we even put on her lipstick.

"What a sight you kids are. Jaden, I believe you're better at modeling than Jenny," our mom had laughed. We were just having fun, but I can remember that even at that age my brother thought I was a sissy. One day we brought out a little table with chairs and set up a tea party. We had our teapot and teacups, along with real cookies Mom had made. I yelled at Brandon who was riding his bike.

"Come to our tea party, Brandon. Pleeeease!"

"I'm not coming to any stupid tea party," he said. "That's for sissys."

"But, Brandon, we have chocolate chip cookies, your favorite!"

"Well, I might have a cookie, but I'm not sitting in those little chairs!"

"Please, Brandon, come be with us." Never one to cheerfully join us, he came over and grabbed a cookie, then jumped on his bike and rode away. I know he probably was thinking that we were just little kids and that there was no way he was going to hang with us. But after he left, even though Jenny and I still had fun, it wasn't the same without our older brother who we looked up to.

A few days later, Dad had us all in the yard with ball gloves.

"It's time you two learned to play ball," he said to Jenny and me. Brandon was playing catch with Jenny, and Dad with me. Granted, not a lot of catching was going on, but at least we were working on throwing.

"Atta girl, Jenny," I heard Brandon say. "Look right at me when you let go of the ball. Follow through on your throw. That's the way!" I wasn't having as much luck as my sister and could tell my dad was disappointed.

Dad would say, "Aim the ball, Jaden. Look where you're throwing, not off to the side. No, not that way, Jaden, use the same hand every time." I'm not sure who was more frustrated, Dad or me. After enduring criticism for what seemed an eternity (but, in actuality, only a few minutes), I was fed up. I finally just put my glove down and started to cry in frustration.

Jenny told me, "Don't worry, Jaden, you can try again tomorrow." After going through that torture for a few days, I finally decided I was tired of trying to please my dad. I just gave up. I think that's when I started carrying around my sister's doll. While they were practicing, it would make me feel better to set up the little table and chairs, put the doll in one and sit down in the other. She and I would have long conversations, and she never disagreed or criticized me. To her, I did everything right. Sometimes Jenny would join us at the table, and other times, she'd just play ball with Brandon.

When Jenny started to abandon me more and more for Brandon, I noticed that the nice lady across the street was outside a lot, and I started going over to talk to her. She was such good company, not at all like an old lady, and she let me help her in the yard. I loved to dig my fingers in the rich soil, and I believe it was during those times that I discovered I had a love for flowers and gardening. She had an awesome yard, and she showed me how to plant and take care of a flowerbed. It was so cool to see a beautiful thing come from a little seed. Before long, I stopped thinking of her as just a neighbor, but as if she were my truest friend.

Chapter 3

Miss Bonnie

*I*felt drawn to Jaden, and I think he could sense it. We talked a lot as we worked in the garden, and he told me about his sadness and frustration with feeling like a disappointment to his dad. On top of that, he idolized his brother, who thought he was a sissy.

"Miss Bonnie, why is Brandon so mean to me?" he had asked. I can remember thinking that he was going to have a difficult time understanding a lot more than just Brandon's attitude, if his situation turned out as I thought it might. But, as hard as things might be for him now, they would have been far harder years ago when very few people were tolerant of those who strayed off the beaten path. These days there is far more acceptance of diversity, even in some churches. I think I was probably the first to realize that Jaden's life was likely going to be different from the norm and more difficult.

When the twins entered kindergarten, they both came home excited after their first day. Not having many kids on our street, they were thrilled to meet so many friends in school and to do so many new things. Jaden came running over, bubbling with excitement, his words tripping all over each other.

"They have a cool playground, lots of books to look at, snacks, kids to play with, and I can already write my name! There is a real oven that we'll get to cook in, and we're gonna make cinnamon toast tomorrow." His eyes were sparkling with excitement at the prospect. I asked him if he wanted to come in and help me make dinner.

"Yes, yes, that'd be great!" I put him to work, scrubbing squash and zucchini, portabella mushrooms, and red and yellow peppers, while I cut up an onion. When the veggies were clean, I cut them up, too. I let him cut a little, under close supervision, but his left-handedness looked even more awkward than it should have. I had him sprinkle the veggies with olive oil, as I was getting some chicken ready for the grill. While it was warming up, I told him to run home to ask his mother if he could stay and cook, then eat with me. During the previous months she had seen me take him under my wing, so, of course she said it would be fine. He ran back, breathless, ready to *grill. He had watched his dad grill many times, but his dad had never let him handle the utensils. He was so excited that he dropped the first piece of chicken on the ground.*

As his lip began to tremble and he started to tear up, I said cheerfully, "Don't worry, Jaden. There's a five-second rule. Quick, pick it up, rinse it off, and start again." Beaming with relief, he took the chicken in the house and was back out with it in a flash. I showed him how to place the chicken and the veggies on the racks. "Come on, we'll set the table while we're waiting to turn the food." He was familiar with what utensils went at each plate, but didn't know the exact placement of each one.

After I showed him, he said," I'm gonna set the whole table for my mom tomorrow, just like you showed me." Turning the food on the grill was an experience in itself, but, after some practice, he could successfully use the tongs with both hands. Only two or three veggies fell through the rack. No harm. He was squirming with excitement when we sat down to eat the meal that he had helped prepare, feeling as though he had done most of the cooking. "I don't usually like veggies that much, but these are good! It must be 'cause I cooked them," he said with a grin. "Can I take some home for Jenny to try?"

"Of course you can, right after we clean up the dishes." I got a small stool to put at the sink, and we both washed dishes. When we were finished, he ran home, carrying his treasure for Jenny.

"Jenny! Jenny! Look what I made! I want you to taste what I cooked!" Everyone in the house was curious and gathered around Jaden.

After having a small taste, Brandon snickered, "Cooking, huh? I guess you'll be sewing and cleaning house next. That's so lame. What are you, my brother, or my sister?" He stalked off. "Come on, Dad. Let's throw the football."

His mother spoke sharply in a warning tone, "Brandon!" But his father said nothing to him as they walked out the door to throw.

As Jaden's face fell, Jenny hugged him and said, "You're a good cook, Jaden. I wish I could cook like that." Her comment took some of the sting from Brandon's remark, but his mom, Alice, could tell he was still upset.

"Honey, what seasoning did you use on these veggies? They're really good!" After smoothing over Jaden's hurtful moment as best she could, she went out to the yard where Brandon and Donnie were passing the football. Calling Donnie over, she told him he needed to praise Jaden for his efforts.

Donnie argued saying, "How is he going to become a real man doing stuff like that? I've tried to teach him to throw a ball, but he's an uncoordinated mess. Regardless, I'm not going to encourage him to cook!" That was just the first of many comments that Donnie would make about his "sissy" son. Alice was at a loss as to what to do. Of course she wouldn't argue with Donnie's views, but Jaden was her little boy. She eased her mind by telling herself that Jaden would grow out of this stage eventually, anyway.

The next day when Jaden got home from school, he told his mom he was going to set the table for dinner. Alice was a little surprised at how well he did, putting everything in its correct place. Then he went out and picked a pretty hibiscus flower. Asking for a vase, he said he wanted to put it on the dinner table. It looked really nice.

When Jenny came in, she exclaimed, "Wow, my favorite flower! Who put it there?" Grinning, Jaden admitted he was the one. It felt great to please his sister! Now, if only Brandon just didn't say anything mean. As if summoned by Jaden's thought, Brandon came in, flushed from midget league football practice.

"Hey, Mom! I made quarterback of the team. I could throw better than anyone there!" He was so wired that he didn't even notice the table or the flower. When Donnie got home, he raised his eyebrows at the fancy table, but said nothing. All talk was about Brandon being quarterback. Even Jenny felt a little left out. She often captured her dad's attention by saying something precocious. Donnie liked to tell people how smart his daughter was. Tonight she tried no fewer than three times to tell her dad about something she had done in school, but immediately the conversation went back to football.

Later in the evening, when Brandon was doing homework and the twins were watching TV, Donnie asked his wife, "What was the occasion with the fancy table and the flower?"

"It was just Jaden, practicing what he had learned over at Miss Bonnie's the other night. Let it be, Donnie. He'll grow out of this stage." Donnie rolled his eyes, but said nothing.

After school the next day, Jenny asked Jaden what he wanted to play.

Jaden said, "Let's play house. You be the mommy, and I'll be the daddy. Let's get one of your dolls, so we can have a baby." While Jenny went to get a doll, Jaden set up a kitchen with a stove and table. Then he got Jenny's doll crib for the baby. When everything was in place, Jaden pretended to walk through a doorway, saying, "I've had a hard day at work, honey. What do you want for dinner? Oh, I know. I'll grill veggies and chicken for you and the baby."

"Jaden, you know the baby can't eat that. Besides, I'm the one who's supposed to cook."

"Well, I want to cook, and besides, you don't even know how." Warding off an argument, Jaden changed the subject. "Let's take care of the baby. Let's paint her nails." They snuck into their mother's bedroom and rummaged through her drawers until they found just what they wanted. Bright red fingernail polish! Sneaking back out to their "house", Jaden painted the doll's fingers, then, Jenny painted her toes. When they were done, the doll looked like it had been in a massacre. There was red nail polish from tip to toe. Looking at the doll, and then at each other, they knew the nail polish had been a bad idea. Afraid of what their mother would say, they snuck the doll to the outside garbage can and buried it deep under some trash. Jenny was a little subdued, because she hadn't had the doll long, but was far more worried about what her mother would think about their "borrowing" her nail polish and getting it all over the doll. They carefully returned the nail polish to their mother's drawer without getting caught. Or so they thought.

At dinner that night, when Donnie got home, talk returned to midget football. Brandon was telling his dad about how they had to raise money for their jerseys this year and was wondering what he might do for extra cash.

Donnie said, "Well, you can do some chores around here, and if you earn half the money needed, I'll match it. After dinner you can empty all the trashcans in the house and take the big garbage can to the street for pickup tomorrow."

As Brandon enthusiastically started shoving his food down, his mother said, "If you choke, you won't be able to do anything, including football. Slow down, big guy!"

"Mom, do I have to eat everything on my plate?" he asked. Never a fan of vegetables other than corn and green beans, Brandon frequently just stirred his food around on his plate, so everything looked as if it had been sampled. Taking advantage of the new football motivation, Alice told him yes, it all had to be eaten if he wanted to gain strength and muscles to play football. After reluctantly eating every morsel on his plate, Brandon asked if he could be excused to do his new chore. Jenny was pleased he was gone, intent on seizing her dad's attention for a while.

"Dad, Dad! Guess what we learned in school today! If someone else if speaking, you don't say anything until they're done. The teacher said you have to be 'spectful. And then we went around the circle, and we all got to tell something about our family."

Jaden piped up with, "I told them what a good baseball and football player Brandon is." Donnie liked the tone of this conversation and smiled at his son.

"What did you tell them, Jenny?"

"I told them that Jaden is learning to cook, and he's already cooked a whole dinner."

"But not by myself, Jenny," Jaden shyly spoke up. He had been so pleased at school when his sister had said nice things about him. Donnie, frowning at this new revelation, was about to speak, when Brandon came back through the door looking perplexed.

He said, "I got all the trash together and was trying to put it in the garbage can, but it wouldn't quite fit. So I dumped everything out to try to make it all fit better. This was at the bottom of the can." He held up a forlorn-looking doll with red splotches all over it, concentrated at the hands and feet. A sly grin played at the corners of his mouth as he looked knowingly toward Jaden and Jenny. The twins looked at each other with shock and horror. As their faces began to redden, Alice stared at them both with sudden realization of what must have happened. Knowing they were probably about to get spanked, tears began to trickle down their faces, until they turned into a rushing torrent.

"Don't just sit there and cry," Donnie said with irritation. "How did this happen?"

Jenny started, "We were just playing house and," Jaden finished, "we wanted our baby to be pretty, so we painted her nails. We didn't know it would get all over her."

"Where did you get the polish?" was the next question. Not wanting to admit they were rummaging through their mom's drawer, they just stared at the ground, silent. Donnie's scowl was deepening. "Go to your room until you're ready to tell the whole story and face the consequences," were his final words. Once in their room they looked at each other again.

"I'm sorry, Jenny. This is all my fault. I should never have said let's polish her nails. I'll go tell the truth."

Immediately, Jenny, who had previously witnessed her dad's wrath upon Jaden's gentle ways, said, "No way. I'll tell Dad it's my fault, that I talked you into it." Even at five years of age, Jenny was beginning to feel protective of her twin. This instinctive mothering and sheltering of Jaden was a harbinger of their teen years when it would occur time after time. Jenny went right out to face the music.

After she explained, trying to deflect responsibility from Jaden, her Dad said, "What you do with your doll is your business, but going into your mother's drawers without permission is wrong. You are both grounded for one week. After school, I expect you to stay in your room. Do you understand? Get Jaden out here." After repeating it all to Jaden, Donnie went into the living room to read the newspaper, while the twins went to their room relieved they hadn't gotten spanked.

Miss Bonnie

When the long, boring week was finally done, Jaden came over to fill me in on what had happened and why I hadn't seen him in days. I had to hold back a smile, listening to the doll story. I asked Jaden if he had learned a lesson from that. Jaden admitted he would rather have had a spanking than to be bored for so long, and that he would not sneak into his mother's room again. Personally, I felt a week was too long for kindergarteners, but who was I to say? It might have been different if they had homework to do or books to read, but at that point their reading abilities were very limited. I was just glad to see him again.

Chapter 4

L ife seemed to snake along for the next few years. Brandon was improving in athletics by leaps and bounds. He began playing whatever sport was in season, with baseball being his favorite. Jenny was becoming a little athlete herself. She played on a city league softball team, and Brandon was the big brother helping her improve. He took his job seriously.

"Come on, Jenny. Let's go play catch." They would throw until their arms were warm, then Brandon would throw grounders and fly balls. Later, he would take a bat and hit balls to her from increasingly farther distances in the vacant field near their house. Jaden would try to join in, but his lack of skill would dishearten him quickly every time. He so much wanted his brother's attention and favor, but the attention he got was always negative. He didn't really like playing ball anyway, but he kept trying, hoping for acceptance. By the time Jenny was eight years old, she and Brandon had become each other's number one fan at their games, and Jaden had given up. Still, he was cheering along with the family at every game.

The fall that Jenny and Jaden entered fifth grade, Brandon was in eighth and was trying out for the Lake Griffin Middle School football team. He had wanted to try out the year before, but Alice had felt he was too small and didn't want him being tackled by big, bruising eighth graders. He had shot up three inches over the summer, so she reluctantly gave in this year. Missing the seventh grade season, he was a year behind most of the other eighth graders, but he got up to speed quickly because of his innate athletic skills. He would come home in the afternoons after practice, tired, but thrilled with learning what almost seemed like a new game. Midget league had been totally different, no tackling, no complex plays, and the athletic kids had ruled the field. Middle school football had opened up a whole new challenge to him, and he was liking it.

"Dad, I tackled the biggest kid on the team today! He dragged me a few yards, but I got him down."

"What position are you trying out for?" his dad asked.

"We aren't trying out for anything right now. Coach Jones has all of us doing all the drills, so he can look at us doing different things. We have three coaches! We have a head coach, a line coach, and a backs coach. Today we tackled a whole lot and learned some defensive formations. I really like the contact!" Alice listened worriedly, but Donnie was all into it.

Jenny said, "I can hardly wait for the games to start!"

"I haven't made the team yet, Jen."

"But you will. You're the greatest athlete ever!" There was no doubt that Jenny revered her older brother.

At school, Jaden had made a new friend. Devon was light-skinned, wore his hair in braids, and was incredibly cute. He had moved in from another school, but had made more friends in a short time than Jaden had made all year. He even had friends in other grades. Jaden felt really special that Devon had made him his friend, too. What made Devon even more awesome was that he could do cartwheels, handsprings, and flips one after the other. He could even do a back flip totally in the air. All the kids would circle around him on the playground at recess to watch. He never seemed to get tired. A few of the other boys would try some his tricks, but none were good like Devon. Jaden was so impressed!

Devon downplayed it by saying, "Aw, it's not a big thing. I've been doing stuff like this since I was little."

Jaden finally worked up enough courage to ask, "Could you teach me, too?"

Devon said, "No doubt! Stop by my house after school, and I'll teach you how to do stuff." After asking his mom that night, Jaden stopped by Devon's on the way home the next day. Devon started by asking him if he could do a somersault. Yes, he could do them backwards and forwards. Next, a cartwheel. Jaden could place his hands down in the right places, but his legs went askew when he tried to bring them over his head.

"That's no problem," Devon encouraged. "When you put your right hand down, then your left, arch your back and stretch your left leg high over your head. The other leg will follow." By the time Jaden had to go home, his cartwheel was looking pretty good. When he got home he ran over to show Miss Bonnie what he could do.

"Boy, your folks need to enroll you in gymnastics! You take to that like a fish to water," she said enthusiastically.

"Why gymnastics?"

"So you can learn to roll and tumble and not get hurt."

"That sounds fun!" Jaden said excitedly. That night at dinner, Jaden asked his parents, "Can I take gymnastics?"

"Now what do you want to go and do something stupid like that?" Donnie said derisively. Like a balloon with the air suddenly let out, Jaden immediately shrank down in his seat, feeling deflated, once again. It seemed that pleasing his dad would never happen.

"It might be good for him, Donnie," his mother defended. "It might help build his self-esteem."

"Yeah, right. I'm not going to see any son of mine put on a leotard and prance around."

Jaden tried one last time saying, "But Dad, Devon can do all those things, and he doesn't wear a leotard." He wasn't really sure what a leotard was, but he was sure Devon didn't wear one.

"Well, Devon probably has a swish when he walks, and that's not going to happen to you. End of subject." Crestfallen, Jaden went to his room after dinner and was soon joined by Jenny.

"Jenny, what did Dad mean when he said Devon probably walks with a swish?"

"I don't know, but it sounds sort of like something a girl would do, and I guess Dad doesn't want you to walk like a girl."

"What's a leotard?"

"It's kind of like a bathing suit. It's what girls wear to dance in or when they exercise so no one can see up their dress or shorts."

"Devon wouldn't wear that!" Jaden said fiercely.

The next day at school, before the tardy bell, Jaden pulled Devon aside and told him about last night's conversation.

"I can't believe my dad said you wear a leotard or have a swish."

"That's 'walk' with a swish, Jay, and no, I don't have a leotard or walk with a swish," Devon laughed. Devon, who was almost twelve and a little more worldly than Jaden, knew what he was talking about. "I'm all guy, Jaden. Nothing to worry about." Jaden, embarrassed because the conversation seemed awkward, laughed, too. Hurrying along, they went inside before the bell rang.

At recess that day, Devon said, "Why don't you come over every afternoon, and I'll keep teaching you stuff."

"Cool," Jaden replied, cheered up at the prospect of learning more stunts and spending time with Devon.

While they were practicing that afternoon, Devon confided to Jaden, "Don't tell anyone, but I'm going to try out for cheerleading in seventh grade. The teacher who coaches the high school cheerleaders saw me doing flips and said I would make a great cheerleader. It's still a long way off, though, so I want to keep it a secret."

"Wow, Devon, do you think you could teach me enough to try out, too?"

"Yeah, we have lots of time before then. I'm sure you could learn everything you'd need to know. Just don't tell anyone. It'll be our secret." Excited by having something private to share with Devon, Jaden swore himself to secrecy.

Thinking again, though, he asked, "But can I tell Jenny? She knows all my secrets, and she won't tell."

"Not even Jenny," Devon said. "Girls can't keep secrets." Jaden silently disagreed, but vowed to do anything that Devon asked. After several days of practicing, however, Jaden could no longer keep completely mum. Over to Miss Bonnie's house he went, and before he realized what was happening, he was spilling out his big secret. He knew she wouldn't tell anyone, though.

"Devon is so good at jumping and twisting. He's really helping me learn, and we're both going to try out for cheerleading. What do you think, Miss Bonnie? Doesn't that sound cool? I wish I could cheer for Brandon! Maybe he'd finally be proud of me." His thoughts were tumbling out non-stop, and she finally held up her hands, laughing.

"Jaden, slow down! I think that's a great idea. These days cheerleading is more of a sport, instead of just 'rah, rah'. A lot of teams even compete against each other!" Jaden's eyes began to shine at the thought of doing a sport. Surely, his dad would like a sport. "You know," she said thoughtfully pausing, "you could come to my pool in the back yard this summer to learn to swim, and then to possibly dive. Diving could make your stunts even better. Diving and gymnastics are very similar in body control."

"Super! Could Devon come, too?"

"Of course, but you'd both have to get your parents' permission first." Excited by the prospect, Jaden went home and willed the time to pass until he could tell Devon in school that next day. After hearing the plan, Devon was visibly excited.

He did a cartwheel, followed by a back handspring, and finished by saying, "That'll be great, Jaden! I can't wait 'til summer. No one in my neighborhood has a pool!"

That fall, while Devon and Jaden were learning all the cheerleading moves, Brandon was practicing with the football team. He had easily made the team, even with all the returning eighth graders. He was a natural. After two weeks of practice, Coach Jones decided that Brandon would be a great wide receiver because of his long, lanky body, his speed, and his ability to catch anything and everything. Brandon loved catching the football and running, but he also wanted to hit and tackle! One of the other coaches, also anxious to use Brandon's athletic ability, suggested that he be a defensive end as well. Coach Jones was amenable to that, and Brandon started defensive practice as well as offensive practice. He was overjoyed.

Within a few days the team would have their first game, and Brandon was sure to play in at least one of his positions. Donnie was equally excited, talking every night about what Brandon did in practice, how many tackles he had made, how many passes he had caught, and asking about every word that a coach may have said. Time crept by until the day of the first game, but finally, the team and coaches were meeting at the high school field in preparation for the big event. The crowd was beginning to form, mostly parents, siblings, and a few friends that could get their parents to drop them off. Of course, the cheerleaders were there warming up too. Jaden was enthralled by them, couldn't take his eyes from them.

The game was really exciting, but while everyone was yelling and screaming for the players, Jaden was glued to what the cheerleaders were doing. If there was a first down, they had a special cheer. If the other team got the ball, they began to yell something else. But, if there was a touchdown, they stood in a line, and one by one, ran down the sideline doing cartwheels and all sorts of flips. Jaden thought that was the most magnificent they did. They all were good. During the try for the extra point, each cheerleader got a partner who climbed into a position using the other as a base. If the point was successful, the top partner got thrown and caught. Jaden's heart was pounding as he imagined himself in the lineup. After the game, he was daydreaming with stars in his eyes. He couldn't wait for middle school. He was not even aware that his brother had made three tackles and had caught a pass that he had run for a touchdown. Brandon was walking on air after his first game, but so was Jaden.

The next day at school, the kids who had older brothers or sisters in middle school told everyone that the Lake Griffin Middle School football team had won their first game the night before. With residual excitement, they repeatedly described all the best plays, especially those that involved their own brothers. Still star-struck, instead of talking about the game, Jaden spent all his time telling Devon about every move that the cheerleaders had made.

Devon was very interested in what Jaden had to say, but he was also interested in what the other kids said about the game itself. When they went out to recess that day, Devon took a football and was throwing to several boys who were running out for passes. Devon can do anything, and he's so cute, Jaden thought while watching. Devon was beginning to fill out and get big. This was not totally unexpected, because he had started kindergarten late and was over a year older than most of the kids in his grade. The whole next week in recess Devon only seemed interested in football, much to Jaden's unease, but after school, he would still work with Jaden on his stunts. Jaden was improving rapidly.

Chapter 5

The next week's game was going to be away and early in the afternoon, so the Hansen family would be unable to attend. Brandon came home from the game with tales of great plays and more playing time. He had really taken to the game, and it seemed inevitable that he would have a great high school career ahead of him. Jaden feigned interest in Brandon's exploits, but was disappointed that he hadn't gotten to go watch the cheerleaders again. Oh well, next week would come soon enough.

Next week did come, and there had been excited talk for days between Brandon and his dad about the big rivalry between the two schools slated to play. Coach Jones had told Brandon he would probably play both offense and defense and be in for most of the game.

"You've really come a long way in a short time, Hansen," Coach Jones told him. "You have a knack for coming up with the ball in the most unlikely situations." In practice earlier in the week Brandon had been playing defensive end. The ball was hiked to the quarterback, who spun around to his left to pitch it to Eduardo, the left halfback. Brandon had eluded a block and was speeding around the player to move in to tackle the QB. Just at the right moment he had seen the pitch, snatched it away from the back's open hands, and then cruised down the open field. He was really becoming a force to be reckoned with.

"Mom, can Devon come home with me tomorrow afternoon and go to Brandon's game with us?" Jaden implored. "His mom won't take him to the games, but she'll let him go with us. He lives too far to walk."

"The car will be crowded, but I suppose we can squeeze him in," his mom said, thinking to herself that this would be a good opportunity to meet Jaden's best friend. Other than Miss Bonnie across the street, Devon was all he talked about. When the two friends walked in the door the next afternoon, Alice was more than a little curious. At first blush Devon seemed like a nice enough boy, but as the afternoon wore on, Alice was even more pleasantly surprised.

The boys went out to work on stunts for a while, and when they came in, Devon asked, "Can I help you do anything with dinner, Mrs. Hansen? I can make the mashed potatoes, if you'd like." He seemed quiet and well mannered, but not shy. When Brandon got home a little later, Devon piped up and asked him if he would throw the football a little with him.

Jenny who had walked home with Brandon, exclaimed, "I want to throw, too!"

"I guess we can throw for a little while. It won't make me tired for the game," Brandon replied. The three of them went out to pass the ball while Jaden set the table for dinner. He was so excited to have Devon there. He wanted to do the job perfectly. While the table was being prepared, Donnie arrived home to see the football being thrown around. Quite well, at that. After watching a while, Donnie was ready to concede that Devon might not be a bad friend for Jaden, after all. He was throwing well and catching everything Brandon threw to him, even if the ball seemed almost out of his reach. Maybe there was hope for Jaden. He had driven home wondering what this Devon would look like, would be like. After hearing his name for weeks and knowing he was helping Jaden with stunts, Donnie had been apprehensive that Devon might be a "wuss." But he seemed like a normal kid. After changing into shorts and a tee shirt, Donnie went back out to join the kids until dinner was announced. Meatloaf, mashed potatoes, and corn on the cob, favorites of the whole Hansen family, were the night's fare.

"Devon, sit here by me," was Jaden's plaintive request. Noticing how Devon seemed to be liked by everyone, Jaden was a little nervous that someone else would command his attention. But Devon cheerfully sat down beside him, taking big helpings of the food being passed around the table.

"For an elementary school kid, you sure eat a lot!" Brandon said, shocked. His own plate of food was half the size of Devon's.

"Maybe you should try to eat more, Brandon," came from Donnie. "You're trying to bulk up for football, and small portions aren't going to do it."

Devon laughed and said, "Mrs. Hansen, you're a good cook, and folks say that if you want to compliment a good cook, you should eat lots. I try to do my part," he said with a playful grin. "Not to say I couldn't eat lots more, but what time are we leaving for the game? I can't wait to see Brandon play."

Donnie looked at his watch and remarked, "We should leave pretty soon. What time is warm-up, son?" As Donnie and Brandon began to discuss the time, with Devon intent on every word, Jaden put more food on his plate and started eating huge mouthfuls, trying to be like Devon. Jenny was watching with an incredulous look on her face.

Whispering, she said, "You'll never be able to eat all that, Jaden. You're gonna throw up!"

He tried to grin with a mouth full of potatoes and mumbled, "Watch me."

Finally, it was time to go to the game. Jenny, being small, had no trouble fitting between her parents in the front seat of the car, and Devon shoved in beside Jaden and Brandon in the back. When they arrived, Brandon trotted over to his team as they were lining up for stretches. As the players were warming up, so were the cheerleaders. Jaden focused on them right away, but Devon was torn between the players and the cheerleaders. Finally, he gave in to the cheerleaders, because he wanted to see if any of them were better than he.

When they started practicing their stunts, he smiled at Jaden and said, "We're in, buddy. We can already do everything they do." That said, he turned his attention to the players on the field. Jaden was disappointed that Devon was more enthusiastic about watching the game than watching the cheerleaders, but soon was so caught up in the girls' routines that he didn't even notice the game was about to start. "Jay, come on over here," Devon called. "We can see the action good from this fence."

Lake Griffin Middle won the toss and elected to receive, and the kickoff return players lined up on the field. The kick, and the game was on. After a few poor attempts to move the ball, the offensive team left the field as the defense ran on. The defense was spot-on and managed to cause the Eagles, the opposing team, to lose a lot of yardage. The Colts of LGMS offense ran back out, in good field position. Recognizing that the defense had gained more yards than they had, they were fired up. However, their excitement didn't buy them much. After a measly seven yards, they gave the ball back up. Brandon, on defense now and watching his player like a hawk, had an idea and backed up from the line of scrimmage. When the ball was snapped he hung back for an instant, making a hole for the offense to send a player through.

On the sidelines, Coach Jones was holding his ball-cap in his hand and yelling, "What are you doing, Hansen? Get up there!" As the quarterback dropped back to pass, his receiver saw the hole and headed for it. Timing it just right, Brandon shot back to the open spot at the same time as the receiver and was able to intercept the pass. He ran like a maniac and scored a touchdown. The opposing players were so surprised by this sudden action that no one could come close to catching him. Suddenly, the Colts were six-zero. The crowd went wild. The cheerleaders went wild. Jaden went wild. Before anyone knew it or could stop him, he raced on to the grass where the cheerleaders were and did a cartwheel-back handspring combination. Watching him, Devon ran out and did the same, only adding a back flip as a finale. The cheerleaders were thrilled and gathered around the two boys, at the same time Donnie was heading down from the stands, red-faced and clearly angry.

Devon saw him first, grabbing Jaden by the shoulder saying, "Uh-oh, bro. Your dad doesn't look too happy. What's up with him?" With no time to try to explain that his dad didn't like stunts, Jaden's arm was seized, and he was dragged away by his dad. Donnie, seething, couldn't speak for a few minutes. Jenny wasted no time getting to her brother to see what was going on.

"Daddy, why are you pulling Jaden?" When Donnie was controlled enough to speak, he did so slowly and forcefully.

"Don't you *ever* do that again! Didn't you just see your brother make a touchdown? Aren't you even watching the game? Not only did you not notice your brother's great play, you then proceeded to embarrass me by jumping and leaping around like a fag. Now no one will remember what Brandon did. Our family will be the laughing stock of town."

Jenny, hardly able to keep the tears out of her eyes, said urgently, "Daddy, Jaden was just excited by Brandon's touchdown. He's just as good as the cheerleaders! Why is that wrong?"

"You keep out of it, princess. Let me handle your brother. Both of you get back in the stands and watch the rest of the game. Don't you leave my side, young man, or there will be greater consequences." Jaden sat with his head down, mortified and oblivious to the rest of the game. Devon came back up and sat with him, but not really understanding what had happened, just watched the game. Later, after dropping Devon off at his house, Donnie told Jaden that he was to come straight home after school for the next two weeks, and then he would decide what would or wouldn't happen next.

The next day was a teacher workday, and the students didn't have to go to school. The night before, after they had gone to bed, Alice had tried unsuccessfully to get Donnie to ease up on Jaden. She felt so bad for him, but didn't want to undermine her husband's discipline. She had tried again to tell Donnie that Jaden was not quite eleven and had lots of interests. Stunts were fun to him, and he would pick up more manly attributes as he grew older. Donnie listened, but didn't give in. His stance was that he loved Jaden and didn't want him to get started on the wrong track. Brandon hadn't had any problem, but some kids just had to be taught to be a man, if it didn't come naturally. After Donnie went to work the next day, Alice woke Jaden up and told him she loved him and not to worry, his dad would come around.

"Why doesn't Dad like my stunts? Don't you think I do them pretty good, Mom? He thinks I can't do anything, but I can do stunts. And now, I can't practice with Devon or do anything. I'm just stuck here in the house." Alice replied that if he wanted to hang out with Miss Bonnie today, it would be okay. It wouldn't be the same as going outside to have fun.

Jenny got up about that time, and since Brandon was still sleeping, dreaming of his touchdown, Alice decided to make the twins their favorite breakfast, pancakes shaped like animals. She knew they were about to outgrow things like this, but she was in no hurry for that day to come.

As she mixed up the batter, they were both excited.

"Can we make the shapes in the pan this time, Mom? I want to make a rabbit."

"I want to make a gosling."

"Where did you learn about a 'gosling'?" Alice laughed.

"Our teacher told us that baby geese were goslings," Jenny said proudly. After breakfast and cleanup of the dishes, Alice sent them in to make up their beds and straighten up their room. While there, Jenny spoke to Jaden. "Jaden, I don't know why Daddy is acting mean to you. You haven't done anything wrong."

"I don't know either. Hey, what is a fag, anyway?"

"I don't know exactly, but I know it's not good. I wish Daddy would act nicer. Maybe you just need to keep your stunts away from him. Just do them at Devon's house." As they straightened their room up, Jaden was thinking maybe she was right, but he would talk to Miss Bonnie about it. When everything was ship-shape, Jaden went out to tell his mom he was going over to Miss Bonnie's house.

"Okay, honey. Just don't bother her too much."

After knocking on her door, as she let him in, he got that familiar feeling he always had at her house. Not completely sure of what it was, he knew he just felt very comfortable there. She was someone he could trust with his thoughts.

"Hey, Jaden, what's up?"

"Oh, Miss Bonnie, I really got in trouble with my dad." With that, he poured out everything that had happened the night before at Brandon's game. Starting with Devon coming over, and ending with his dad's words, the tears were coming down his cheeks by the time he finished. Then he said, "Do you know what a fag is?" Looking up at his older friend, he saw a myriad of emotions go across her face, which ended with a tender look.

Miss Bonnie

In a few short seconds it had all come back. I hadn't planned on dealing with those feelings again, but here they were, as raw and hurtful as they were the first time. Memories of being on the playground in sixth grade... there was that fat boy, with poor self-esteem, always trying to bully others to compensate for how he felt about his body.

"Queer! Dyke!" He had taunted me. I quickly pushed those feelings away. With Jaden still in fifth grade, I felt that he was he was too young to understand such harsh words. I told him fag was just a word that people used sometimes to let their emotions out when they were angry.

"Honey, have you heard your dad use words before that your mom says you shouldn't use? This is just one of those words. Your dad probably will be fine when he gets home from work this evening. Maybe you should just practice your stunts at Devon's for a while. Now then, I'm glad you came over; I could use a little help." The day zoomed by, because Jaden always had fun at my house. He couldn't believe it when I said, "You'd better scoot! Your dad will be home in a little while."

The rest of the weekend passed uneventfully, and Monday, getting ready for school, they all noticed a chill in the air. Fall was fading, and winter was coming on.

Football season for Brandon was coming to a close, and the two weeks of isolation were passing for Jaden. Donnie had let the restriction end without adding anything to it. Soon Jaden was having fun with Devon again, and life in the Hansen family rolled on uneventfully as the months passed.

———————

As summer approached Alice decided it was time that Jaden and Jenny each had their own room. By their own choice, they had been sharing a room since they were little. As a toddler, Jaden had experienced terrible nightmares, and Jenny had soothed his fears as if she were his *older* sister, not his twin. Now that time had passed, and Jaden's nightmares had grown farther apart, he was confident that he could be comfortable in a room of his own. Besides, as they grew up, each of them was expressing distinct and different tastes. They thought it would be fun to decorate in their own styles.

Chapter 6

That summer, as promised, I invited Jaden and Devon over for swimming lessons. Having been a swimmer in my youth, I knew all about the strokes and how to teach them. The two boys were both naturals and not afraid of the water one bit. Finally, Jaden was as good as Devon at something, and in some ways even a little better. Devon took to the water as a budding athlete, but Jaden really paid attention to the little things that eventually make a swimmer excel. At the end of the summer, Devon could power his way down the pool to get ahead of Jaden, but Jaden's turns were so precise that he would catch back up. They had so much fun competing! Sometimes when Devon would get a little ahead, Jaden would grab his foot to slow him down. Then, the horseplay would start. The splashing and dunking and giggling would make them come up gasping for air. When I told them that swimming was a varsity sport in high school, they were thrilled, vowing that they would certainly join the swim team. High school couldn't come soon enough.

During the next two years things went fairly well for Jaden with his dad and brother, and when he came over to see me, it was not always traumatic. With the swimming, cooking, and the occasional bike ride, we had a lot of fun together. Never having had children, I loved spending time with him. I was overjoyed that Alice felt she could share him with me. Jenny would come over a lot too, but as the years passed, she drifted away as Jaden got closer. Jenny had become very interested in Young People's Theater and was spending a lot of time with it.

Brandon was a know-it-all sophomore in his second year of high school when the twins started their second year of middle school, seventh grade. Right at the beginning of school that year, cheerleading tryouts were announced and open to any student in the seventh or eighth grade.

Devon turned to Jaden and gave him a high five.

"We have to make that team, buddy," he said. "We should have it in the bag. We know we can do all of the stunts they can."

Jaden grinned, and said, "Listen to the announcement. We need to know how to sign up." After hearing there would be a meeting that afternoon for everyone interested in trying out, the boys were set to go. At the meeting, the cheerleading sponsor gave everyone paperwork that had to be filled out and signed by a parent before the tryouts. There would be a week of practices, and then tryouts would be the following week on Monday. Jaden rushed home after school with the news. Alice smiled at him, and then was a little quiet.

She said, "Let's talk to your dad when he gets home. I'll talk to him first." Jaden's heart sank, as he realized his dad would be an obstacle that he may not be able to overcome. He knew how his dad felt about his stunts, and even after two years, he acutely remembered the tongue-lashing he had received after running onto the field with the cheerleaders at Brandon's game. When Donnie did get home, Alice pulled him into the bedroom where they could talk privately. At least, it started out privately.

Before they came back out, everyone could hear Donnie's loud voice saying, "There is no way my son is going to be a cheerleader! Don't you people get it? I don't want my son to turn into a fag." Alice's murmuring response was so low it couldn't be heard, but Jaden felt his world was being turned upside down. He knew then his dream of being a cheerleader with Devon was smashed to the ground. He might as well give up on living.

When Donnie emerged from the room, he said, "I'm not signing your paperwork, Jaden. You can find something else to occupy your time in middle school. It's not going to be cheerleading!" Tears welling in his eyes, Jaden went to his room and lay face down on his bed. Jenny followed and tried to cheer him up.

"It'll be okay, Jaden. We can both do something else together." Inconsolable, Jaden began to cry in earnest. Jenny sat down and began rubbing her twin's back. "Dad just doesn't understand how much it means to you. If he did, I'm sure he would let you try out."

"Jen, I think sometimes Dad doesn't even like me. He keeps calling me names, and it seems like he never stops criticizing me." Upset by her brother, Jenny began to cry, too. When dinner was ready, neither twin went out. Both had lost their appetites.

Brandon yelled, "Come on out here, you cry-babies. It's dinner time." Alice told him to leave them alone.

With eyes swollen from crying, Jaden went to school the next day and gave Devon the bad news.

"What's up with your dad?" Devon wondered aloud. Jaden was too embarrassed to tell Devon the real story, so he just said his dad wanted him and Jenny to concentrate on school work and bring their grades up higher. "Well, I'll learn the ropes this year, and next year we can both do it." Devon felt really bad for Jaden and put his arm around his shoulder. "Chin up, buddy. It's not the end of the world. There's always next year." After school, Jaden rushed over to Miss Bonnie's house.

"Miss Bonnie, my dad keeps on saying he's not going to let me turn into a fag. Now, I get it that a fag is a gay guy, but I still don't see how someone would turn into one, or why he thinks I'm going to."

Miss Bonnie

Oh, my goodness. Am I the right person to talk to him about this? What would his parents think? Surely I'd be better at talking to him about it than his dad would be, though! He needs to find out in a gentle and unbiased way. I guess it's me. I'm going to have to tell him something this time. He's in seventh grade. Maybe he can handle it.

"Jaden, you know that a fag is a mean, slang term for a homosexual. Do you think you complete understand what that is?"

"I'm not sure."

"Come over here and sit on the couch with me. Let's talk about it in terms of families, rather than just the typical guys who like guys or girls who like girls. You know how your mom and your dad and your sister and your brother make up your family? Well, that is a heterosexual family. Hetero means opposite. A homosexual family might have two dads or two moms instead. Homo means the same. Most homosexual families live their lives just like your family, with kids and activities and church. Unfortunately, a lot of people think that kind of family is weird and wrong. They think a family should only have a mom and a dad. Some even think it is against the teachings of the church, so it can really cause problems for the people involved. Your dad probably just doesn't want you to have to face those kinds of problems in case you were gay and wanted to have a family with your partner."

"I'm not ready to have a family with anyone," he said firmly. "And what does it all have to do with cheerleading? There are lots and lots of girl cheerleaders. Why is it that just guy cheerleaders could turn out to be gay?"

"Jaden, both guys and girls can be gay. It doesn't matter what their interests are. Do you know what the word stereotype means?"

"No, ma'am."

"It means that people think everyone who is a certain type of person will act the same, dress the same, and have the same beliefs. For instance, what do you think about preachers?"

After pondering it a bit, he said, "I think they are Godly, never get mad, are always worried about other people, and don't cuss or drink."

"That's stereotyping, Jaden. Preachers are human just like the rest of us, and they get mad, some of them drink, and some are self-centered. Another example of a stereotype is that many people think boys should play rough and girls shouldn't, because they are dainty. Your dad is stereotyping male cheerleaders as being fags. That's a good example of the narrow thinking that some people have about homosexuals, or gay people. A lot of people think all gay men act feminine, and all gay women act masculine. But there are gay people of all kinds in all walks of life. There are even gay professional football players. That's about as non-feminine as you can get."

"Football players? Wow. This is a lot to think about Miss Bonnie. You know just about everything, don't you?"

Jaden went home with a lot on his mind.

When Alice asked him if anything was wrong, he said, "No, just thinking." She was sure he was still upset about not getting to try out for cheerleading.

"Try not to let it get you down, honey. Maybe your dad will come around next year."

"What? Oh, okay." With that he went into his room, lay down on his bed and stared up at the ceiling. When Jenny walked in a while later, he was still staring at the ceiling.

"Whatcha thinking about, Jay?"

Confiding in his twin, Jaden said, "Jenny, I need you to keep a secret. I talked to Miss Bonnie about gay people."

"What? What did she say?"

"I asked her about Dad always saying he's not gonna let me turn into a fag, and she explained things to me that I didn't get before. She told me a fag and a gay person are one and the same, and that fag is a hurtful word to label somebody, which I knew. She also talked about how gay people can form families with two moms or two dads, which I hadn't really thought about before."

"What do you mean, Jaden? You obviously have to be a woman to have children," she said earnestly.

Jaden said, "I guess that wouldn't be too hard for the two women, but I don't know about the two guys. I guess they could adopt kids."

The next day after school, sure enough, Jaden was at Miss Bonnie's house brimming with questions.

"Do gay guys adopt children? Do gay people get married? Are only grownups gay? How do people find out they are gay?"

"Whoa, whoa, my young friend. One question at a time. Where do I start? Jaden, a person of any age can be gay, adults or young people. It's not a choice one makes. A lot of people think it's a choice and that you can change your mind. But it's not. If you are gay, you were born that way, and that's backed by tons of research. Some people know they are gay by the time they are eight or ten years old. Others don't know until much later. Some know it, but never admit it, because they are afraid of what the world would say about them."

"How do you know if you're gay?"

"Sometimes, at first, you just feel like you're different from others. All your guy friends have crushes on girls, but you don't. After a while, you may discover that there is a boy that you think is cute, and all you want to do is hang out with him. That's a normal thing in adolescence, but if you discover one day that you're attracted to him physically, then you may be gay."

"That's sort of how I feel about Devon. Does that mean I'm gay?"

"Let some time pass, Jaden. Don't try to classify yourself while you're in seventh grade. Let's talk about some of the other questions you have. Gay people can get married, but in the United States, only in a few states. If they have a lifetime commitment to each other, a lot of gay people travel to get married in a state that allows it and then go back home."

"That seems kind of crazy to go to all that trouble."

"It means a lot for gay people to get married, just like straight people. As I'm sure you know, straight is another name for heterosexual. Gay people kiss and hold hands and are intimate, just like straight people. But being gay isn't just defined by whom someone is sexually attracted to. Being gay is very much about whom a person can form an emotional *attachment* to. Straight people naturally form emotional attachments to people of the opposite sex, and gay people form emotional attachments to people of the same sex. A gay person can be in a relationship with someone of the opposite sex, and even live out his life that way, but despite loving his mate, may never be able to develop a complete emotional attachment. And so, he may always feel that something is missing, despite living a full life in every other way. Is this conversation embarrassing to you, Jaden?" she said, as she saw him squirming a bit in his chair.

"Yes, ma'am, a little. But not near as much as it would be with my mom or dad. I could never talk to them about this. Plus, I'm the one who asked you all the questions."

She continued the conversation with, "Let's talk about babies next. Some people, gay and straight, decide they just don't want babies. That is an option for anyone. For those gay people who do want them, there are several things they can do. Some women get a donor sperm to fertilize their egg and have the baby naturally. On the other hand, some men donate a sperm to a woman who will carry their child for them as a surrogate mother. They pay all their expenses, and when the baby is born, it goes home to its gay family. Some people already have children before they realize they are gay, and some people just adopt. There are plenty of kids in the world who need homes." Standing up, she said, "Okay, Jaden, I think that's enough education for one day. Want to help me plant some flowers?"

Jaden seemed content with his newfound knowledge. He understood that his dad was just trying to protect him, even if it was hurtful. He told himself he would try not to get so upset when his dad fussed at him about his stunts.

When Jaden got home, Jenny was eager to hear about what he had learned, so they went into his room, and he told her what Miss Bonnie had said.

"Jen, I really like Devon. Do you think I'm gay?"

"I don't think so Jay, but I don't care if you are. I'll love you just the same." Then they went out to set the table for dinner.

Chapter 7

After being in seventh grade for nine weeks, both Jaden and Jenny felt they were seasoned scholars. It was nice to have a grade behind them, and now they were well into the next. One day when Jenny saw her brother after school, she was bubbling with excitement.

"Jaden! The Young People's Theater group is going to produce your favorite story, *Peter Pan*. And, they're going to reach out to the seventh grade for some of the parts. Why don't you try out to be a pirate? You love pirates, and you'd be great!" Jaden was immediately interested, because he had become obsessed with being a pirate since the release of several popular pirate movies. For days after the last one he had seen, he had worn a bandana and had gone around saying, "Ahoy, Mate."

"That would be so fun, Jenny. Count me in!" The next week the theater posted signs at the middle school asking that all interested students show up Saturday to audition for various parts, including pirates, Indians and the Lost Boys.

Jaden and Jenny were among the first to arrive at the theater that Saturday. Jenny wanted to be Princess Tiger Lily, and of course Jaden wanted to be a pirate. By the appointed hour lots of kids were there, some they knew and many they did not. Apparently the signs had been posted at several schools. There was a ripple of excitement everywhere, and tension filled the air. Many of the young would-be actors and actresses had never been in any kind of production. When it came time to begin auditions, for many it was pretty intimidating to have to get on stage, state your name and school, and then tell what part you were interested in. The judges were concerned with voice projection, ease on the stage, and eye contact, none of which Jaden felt he had. Jenny got up there like a seasoned trooper, and everyone knew she was a shoo-in. She had been in lots of plays and had stage presence. When Jaden's turn came, he wished he felt as relaxed as Jenny had appeared. But he did his best, and when asked what part he wanted, he suddenly felt at ease.

He said, "A pirate, of course! Ay, and it's me peg leg that suits me for me part, Mate." With that, he hobbled across the stage, as if he had a peg leg, and the judges loved it. At the end of all the auditions, the judges explained that a list of chosen cast members would be posted at all the schools the following Monday.

When Monday arrived, more than a few kids were gathered around the theater's posting. Shouts of excitement arose, but there were a few disappointed faces as well. From all appearances, though, it seemed that more kids were chosen than not. Not everyone had specific parts listed by their names. Some, like Jaden, did, and he was thrilled to learn he would indeed be a pirate. Jenny, on the other hand, had TBA beside her name.

"I wonder what 'to be announced' means, Jaden. Do I have a part, or don't I?"

"You'll just have to show up to find out," Jaden said gleefully. He wasn't worried, because he had *his* part. The notice also said that all cast members were to meet at the theater Wednesday after school.

When Jaden and Jenny arrived at the theater that Wednesday, some kids were milling about, while others were sitting in the audience seats. A few minutes later, the director, Ms. Julia, clapped her hands to get everyone's attention. They all settled down in the seats, and she began to pass out the scripts. At the top of each script was the actor's name and assigned part.

"Jaden!" Jenny called, looking for where he was sitting. "Jaden! I'm going to be Wendy! I can't believe it! I'm going to be in most of the scenes, and I get to fly away with Peter Pan!" Talk about a primo part! Jenny was walking on air as she turned from friend to friend excitedly talking about her news.

"Peter Pan's" name was Trevor, and he was a thin boy about thirteen or fourteen years old. He seemed very limber, and he had been practicing doing splits and jumps while everyone was arriving. He seemed very capable of controlling and maneuvering the harness that would be hooked to a wire that would allow him to "fly" through the theater during parts of the performance. (Jaden had noticed that harness when he was looking around backstage and envied whoever would get to use it.) "Peter" had a beautiful face and when he spoke, his voice still had the higher-pitched voice of a child. Jenny was immediately in love, and Jaden was intrigued as well. What was the talented boy like, as a person? Hopefully, through the passing weeks they would find out.

Jaden's attention was drawn back to Ms. Julia as she began to call out the names of people who were in specific groups. Jaden was going to be in a group made up of pirates and Indians. He was excited because he was told he would be allowed to suggest a name for his character, and if appropriate, it would be used. He was mulling this over while he and the other pirates were getting acquainted. Captain Hook was a fifteen-year-old seasoned veteran. He would obviously be the group leader.

Next, Ms. Julia told them about the practice schedule. Jaden's group would be meeting on Saturday afternoons and would be practicing with the entire cast. Jenny, along with the other main characters, would have extra practices on Saturday mornings and on other afternoons during the week.

After being told what time to show up for Saturday practices, everyone was released to go their separate ways. The twins talked excitedly all the way home.

"This is going to be great, Jen. If I can't be a pirate in real life, what better place than on stage. It is kind of scary up there, though. But you looked great, totally relaxed and all." Jaden was complimentary to his sister.

"Maybe Peter Pan and I will fall in love and live happily ever after in real life," she added, laughing.

They both vied for their mother's attention while they proceeded to tell every single moment of that day's meeting. Alice was pleased that they would both be doing something fun together. Maybe it would help Jaden to be less upset about cheerleading and help him come out of his shell of low self-esteem. Poor kid never felt as if he could compete with his siblings.

"Mom, what do you think of Bonesy for a pirate's name? Or how about Captain Jay? Or Skullcrusher? What do you think, Mom?"

"I don't like Skullcrusher, honey. Sounds too violent. How about Captain Jayhawk? It has a certain air about it that makes it seems like you have an eye for what is going on around you."

"Perfect, Mom, I love it! Captain Jayhawk, pirate extraordinaire. Ha,ha,ha." Then he ran across the street to let his friend in on the fabulous news. "Miss Bonnie, I am Jayhawk, pirate extraordinaire!"

"Why, that's wonderful, Jaden. Tell me everything."

Meanwhile, Jenny was telling her mom all about the part of Wendy and how good-looking Peter Pan was.

"I have a lot of practices, Mom, but I promise I'll get all my homework done. Trevor - he's Peter Pan - is so cute. And, I get to spend every week until show time with him. It's going to be great! I can't wait to start."

"I'm not worried about your homework, sweetie. You're always on time with everything."

"I wonder if Trevor has a girlfriend....oh, well, it doesn't matter. I get to spend tons of time with him no matter what."

When the Saturday of the first practice rolled around, both twins were chomping at the bit to get started. Jaden decided to go to the theater with Jenny that morning, even though he wasn't due to practice until the afternoon. Alice had packed them both a lunch, preparing them for a long, fun-filled day. Even though they arrived a few minutes early, almost everyone was already there and had gathered around Ms. Julia. All the kids seemed as eager as the Hansens were to begin. It was all Jaden could do not to run up to tell Ms. Julia the name he had picked out for his character, but he remembered his mother saying that if he was going to be there during his sister's practice, he had to sit quietly until his practice started. As he sat, he decided to listen and learn from everything Ms. Julia had to say.

She began by reminding the actors about stage directions. Most of them had experience, and to them it was just a review, but it was a new world of commands to Jaden. He was glad he was there early and could get a head start on how to do things. Next, Ms. Julia said they would block out the action of Wendy and her brothers, Michael and John Darling, in their home before Peter Pan and Tinkerbell arrived at their window. Curious, Jaden watched as she showed them different places to stand and move on the stage. So far, they were not speaking lines.

While Jaden was watching, Trevor(Peter Pan), came over and sat beside him. Surprised and pleased, Jaden told him he was trying to learn about the stage stuff. Trevor started explaining to Jaden how Ms. Julia was trying to get the Darling clan to feel comfortable with their movements before they began to speak their lines.

He said, "We'll all have our acts blocked out before we start speaking our lines. It helps a lot, not having to learn where to go, while you learn what to say." Jaden immediately thought that Trevor was as smart as he was cute.

"I haven't seen you around before. Where do you go to school?" Jaden asked.

"I go to Holmes Academy. My parents think I'll get a better education there, but I'm trying to talk them into letting me switch to public high school when I finish eighth grade."

"How long have you been in theater?" Jaden was full of questions.

"Ever since I was born," he grinned. "My mom and dad are in the community theater, and they've been taking me with them my whole life."

"How fun!" Jaden expressed. "I wish my parents had been interested in theater and had done that with me. Then, I might be as good as you," he said wistfully.

"All you need is a little experience under your belt. You'll do great." The two boys sat and talked about Trevor's acting experiences until Ms. Julia called Trevor to come to the stage.

Now that Jaden felt like he "knew" Trevor, he couldn't keep his eyes off of him. His movements seemed so effortless, and he always seemed to anticipate his next position on the stage. From the part where he came through the open window, doing a somersault and landing right at Wendy's feet, to the part where he finally led them back out the window, Trevor was a natural. It was obvious that this wasn't Tinkerbell's first play either. She followed Trevor's lead, seeming to know just what to do. The others took their cue from the two of them and seemed to relax as Trevor led them through their paces. By the time Ms. Julia had blocked in the Lost Boys and Peter with Wendy and her brothers, it was time for lunch break.

Jaden was amazed at how a play came together. When he saw movies and shows on TV, he had no idea what it took to make things look so natural. Inviting Trevor to sit with them at lunch, Jaden was content to just listen while Jenny talked on and on about the morning. She gave Jaden a look that expressed how pleased she was about Trevor's sitting with them. After eating his lunch, Jaden spotted Ms. Julia by herself for a minute and hurried over to tell her his pirate name.

After hearing what he had to say, Ms. Julia said, "But, Jaden, we already have Captain Hook. There can only be one captain in a bunch of pirates." Seeing his crestfallen face, she added, "But Jayhawk by itself is a wonderful name. He can be the one who scouts out situations for the captain." Disappointed, Jaden went back to his seat to wait for his practice to begin.

"What's wrong, Jaden?" Trevor asked, with a concerned look on his face. After Jaden told him, he said, "Don't worry about that! It's just a name.

You'll still be the same pirate, no matter what your name is." Somehow Trevor's words took the sting from his disappointment, and he realized he was right. It was just a name.

After working with the Indians for a little while, Ms. Julia came over to work with the pirates. She told them that every time they came on stage, they would move their feet in unison, doing a menacing skulk, so that the audience could tell by looking that they were up to no good. It would be the pirates' trademark move. The pirates went to work immediately, trying to perfect the steps that Ms. Julia had shown them. Captain Hook led, of course. It reminded Jaden of the teamwork that cheerleaders needed to do their cheers in unison. This was a great way to start being a pirate, he thought. After a lot of giggling and a little shoving and pushing, the pirates were beginning to get the hang of the walk. Meanwhile, on the other side of the stage, they could see the Indians engaged in some sort of walk of their own.

After practice, walking home, Jaden remarked to Jenny, "I'm so glad you asked me to do this, Jen. I think I'm gonna love the theater as much as you do."

"Well, we've only just started, and there'll be lots of practices. I hope you don't get tired of it."

"No way! It's fun, and the kids there are really cool, especially Trevor."

"I know! Isn't he just the greatest?" Jenny raved.

As they walked into the house Alice asked, "What did they think of your pirate name?"

"Oh, they already have a captain, so I'll just be Jayhawk. No big deal. I'm still a pirate."

"What a mature attitude, honey."

"Trevor said it didn't matter, it was just a name. Trevor's parents are in the community theater, and he's been in plays with them before. He's such a good actor, and he knows everything about theater. He had on some really cool shoes today. Next time we go to the mall I want to get a pair just like them. And, can I get a tie-dye shirt? Trevor wore one, and it looked really good on him."

Jenny was able to finally break in to say, "I want a tie-dye shirt like Trevor's too."

"Trevor must be some sort of character if he has both of you wanting to be just like him," Alice noticed.

"He's really nice and fun, too," chimed in Jaden. "I want you to meet him, Mom."

"So do I, Mom."

"I'm just glad you both had a good time and met new friends today," said Alice. "I'll be looking forward to seeing the play when it's ready. When will the performances be?"

"Some time around Thanksgiving."

"Okay, enough about the play for now. How about getting the table set for dinner? Your father is grilling hamburgers."

———

The next day, Sunday, Alice was taking special pains to make everyone look their best for church.

"Mom, enough already! We're old enough to know how to dress for church." A photographer was scheduled to go around to all the Sunday school classes and take group pictures for a display in the sanctuary. This was the final Sunday of the class competition for having the most people in Sunday school each week. The winning class would have its picture prominently displayed for a whole month, and they would be recognized in a future church service. Since Alice had been raised as a "pk" (preacher's kid), this was especially important to her. She wanted to report back to her dad, the Reverend Brooks, that at least one of her kids was in the winning group. Donnie attended church, but didn't get involved like his wife did. He had been raised Catholic, was even an altar boy, but when he married Alice, he was more than happy to raise the kids in her Baptist faith, despite the differences in doctrine. He felt there were things in his past as a Catholic that were better left alone. Alice had just been happy that religion had not been an issue. Her parents would have pitched a fit if she had wanted to raise her kids in the Catholic Church.

"Is church ever going to be over today? I don't think the preacher is ever going to stop," Jaden whispered to Jenny. When the service was finally over and the family had arrived back home, Jaden raced over to Miss Bonnie's house to tell her all about theater practice, and all about Trevor.

Miss Bonnie

When I let Jaden in I could tell he was particularly excited, even for him. He told me all about the pirate skulk, how his pirate name had changed somewhat, all about the stage directions, but mostly he talked about Trevor. How smart Trevor was. How wonderful Trevor was. What a good actor Trevor was. How Trevor could bend and stretch in all directions. I teased him that it sounded like he had a little crush on Trevor.

"Oh, no, Miss Bonnie! Girls have crushes. Jenny has a crush on him. It's not like I to want to kiss him. I just like him. He's cool."

"Okay, Jaden, whatever you say," I said smiling, but thinking to myself, he has a lot to learn, and I hope he doesn't get hurt."

As it turned out, Devon didn't become a cheerleader after all. He had begun to wonder if he wanted to be the only boy on the squad since Jaden couldn't try out, and when the sponsor discouraged him by saying rarely do they pick seventh graders, he decided not to try out either. He did begin thinking about trying out for basketball, though.

The next time he met Jaden on the playground, he said, "Hey, Jaden! Let's try out for basketball!" While saying the words, he suddenly remembered why Jaden had said he couldn't try out for cheerleading. His dad had been a real bear about his grades. "Oh, man, I'm sorry, buddy. I forgot you...."

Interrupting him, Jaden said, "No big deal, Devon. I probably wouldn't be any better at basketball than I am at baseball. Besides, you see me in P.E. class. I can't even make a basket up close. But I found something fun that I am good at. I'm in the Young People's Theater play of *Peter Pan*, and I'll be going to practices a lot. It's going to be great! But I'll come watch you play basketball, if you'll come watch my play."

"Deal, buddy. When is it?"

"Not 'til around Thanksgiving. I'm not sure of the exact days."

Chapter 8

As the younger kids were getting into the groove of middle school and theater, Brandon was making his way through high school. Having finished his freshman year, he felt he knew his way around. He had made new friends who were very different from his old friends. Before high school, the majority of his friends had been athletes and played on teams with him. Sure, he was friends with several of the football players now, but his base of friends was expanding. Being a smart kid, when it wasn't football or baseball season, he had gotten closer to some of the brainiac kids and had joined two of their clubs, the Hi-Q Team and the Computer Club.

The Hi-Q was an academic team that competed against other high schools, answering questions in multiple categories. He was good at it, and it was fun to show off what he knew, but it was the Computer Club where he felt more at home. The kids there had it going on. They were smart people who were smartasses, as well. He was learning to further his knowledge in designing computer games and might be able to enter at least one of his games in a contest, the winner of which would get to submit his game to a manufacturer. He didn't know if he could ever make one good enough for that, but gaming was fun. On the Hi-Q Team, most of the members were just regular, polite nerds who knew a lot, but the kids in Computer Club were both smart and quick witted. Learning to verbally spar with them was a challenge Brandon was enjoying. They had no qualms about taking you down a notch or two. Sarcasm was their friend. As time went by, he participated in competitions with Hi-Q, but hung out with the gamers. Of course, all of that was pushed aside when it came to sports seasons. But it took up time between the late fall and early spring when there was nothing else going on.

Devon had made the basketball team, and the season had started. True to his word, Jaden showed up at every home game to cheer on his friend from the stands. He knew a lot about the game from P.E., but it didn't take an expert to see how well Devon was playing. He was a seventh-grade starter on a team of eighth graders. He could dribble, jump, and shoot. As he watched his friend play, sometimes it was hard not to compare the qualities of Devon and Trevor. He loved being with Devon, and he loved being with Trevor. They were both very good at what they did, but what they did was so different from each other. He was glad he didn't have to make a choice about who was his best friend. Trevor went to a different school and was in a different grade. Jaden could spend all his time with Devon while at school and still have time with Trevor at the theater.

While Devon was improving his basketball skills, Jaden was learning about acting from Trevor. The play practices went well, and Jaden was thrilled when Trevor watched him act, giving him suggestions and tips. He was going to be the best pirate ever! He even had a few lines to speak. He said them over and over to Trevor until his friend had to laugh.

"You've got it, Jaden. Ease up."

As the time for the performances got closer, Trevor was getting to fly in his harness more often. He had to arch his back and hold his legs up behind him. It looked a little scary, but he didn't seem to mind. Making his body go where he wanted took some practice, but he was getting used to it. One day, as Jaden and Jenny were both watching, their smiles turned to looks of horror as they saw Trevor flying headfirst into a wooden backdrop. Crash! It made an ominous sound that got everyone's attention. He was quickly lowered to the stage floor while everyone ran up to see if he was hurt. Of course, the twins were the first ones there, because they had started for the stage as soon as they had seen it coming.

"Trevor, are you all right?" Ms. Julia got there just a split second after the twins.

"Are you hurt?"

"Can you move?"

"Where does it hurt?" Questions were flying.

He responded, "I think I'm okay, but my back hurts a little. When I saw the backdrop coming, I turned myself around so it would hit my back. I'm not sure that was such a good idea," he said ruefully rubbing his back. After checking him over, Ms. Julia decided that it was only going to be a few sore muscles and some bruises.

She said, "Go offstage and rest a little, then we'll see how you feel. I don't think you've actually done any damage. We'll go on with practice, but let me know if anything starts to hurt worse." Trevor headed for the left wing with Jaden and Jenny right behind. "Jenny, come back. I need Wendy's character out here right now," said Ms. Julia's insistent voice. That left Jaden alone with Trevor.

"Hey, Trev, why don't you lie on your stomach, and I'll rub your back so it doesn't tighten up."

"That'd be great, thanks," Trevor replied as he lowered himself to the floor and gingerly pulled his shirt up.

"Does it hurt here?" Jaden could see a red mark.

"Yeow! Yeah, right there," he winced. Jaden began gingerly massaging Trevor's upper back, until he could feel Trevor relax beneath his hands. "That helps a lot." Jaden began moving to different places on his back and was surprised to find that he liked touching Trevor's skin. He thought Trevor must like it, too, because he began to make little groans and sighs. And then it got very quiet on stage.

"What's going on back here?" Ms. Julia demanded walking to the wing.

"Nothing!" Jaden said defensively. But, he jumped up quickly, wondering why he suddenly felt guilty. "I was rubbing the sore muscles on Trevor's back. He says it feels better now."

"You two come on back out. That should be enough rest for Trevor's back." As Trevor got up, he made eye contact with Jaden, rolled his eyes toward Ms. Julia then, winked at him.

That night, Jenny cornered Jaden and asked a little jealously, "What was going on back there in the wings?"

"Nothing was going on, Jen, really. I was just rubbing his back. I know you like him. I like him, too. We can all be friends." Taking a deep breath, she thought maybe things would be all right. But, maybe not. She wasn't sure what to make of this little turn of events.

Miss Bonnie

A few days later, at my house, Jaden told me about the backrub and the wink.

*"Miss Bonnie, when Trevor made little noises while I was rubbing his back,
I had a funny feeling way down in my stomach. It got me to thinking about the gay
thing again."*

"Did it make you uncomfortable?"

"No, it was nice," he quickly responded.

*"I don't think you should worry about it, Jaden. Nothing in your life has to
change now, maybe ever.*

*"I don't think I'll tell anyone, not even Jenny. I'm afraid that she's jealous of
Trevor and me." After a pause, he asked, "Do you think Trevor might be gay?"*

*"I don't really know, Jaden. Those things will sort themselves out. But, I want
you to know that whatever you may go through, you can come over and talk to me
about it anytime." He gave me a big hug and went home.*

At home, Brandon had begun to use a little of the sarcasm he had
been using with his friends at school. Alice and Donnie weren't particularly
thrilled by it.

One afternoon while Jaden was helping Jenny learn her lines, Brandon
said with a sneer, "Well, if it isn't the little stars of the kiddie show."

"Not me, I'm just a pirate." Jaden played it off.

"And, if I hear correctly, there is a little budding romance between you
and Peter-the-Pan, Jenny. Next thing you know you'll be interviewed by the
newspaper and go off to Hollywood to be a star with your little boyfriend."
Jenny wasn't as easy-going as her brother.

"Brandon, that's not fair. We work hard to learn our parts. We don't
make fun of stuff you do. And, he's not my "little" boyfriend!" Jenny's voice
was becoming shrill.

"Brandon, that's enough!" Alice said sternly. "Leave them alone."

"Leave them alone," he mocked, as he stormed to his room, muttering
under his breath. Jenny was truly upset.

"Mom, Brandon used to cheer me on in everything. Why is he so different now? On top of that, Trevor won't even look at me. I feel like Jaden
took him away from me. All he does is hang out with Jaden at practice." Ball-
ing up her fists, she cried, "Why is Brandon being like this?" With that, she

burst into tears. Following her into her room, Alice thought the boyfriend thing was the crux of the issue, not Brandon.

"Honey, I know your feelings are hurt, but Brandon was just being a teenage boy. He didn't mean anything by it. Do you want to tell me about Trevor?" Still crying, she let her mom put her arms around her.

After a bit, she sniffled, "Trevor is the first boy that I have ever really liked. I thought he liked me, too, but he was just being friendly. He acts the same to everyone. And now he likes Jaden."

"Well, of course he likes your brother, dear." Alice was guileless.

"No, I mean...never mind," Jenny decided to keep her thoughts about Jaden to herself.

"Anyway, honey, plenty of boys will come along in the next few years. I know it's hard with your first crush, but it's not like he has some other girlfriend instead of you. He's just not ready to have any girlfriend yet."

Chapter 9

Winter roared in and blew fall away, along with the dried leaves that were once such beautiful colors. The gym stayed lively as basketball season continued, and the theater was being spruced up as last minute changes and corrections were made to the play. Jaden and Jenny could hardly wait to get their costumes and makeup! It was old hat to Jenny, but Jaden was thrilled to learn that everyone on stage would wear makeup. Dress rehearsal was to be the next Friday, with the play starting on Saturday and running for two more performances the following Friday and Saturday. Ms. Julia called the whole cast to come in the Wednesday of that week to be fitted for costumes and to learn the curtain call. Jaden hadn't expected that he would get to come out and bow to the audience at the end of the play. He thought only the main characters would do that. He was thrilled.

Thanks to Trevor, he had lost almost all of his stage shyness and was even becoming somewhat of a ham. Ms. Julia had to tone him down more than once. Jenny spent the whole weekend prior to the play telling all her friends to come see it and when the dates were. Jaden only told Devon and Miss Bonnie, who both promised they wouldn't miss it.

On the day costumes were handed out, Jaden put his on and immediately ran to a mirror in the boys' dressing room.

"Oh, wow! I really do look like a pirate," he said to no one in particular. Most of the boys were crowded in there, trying on their costumes, too.

"Man, you look great!" Trevor said enthusiastically as he came in the door. "You're going to be the hit of the pirates. Your costume is awesome!"

"I like yours, too. You look like a pixie or an elf, just like Peter Pan did in the movie. That's such a cool hat. But the shoes, not so much," Jaden said teasingly. In the other dressing room, the girls were delighted, as well. Jenny's outfit didn't fit exactly right, though, so she went out to show Ms. Julia.

"Oh, that's no problem, Jenny. I can take a nip and a tuck here and there, and it will fit you perfectly. Let me feel the waist to see how much it needs to be taken in." Relieved, Jenny let her take some tucks and make all the necessary adjustments.

After everyone had tried on their costumes and commented on how great each other looked, Ms. Julia called them out to practice the curtain call. Jaden learned that the smaller parts went out on the stage to bow first. All of the Indians went out together, followed by all of the pirates. The Lost Boys had bigger parts, so they went out just before the younger Darling children and Tinkerbell. Each group stood in a horizontal line, and bowed at the same time. Last, it was time for Peter and Wendy. They went out holding hands and bowed together. Then, Wendy was instructed to step back and let Peter take a bow alone, since he was the main character. Jaden felt a pang of jealousy when Jenny was holding Trevor's hand. Right away he thought, crap, I really must be gay if I want to hold his hand. Momentarily dismissing that thought, he began to join the other cast members in clapping long and loud for Trevor.

Jenny and Jaden could hardly sleep Thursday night, because Friday's dress rehearsal would be just like a performance. School the next day was endless, but Friday night finally arrived. Ms. Julia had told them that they had to be made up before they put their costumes on. She had recruited several members of the high school drama club to help with that task. As Jaden was standing in line waiting, he was impatiently shifting his feet. Finally, it was his turn. They put a makeup base on his face, then, started making scraggly whiskers using a tube of black cream and a small brush. After adding big eyebrows, long sideburns were the final touch. After seeing himself in the mirror, Jaden couldn't believe it. He looked so mean! His Mom and Dad wouldn't even recognize him. Then he went to find Trevor. Trevor's makeup was just being finished, and he looked terrific. He was even more beautiful than usual, if such a thing were possible. Breathless, Jaden wanted to grab his hand and run back to the wings to hug him. Fortunately, at that very minute, Jenny walked up to look at both of them and to show off her own makeup.

After talking excitedly a few minutes, they heard Ms. Julia announce, "Time to start!"

The dress rehearsal had a few snafus, but Ms. Julia told them that was to be expected, and that was what dress rehearsal was for. She hadn't stopped the action at any time, because they were such small mistakes, and she didn't want to interrupt the flow of the play. She took notes, instead, and went over them with the cast at the end. When she finished, everyone clapped and cheered. *Peter Pan* was going to be great!

At home, Jaden and Jenny couldn't quit talking about the practice performance to anyone who would listen. Neither of them had made any mistakes, and each was filled with visions of greatness. They stayed up talking well past the time they usually went to bed. Tomorrow was Saturday, after all. When they finally did turn in for the night, Jaden's thoughts turned to Trevor only. He lay in bed thinking about him and his reaction to how great he looked.

"I really did want to hold his hand, but I know I never could have. Everybody would have freaked out." While Jaden was telling his thoughts to Miss Bonnie the next day, she sadly noted to herself that it was already starting.

"Jaden, there are some people who think that anything other than the norm is wrong. On the other hand, more and more people, especially young people, are accepting differences like never before. If you had held Trevor's hand at play practice, chances are most of the teenagers there would have been surprised, but wouldn't have made it a big deal. I'm not sure about some of the younger kids or your director. Who knows? These days a lot of gay teens are open and out with their parents and friends."

"Well, Miss Bonnie, if it turned out that I was gay, you know that I could never tell my dad! He would go ballistic!"

At school on Friday, Brandon told his computer friends that his parents were making him go to his little sister and brother's play on Saturday night.

"What a drag," he said. "Why don't you guys go with me? That would at least make it tolerable."

"What play is it?" asked Dan, slightly interested.

"*Peter Pan.*"

"*Peter Pan?* Give me a break! A little kid's play? Not in a million years!"

"They're only in seventh grade, butt-head. They *are* little kids," defended Brandon.

"Don't be snarky, Dan," said Evan, joining in. "We might find a way to get some fun out of it, anyway," he said with a sly smile. Nodding at each other with knowing looks, and then glancing at Brandon, they both agreed to go.

On Saturday Alice noticed that Brandon seemed to be in a good mood. Thinking about the fuss he put up about going to the play, she was surprised that he seemed okay about it today.

"Hey, Mom, Dan and Evan are going to the play with me tonight. Is it all right if I ride with them? Evan has his license." So that was the change of heart.

"I guess it's okay with me, if it's okay with your dad. But, don't be late to the play!"

Finally, it was time to go to the theater. Having tried to will the hours to pass all day, the twins had been sure they would die before it was time to leave the house.

"Mom, do you know it actually costs money to get into our play? Just like at the movies, or a community theater play."

"I know, hon, I saw it in the paper."

"Our play was in the paper?" they both screamed. "Wow! I'll bet lots of people come, then," said Jaden, excitedly.

Getting into the car, Jenny asked, "Where's Brandon? Isn't he coming?"

"Yes, two of his friends are coming, and he's riding with them."

"Cool!"

The actors and actresses immediately went backstage to be made up, while the parents and friends settled themselves into cushioned theater seats.

"At least it's more comfortable than I thought it would be," Donnie remarked. "I thought it might be seats like at the ball field." Thirty minutes before the play was to start, Brandon and his friends weren't there yet. Alice was nervous until about ten minutes before the curtain went up, when she saw them come in and get seated in the back. They were acting aloof, as if they were too cool to be there. At almost the same time, Miss Bonnie arrived and took a seat in the middle section. A few minutes later, Devon came in and sat near the front.

As the show began, when Wendy came out, Brandon said, "That's Jenny."

Fanning himself, Dan said, "You go, girl. She's pretty hot for a seventh grader, Brandon."

"Hey, now, that's my sister. I don't want to hear it," Brandon shot back at him.

"Even so, she could light my fire. You'll have to introduce me to her after the play," he said teasingly. He knew he wouldn't date a seventh grader, but he was trying to get Brandon going.

It worked, because Brandon fired back, "You aren't getting anywhere near my sister! You'd have to come through me first!"

"Okay, okay, just kidding," Dan said, laughing, trying to appease Brandon. Surely there would be more to razz him about before the night was up.

"Look at that hat, and those elf shoes on Peter Pan!" Evan snickered. "What a queer."

Dan added, "Wow! Look at him fly! He's such a fairy, pun intended." A few aisles away Donnie was having the same reaction, but thought better of saying it out loud.

"I know," said Brandon. "I wonder what my Dad thinks about it."

Unlike Donnie, Dan and Evan felt free to make comments about everyone on stage. They made fun of the costumes and makeup and mimicked the voices of some of the boys. After a bit, Brandon joined right in. The teens were having a fine time in the back of the theater. No one was in the row directly in front of them, but from time to time, people in other rows would try to shush them, as they got a little loud. When the pirates came on stage for the first time, doing their skulking walk, the boys in back laughed out loud. Suddenly feeling conflicted, Brandon didn't know whether to laugh with them, or be indignant because his brother was a pirate. As it turned out, he laughed with them, but felt a little ashamed doing it.

As Donnie watched, he could finally contain himself no longer.

Turning to Alice, he whispered, "Is this what all those weeks of practice have been for? For my son to do a little dance on stage, in front of everyone, and humiliate himself?"

Tired of months of trying to appease Donnie, Alice whispered back with annoyance, "Donnie, that's enough! Our son is who he is! He already thinks you don't love him, and if you don't praise him for his performance tonight, he'll be crushed. See if you can find something to like about his play!" Donnie sat back, quiet again.

Miss Bonnie had been sitting in a middle row, but after hearing raucous laughter from the back, she changed her seat during the intermission. She had seen teenagers sitting back there, but was a little surprised to see Brandon among them. Feeling she was a stakeholder in the Hansen family, she wanted to hear what was going on. Devon came back with a Coke, saw her there, and decided to sit with her. After all, this was Jaden's friend who had taught them how to swim. She didn't need to be sitting there alone!

When the next act started, every time the pirates or Indians would come on, Devon would laugh in delight, along with the crowd, because he thought they were funny. And then, when Captain Hook and Peter Pan were looking for each other, the audience screamed as they almost collided back to back. This happened several times, with more screams, before the two exited the stage without seeing each other. About that time, Devon noticed that the boys on his left, a few seats over, were holding up limp wrists and totally making fun of the actors. Devon couldn't believe his eyes when he saw that one of them was Brandon. How could he make fun of a play where his own brother and sister were actors? This was really un-cool, and he planned to confront Brandon about it as soon as he ran into him. He didn't want to start something in the theater, and as it turned out, the boys left before the curtain call anyway. Just as well, Devon thought, less for them to make fun of.

Miss Bonnie had planned to shush the boys if their antics got loud, but the rest of the audience had gotten loud, too, so it didn't matter as much. She, too, was relieved to see them go.

After the curtain call and much clapping, the lights came up, and Devon asked Miss Bonnie, "Did you notice that Brandon was in that group of rude guys? As much as Jenny and Jaden cheer for him in his games, I can't believe he acted like that! I used to think a lot of him."

She replied, "I can't believe it either. I know he's been raised better than that," she replied as they walked down the aisle to congratulate the cast. As parents and friends were moving toward the stage, the young actors and actresses were still shining in the glow of the audience's applause. Coming down the stage stairs, they heard praise everywhere.

"You were wonderful, honey! I've never seen such a good Indian."

"Wow! Who did your makeup? I didn't recognize you."

"I can't believe Peter Pan really flew!"

"Where do you want to go to celebrate?"

Everyone seemed thrilled with the production, cast and audience alike. As the groups started to break up, Jaden and Jenny joined their parents, but soon started looking around a little disappointed.

"Where's Brandon? Didn't he come tonight?"

"Of course your brother was here. He wouldn't miss your performance," said Alice, who had been wondering a little herself about where he had gone. Devon, standing nearby, spoke up.

"He was in the back row and left with his buddies before it was over." His tone of voice indicated he was not pleased.

"What's wrong, Dev?" asked Jaden.

"Nothing you need to be concerned with right now," he replied, with a funny look on his face. Then, trying to sound upbeat, he said, "The play was great and you were an awesome pirate! I'll see you in school Monday." With that, he turned and left.

Riding home with their parents, the twins were wired. Jenny was euphoric, because she hadn't made any mistakes or forgotten any lines in her first show with a major part. She was chatting nonstop with her mom and dad, so glad that they finally had been able to see how great the show was. Jaden was pretty happy too, but not only was he thinking about his part as a pirate, he was also re-living the brief moment backstage when he had been alone with Trevor. After a bear hug from Trevor, who said he couldn't wait to see him again, a small piece of paper was pressed in his hand. It had Trevor's telephone number on it. Right under the number, if he had made it out correctly, was a tiny little heart. Jaden had that piece of paper clutched in his hand, all the way home.

Chapter 10

Monday, at school, Jaden found Devon right away. "What was that deal Saturday at the play? You were acting so weird when it was over."

"I don't even really want to tell you, but I think you need to know," was his response. "There was a small group of guys in the back of the theater who were making fun of all of you on stage."

"Making fun of us? In what way?" Devon slowly poured out the whole story, including the limp wrists and the 'fag', 'queer', and 'fairy' names they had used.

"The worst part is - Brandon was with them." A sudden chill made the hairs on Jaden's neck rise up. His own brother joining in with others to make fun of him? Steadying his emotions, he thought, at least Devon is on my side. As the bell rang, Devon said, "Don't worry, I'll take care of it."

That whole week after basketball practice, Devon purposefully walked past the high school to see if he might run into Brandon. He was about to give up when, on Thursday, he saw a group of five or six guys standing near a car in the parking lot. One of them was Brandon. Hanging back, out of sight, he watched them for a few minutes. When he saw Brandon finally break away from the group, Devon quickly walked in his direction.

"Hey, Devon. What's up?" Brandon seemed relaxed.

"You tell me what's up!" Devon shot back at him.

"What are you talking about?" Brandon looked a little puzzled.

"I'm talking about Saturday night at the play when you and your friends dissed your own brother."

"Oh, that," he said. "That was just a stupid, juvenile play. I can't help it if they're all little fairies." Devon took a step, as if to hit Brandon. Even though Brandon was older, Devon had filled out quite well. Brandon, backing off, said with a smirk, "If you want a piece of me, bring it on, but I don't want my little brother to know I beat up his best friend." With that, Devon swung, making contact with Brandon's left jaw. He followed with a jab to the right, and just like that, the skirmish was over with Brandon on the ground, wondering what happened. Brandon looked around, embarrassed and hoping no one had seen. He considered going after Devon, but gingerly touching his sore face, he thought better of it. Devon strode off, satisfied that he had restored his friend's honor.

Brandon took his time going home, hoping his face would look normal when he arrived.

It didn't, and when his mother saw him, she said with alarm, "What happened to your face? You have the beginning of a shiner on your left eye, and your right cheek is all red."

"We played dodge ball in P.E. today, and I got hit in the face," he said, thinking quickly.

"Well, I don't think that's a good game to play if people get hurt. I'm calling the school."

"No, no! Mom, don't do that. It's fun and the balls are foam; it didn't even hurt. I've been hurt much worse in football, even baseball. I just wasn't paying attention for a second."

When she relented and agreed not to call, Brandon breathed a sign of relief and headed for his room. He saw Jaden in the hall, but he breezed right past him and shut his door. Noticing Brandon's face, Jaden had a sudden recollection of Devon's words: "Don't worry, I'll take care of it.

———

The next week, time went by slowly as Jaden wrestled with the decision about whether or not to call Trevor. He really wanted to, but something was holding him back. Several times he picked up the phone, but thinking about how his brother and his brother's friends had acted at the play, as well as Devon's fight with Brandon, he always hung it back up. Was what he felt toward Trevor worth the whole world being upset about it? And, of course, there was always the matter of his dad. He really wanted to please him and felt he never had. *It feels awful for people to make fun of you. I hate that my brother and my best friend had a* fight *about it*, he said to himself. Feeling torn between trying to please his family and trying to believe that what he felt about Trevor was okay, Jaden put off the call, knowing he would see Trevor at the final performance of the play the next weekend anyway.

The weekend came, as it always does, and the twins went to the last show feeling a little conflicted.

Jenny spoke up, "I don't really want it to be over. This is my first big part, and it's been so much fun." She reveled in the glory of being a major player. "But at the same time, I need a break, and the next play will come around soon enough."

"I feel the same way, Jen, except this is my first play, and being a pirate is so awesome. It's so natural for me. I'm not ready for it to be over." Without voicing his other concern about not being able to see Trevor much anymore, he said, "I guess having some Saturdays off with no practices will be nice."

The performances came and went, and the actors and actresses were backstage after Saturday night's finale, having a cast party. They were patting themselves and each other on the back for doing so well, while they ate cookies and drank soft drinks.

Everyone was mingling, asking, "Are you going to be in the next show?" and "Sign my program beside your part."

"I'm going to miss you so much until we start practice again." Many were exchanging telephone numbers. There were a fair amount of tears, too, because "Tinkerbell", Emily Shreeve, had announced that she had to move to another state right after Christmas. She would start the next semester in a new school without knowing anyone. Everyone individually had to give her a hug, telling her they would really miss her, and urging her to write. Taking advantage of the crowd around Emily, Trevor and Jaden took a moment to disappear to the boys' dressing room.

Sitting on a makeup bench, Trevor began, "I'm going to miss you lots, Jaden."

As his eyes began to tear up, Jaden said, almost in a whisper, "You have no idea how much I'll miss you."

Trevor quickly started speaking again, "We don't have to miss each other for long. I'll be sixteen in February, and I'll be able to drive. I can come to your house." Jaden seemed to visibly sink down in his seat. "Jaden, what's wrong? Don't you want me to?" Trevor was confused.

"My dad thinks I'm a fag, and I don't know what to do," Jaden said sadly.

"If you're a fag, then so am I," Trevor said gently. Then he leaned forward and gave Jaden a tender kiss on the mouth. It was over as soon as it began. "Let's go back out there before the others miss us."

Jaden followed him out, stunned. What had just happened? He couldn't think. Thankfully, the crowd, although diminished, was still around Emily. No one had noticed their absence. The two friends took their place in the group to wish Emily well. Jaden tried his best to appear normal, but felt like everything about him had just been irrevocably changed forever. The kiss had felt so right. For the first time, Jaden felt he understood what it was to be gay.

"Dad's here, Jay," said Jenny, bringing Jaden back to reality. Even though he was shaken, he couldn't quit thinking about how good, how sweet, Trevor's kiss had been. Trevor must be gay, too, he thought. The idea both excited him and frightened him, but he was still worried about his family. He knew they would not approve of Trevor coming over to the house, at least his dad wouldn't, and he didn't know how or when he could see Trevor again.

Proving that Jaden's worry was valid, when the kids got in the car Donnie remarked, "Well, I'm glad that's over. We can get back to the business of being a normal family, instead of being in the midst of a bunch of actors prancing around the stage." Thinking back to what Alice had said the week before, he did concede, "You both did a good job, though. I give you credit for that." Jenny smiled, but the praise left Jaden feeling a little hollow.

The basketball team had four more games, and Jaden tried to get enthusiastic about Devon's playing. He really did think Devon was great, but something wasn't quite right. Outwardly, he still cheered and clapped, but he was feeling a little sad and empty all the time. Devon didn't appear to notice. He seemed to be caught in the thrill of a winning basketball team and wanted to talk of nothing else.

Chapter 11

Miss Bonnie

When Jaden finally came to see me, I noticed he was a little down. He just sat on the couch without a word. He opened his mouth several times, but nothing came out.

I let him sit there with his thoughts for a while, then said, "Come on, Jaden. Out with it. What's on your mind?"

"Miss Bonnie, Trevor kissed me the last night of the play. All I can think about is that kiss." I was surprised, and not surprised, both at the same time.

"Yes, your first kiss is very momentous." To this day I can still remember my first kiss. "How do you feel about it?" I asked him.

"When I think about that kiss, I want to do it again. It felt scary, but good. But I don't know if I'll get to see Trevor again."

"Why not?"

"My dad will never let me be gay. If he finds out, he'll forbid me to see Trevor. I'm pretty sure he won't allow Trevor to come over, as it is. He made comments about him when he saw the play. And, Brandon and his friends made fun of us."

"I know, dear, I heard them."

"I just don't know what to do," he said mournfully. "I don't want my family hating me." Sitting there on the couch with this sad boy brought back my early years. My first kiss was when I was in college, the summer when I was nineteen, almost twenty. Going down memory lane of my college days was almost always pleasant, and today, remembering the thrill, the ecstasy of that kiss, awakened in me feelings that have long been dormant. Startled when Jaden spoke, I put my thoughts away and came back to the present.

"Jaden, honey, your dad can't forbid you to be gay anymore than you can forget about your feelings for Trevor. You are what you are. Your dilemma, however, is how, and even whether, you ever act on it. It's a tough decision. Do you try to appease your family by acting as if you are straight, maybe getting a girlfriend, or do you let your feelings take you wherever they lead, perhaps being open to the world? I've told you *before, Jaden, that you are young. You don't have to do anything at all right now. Just live each day as it comes, and maybe your decision will be made for you at some point.*

Jaden returned home feeling a little better about his situation and about himself. She's right, he thought. I don't have to make a decision now or ever, if I don't want to. He felt a heavy weight come off of his shoulders. I shouldn't worry about this all the time.

The next couple of weeks, as middle school basketball came to a close, Jaden watched Devon, and thought about Trevor. Jenny was excited about the next play coming up, *Aladdin and His Magic Lamp*. Practice wouldn't start until after Christmas, but Ms. Julia was going to pick the cast in December.

This might be my answer for now, Jaden thought. I can see Trevor at practices, and no one will think anything about it. He decided to call Trevor right then and there.

A woman's voice said, "Hello?"

"May I speak to Trevor?" His voice was shaky.

"Trevor! Telephone."

When Trevor answered, Jaden blurted out, "Hey, it's me."

Trevor said in a hushed voice, "This isn't a good time to talk. My mom's coming back into the room."

"Wait, don't hang up yet!" Jaden implored. "Just tell me quick if you're gonna be in *Aladdin*."

"No, my parents want me in the community theater with them for their next play. Call me later." He hung up abruptly. Disappointment was all over Jaden's face as he walked down the hall to the bathroom that he shared with his brother and sister.

Seeing him pass her room, Jenny said, "Hey, what's wrong?" She was concerned.

"I'm not sure if I want to be in *Aladdin*," he said.

"Why not?" Jenny was mystified, because she knew Jaden had come to love the theater. Jaden decided to be honest with his twin. They had always shared almost everything.

Stepping into her room, he said, "Trevor can't be in the play this time, so I don't think I want to either."

Jenny said, "You have other friends in theater, Jaden."

"Will you promise to keep a secret if I tell you something, Jenny?"

"You know I will. We're closer than anyone else."

"I think I like Trevor more than just a friend. More like a boyfriend," he confessed. Jenny's eyes widened as Jaden continued talking. "We kissed the night of the last performance."

Jenny gasped, in surprise. I guess that's why he wouldn't pay attention to me, she thought to herself.

"Jen, I really don't know exactly what to do. Miss Bonnie said I don't need to do anything if I don't want to. I don't want you and Brandon, and Mom and Dad to hate me, but I have feelings for Trevor."

"They won't hate you and you know I won't! I told you a long time ago that I'll always love you no matter how you are." Jenny was remembering back to the day she had cried over Trevor. She said, "I don't even have a crush on Trevor anymore. And don't worry, I won't tell anyone."

Later that evening, emboldened by Jenny's reassurances, Jaden called Trevor again. This time Trevor quickly answered on the first ring.

"Hey, I'm so glad you called me back," said Trevor, after Jaden had identified himself. "I didn't want to hang up on you this afternoon, but my mom says I'm on the phone too much, and I didn't want to get in trouble. Play practice is on Mondays and Thursdays, so I can't talk then, but it doesn't start 'til next week. My parents usually go out for walk around seven every night we're home, so that would be a good time to call each other." Trevor seemed to go on and on.

Jaden finally interrupted to say, "It's nice to talk to you again. I've missed you."

Jaden and Trevor talked every evening that week for a few minutes. Neither wanted Trevor to get in trouble, so they kept it short. Plus, Jaden didn't want his dad catching on to the fact that he was talking to someone every night. He would be sure to ask who was on the phone.

During the weeks leading up to Christmas, all three Hansen kids wanted the time to pass. Sure, everyone looked forward to the holidays and being off from school, but Jenny was looking forward to play practice starting again, Brandon was looking forward to baseball starting, and Jaden was looking forward to Trevor's getting his driver's license. They were all eager for the new year to begin.

Chapter 12

Christmas and the holidays were fun, but passed quickly, and January arrived. The first day back to school, January fifth, the Hansen kids were psyched about seeing their friends and finding out what they got for Christmas. Everyone seemed to have on new clothes, and a few kids were sporting new iPods. Loads of middle school kids, including Jaden and Jenny, had gotten cell phones for Christmas and were comparing them with each other. Jaden was especially thrilled with his, as it meant he could contact Trevor any time, as long as his dad didn't see him. When the teacher made them put the cell phones out of sight, they reluctantly did, but would sneak a peek at the phones on their laps as often as possible to see if they had gotten a text.

Conditioning for baseball started on January sixth, and practice revved up the following week. Brandon had played junior varsity last year as a freshman, but this year he was trying out for varsity.

Donnie had talked him into it, saying, "You might as well try to get a varsity letter for three years in baseball. That would look really good on your college resume." Brandon figured he would try out for third base, since that's where he had made the All-Star team in Little League and where he wanted to play in college. Last year the coach had tried him in several positions. He did well in all of them, but never landed in a secure spot. Donnie had said, "Take a chance, Brandon. Make them notice you. If you can learn all the ins and outs of third base, you'll be ready for college." The varsity coach was noticing him, all right, but the fact of the matter was that Jason, a graduating senior, had played third base the last two years and had no intentions of giving it up. Brandon realized he just had to work that much harder.

Jenny had been given a starring role in *Aladdin*, as the genie of the lamp, and play practice had started in earnest. Once again she had the lion's share of practices, but loved it. Donnie was relieved that Jaden didn't want to try out this time. While Brandon and Jenny were otherwise occupied in the afternoons, Jaden would sneak off somewhere to call or text Trevor whenever he could.

One evening when they were talking, thinking of Trevor's beautiful face, Jaden was having trouble concentrating on what Trevor was saying. Suddenly, it came to him that Trevor was saying his birthday was coming up in a few weeks.

He followed with, "And then, I get my license!"

"Are you going to get a car?" Jaden asked hopefully. When no comment was forthcoming, Jaden disappointedly realized that the answer was no.

"I don't have enough money for a car, and my parents have said that if I want one, I'll have to earn it myself. My mom did say I could drive hers sometimes, when she's not using it. And, I have a little money saved. Maybe I could earn some more and get a 'beater'."

"What's a beater?" Jaden wondered aloud.

"You know. It's a car that's older and has some dents in it, that you can buy pretty cheap."

"Where would you earn more money?"

"Maybe I can get a part-time job. I heard the YMCA is looking for lifeguards on weekends."

"Really? You can be a lifeguard? Are you a good swimmer? Have you been a lifeguard before?" Jaden, excited again, was firing off questions, exhilarated that Trevor liked to swim, too. "I wonder if I could be a lifeguard, too?"

"Sorry, you have to be in high school first, and pass the lifeguard course. In the meantime, at least I can get a job, save money, and get a car. Then we can do stuff. We'll be free!"

When Jaden hung up, he was thoughtful. I wish I was in high school. It seems like the rest of this year, and next, will never go by. But if I can do stuff with Trevor, I guess it doesn't matter. Right now I'd better be thinking of a birthday present.

Trevor cornered his mom as soon as she and his dad got back from their walk.

"Mom, do you think I could be a lifeguard on the weekends? It wouldn't interfere with school or the play, and I could earn some money! The YMCA is hiring."

"Hmm, I guess you're getting to the age where a part-time job could be good for you. That should be okay, sweetheart, go ahead and apply."

"I'll have to get certified, but the Y provides that training, too."

His mom replied, "You'd better check into that right away. You wouldn't want to miss the training and then miss out on the job." Trevor, after looking at the YMCA's website, immediately called to register for the lifeguard class. It would only take a day, and at the end he would be certified in lifeguarding and CPR. He felt lucky that the class happened to be on the very next Saturday, so he wouldn't even have to wait a week to get his certification.

At the beginning of the class, Trevor and other hopefuls filled out employment applications, contingent upon passing the class, of course. At the end of the long day of swimming and learning rescue techniques, Trevor was pleased to find out that he had passed all the tests.

"Trevor Kinney! Come up here. I need to talk to you about your application," said the head lifeguard, staring at it. "This application says you're almost sixteen, but you are only in ninth grade. What's up with that? Have you failed a grade?"

"Oh, heck, no!" Trevor replied earnestly. "My parents wanted me to get a real-life education, so they took me out of school for a year, and we traveled all over the place. We even spent a month in Europe. When that year was over, I started back in the grade that I had missed while we were traveling."

"Oh, gotcha. That's actually pretty cool. Anyway, you did a great job today, and you're hired for ten hours a week on weekends at minimum wage. The job starts the first weekend in February. I'll email you your schedule for the coming weekend on Monday of each week. Congratulations."

Trevor went home that evening, exhausted, but daydreaming about the car in his future.

"I got the job, Mom! Ten hours on weekends, and they said I did great!" He texted Jaden to ask if it would be a good time to call. Jaden texted back "not really", so Trevor kept texting him instead and told him all about the class, and that he was hired.

Sunday, after church, Jaden asked his parents, "Can I join the YMCA?"

Donnie, pleased that Jaden was interested in something other than theater, said, "I don't see why not. Are you going to start working out? Or maybe play on one of the teams?"

"Actually, Dad, I want to swim. I want to be on the swim team in high school, and it would help me get better. Devon wants to be on the swim team, too," Jaden quickly added, knowing his dad likes Devon.

"All right, son, see how much it costs."

Jaden went to his room and excitedly texted Trevor. They texted back and forth for over an hour about the prospect of being able to see each other every weekend while Trevor was lifeguarding.

Chapter 13

Jenny heard some girls talking about softball one day at lunch. Curious, she sat down in an empty seat at their table, smiling shyly.

The one who seemed to be the leader, who Jenny recognized as a girl named Liz, rudely said, "What do you want?"

"I, uh, I heard you talking about softball, and I want to be on the team," Jenny said, taken aback by the girl's tone of voice.

"You don't look much like a softball player," she said critically, and continued with, "besides, we've all played on a traveling team together since we were ten. You can try out, but you probably won't make it. In fact, go to tryouts, so we can watch you *not* make it." Looking smugly at the other girls, Liz saw them snicker and nod in agreement.

Walking back to her own table, Jenny began to tear up a little. She could hear the girls at the other table laughing. Her friend Dena asked her what had happened.

"Why do they have to be so ugly to me? I haven't done anything to them. I just wanted to hear what they were saying about softball. I don't even know if I want to try out now." By then, the tears were brimming over.

Dena, hugging her, said, "Don't listen to those snobs. They think they're so great. Wait 'til they see how good you are! I know you'll make the team."

Trying to regain her composure, Jenny sniffled, "You're sweet to say that, but I'm probably not as good as they are. It's not like I've been on a traveling team." Dena continued to try to make her friend feel better.

"You're as good at softball as anyone else," she exclaimed. "You told me your brother has worked with you for years, and that's got to count for something!" Somewhat mollified, Jenny decided to talk to her dad about it.

At dinner, Jenny was so quiet that Donnie asked, "Jenny, is anything wrong?"

"Dad, do you think I'm a good softball player?"

"Of course you are, honey. What's the matter?"

"The girls at school have all played on a traveling softball team, and they said I'm not good enough to make the team."

Donnie fumed, "How dare they say that to you! Who do they think they are? They have no idea how well you play." Donnie was fired up. Brandon was irritated, too. He knew his little sister was good. He had worked hard with her. Even Jaden was angry. He thought he might have a word with them.

"Who are they, Jen?"

"I only know one girl's name. It's Liz. She's the one who was the meanest. You don't know her because she has a different lunch period."

Although sympathetic, Alice said, "Sweetie, how will you have time for softball anyway, with your play practice?"

"That won't be a problem, Mom. The high school gets to use the field first, and middle school doesn't get it until five o'clock. I'm through with play practice by then."

"Don't you think that play practice and softball practice all in the same day is a bit much?"

"Brandon doesn't get home from baseball practice until six or after. He still gets his homework done. I'd be home by then."

"Let her try it, Alice. If we see she's getting too tired or behind in schoolwork, we can put a stop to it then," Donnie reasoned.

"Yeah, Mom, please...my hard play practices are on Saturdays anyway."

"I'll think about it and talk more to your dad. We'll tell you in the morning. When are tryouts?"

"It's not a long season, Mom. Tryouts are in February, and the season is over the first week in April."

"We'll see, Jenny, we'll see."

The next morning, after being told it was okay to try out, Jenny and Jaden walked to school, each preoccupied with his own thoughts.

After walking a while, even though softball was foremost on her mind, Jenny wanted to know, "How is it going with you and Trevor? You haven't said much lately."

"It's going good. We talk and text a lot, and now that Dad said I can join the Y, I'll get to see him on weekends. He'll be lifeguarding there."

"So that's why you were so psyched about joining the YMCA. It makes sense now," she smiled.

"Yeah, it'll be great, but right now I'm still mad about those girls who were mean to you. If we see them before school, I want you to point them out. Do they always hang out together?"

She replied, "I don't know. Every time I see them, they're together, but that doesn't mean they're always together."

As if on cue, as soon as they stepped onto the school grounds, Jenny saw Liz with her little entourage right in tow.

"There they are right now." Jaden instantly broke away from Jenny, heading toward the girls. Jenny followed him, saying," Wait! What are you going to do?" Jaden was already there.

"I heard you've been giving my sister grief," Jaden began.

"What do you think you're going to do about it, you little fag?" sneered Liz. As soon as Jenny heard that, she stepped up and pushed Liz hard. Erica, seemingly second in command, rushed over and grabbed Jenny by the hair, pulling her away from Liz. Jaden really wanted to swing on Erica, but instead just pushed her. By then, Liz was enraged and heading toward Jenny with a raised fist. Luckily, some kids standing nearby heard the ruckus and began pulling everyone apart. Devon, who had just arrived at school, saw what was going on and ran over to them.

"Hey! Hey!" Devon was talking loud. "Do you guys want to get suspended? If a teacher sees this, you know you'll go home for at least three days. Just break it up, and everybody go their own way." Even as the combatants began to breathe slower and settle down, they continued to glare at each other menacingly. Eventually, the kids who were holding them back released their grip.

As Liz and her group started walking away, another of her pack, Janine, warned, "It's not worth getting suspended and then not being able to play softball, Liz." They continued to walk away out of earshot.

"What the heck?" Devon was all about wanting to know what started that confrontation.

Jaden, still angry, said, "They've been talking trash to Jenny. I was just going to tell them to shut up."

Jenny added, "Then they called Jaden a fag. I'm not letting anyone get away with calling my brother a fag." Devon grinned at her and nodded in complete agreement.

"I'm just glad no one got in trouble. School wouldn't be any fun without my bud, here."

As it turned out, one of the kids who had seen the whole episode reported what had happened to the assistant principal, Mr. Anthony, He called the girls in, one by one, to hear each of their stories. When he called Jenny in, she was petrified. She had never even had detention, much less been called to the office. Her insides were so shaky that she didn't know if she could speak. Mr. Anthony had a stern look, but his words belied his face. His voice was kind.

"Jenny, you're not in trouble, but we do have a problem." Jenny continued to look stricken. "No need to be so upset. From what I understand, there was a little pushing match on the campus this morning before school. Let me hear your side of it." Finally getting control of her emotions, Jenny spoke up.

"Mr. Anthony, I just want to play softball. Those girls have said horrible things to me, and then they called my brother a fag. I couldn't just stand there and let it be."

Mr. Anthony replied, "I can understand your feelings, Jenny, but we can't have physical violence on school grounds. Fortunately for all of you, no teacher witnessed any of it, so you won't be suspended. However, I seriously urge you to consider having respect for everyone, teachers and students alike."

"Oh, I do! I do, Mr. Anthony. I would never be mean to someone else. They were just so ugly to call my brother a fag."

"I realize that you felt that you were defending your brother, and name calling is very wrong, but there are ways to handle a situation other than fighting. All students at this school need to have respect and learn tolerance, and that's a primary goal of mine. The next time you feel that you're losing control, step back, take a breath, and walk away. Then report it to a teacher or to me. I can, and will, take care of anything that happens here at school. Lastly, I'd like you to consider joining the new after-school group called TEAM Club. Mrs. Cohen is just starting it up. It stands for Tolerance, Empathy, Acceptance, and Morality. You can learn how to deal with intolerance in a peaceful way and perhaps make a difference here on campus."

"Did you talk to Jaden about it, too?"

"I haven't talked to Jaden yet, but I certainly plan to bring it up."

As Jenny left the assistant principal's office, she thought about what he had said. Sitting back down at her desk in the classroom, she whispered to Dena, who was in the row next to her.

"Mr. Anthony called me in about the 'fight' this morning. I was so scared, but I didn't get in trouble. He told me to tell him or a teacher about things before they get started, but I don't think I can be a tattletale. He asked me to join the TEAM Club. Will you join with me?"

"That's enough talking, young lady," Mrs. Walker was glaring at Jenny. "Didn't you just get back from the principal's office?"

"Yes, ma'am, I'm sorry," said a red-faced and meek Jenny.

Sitting down by Jenny at lunch, Dena started in, "Boy! That was a close one in Mrs. Walker's class. She loves to give detention, and she'd have given it to both of us. Detention's not so bad, but she also calls your parents. I would get killed at home."

"Oh, wow. I didn't think of that. I hope Mr. Anthony doesn't call my house! I'd be grounded forever."

Chapter 14

When the twins got home after school, Alice was waiting for them, and she was not smiling.

"So, what happened at school today?" They had never seen their mother look so stern. "Brandon is in tenth grade, and you two are in seventh. In all these years, I have never had a school official call me. I just can't imagine the two of you fighting in the school yard, like hoodlums, as if you had never been taught respect for others." Starting to speak at the same time, Jaden gave way to Jenny.

"Mom, remember what I was telling you last night? About the girls who were mean to me? They're the ones who started it. They called Jaden a name."

Alice responded, "I don't care who started it, and I don't care if they called you a name, flipped you off, or anything else. You don't fight in school, or elsewhere for that matter. There are ways to handle things without fighting."

Jenny replied, "That's what Mr. Anthony said. He said I should join the TEAM Club at school to help me. TEAM stands for tolerance, empathy, acceptance, and morality."

Jaden piped up, "He told me that, too."

"That's probably a good idea, but in the meantime, go to your rooms and think about what you've done. I'm not waiting for your father to get home. You two are grounded for two weeks."

When Jaden got to his room, he quickly texted Trevor, fearing his phone would get taken away, too. Briefly, he told Trevor the details, and that he would text him again later if he could. Then he began to think of all the ramifications of being grounded, especially these two weeks.

With a low groan, he thought, I can't get Trevor a birthday present. And, I won't be able to go to the Y the day Trevor starts his job. Dad might even take my phone away. Geez, I hope that doesn't happen. That would be even more horrible. Jaden sat there and worried for almost an hour before starting his homework.

Jenny was feeling the same pinch in her room down the hall. Thank goodness softball tryouts aren't until February, she thought. But, I don't know what I'll do about play practice. Ms. Julia doesn't deal with missed practices so well. Why did I get into a stupid fight! What those girls said wasn't worth messing my life up for. I sure do wish I'd thought before I acted.

True to form, Donnie was angry, with good reason, when Alice told him what happened. He was surprised, though, when Alice told him she had already grounded them.

"Since when did you become the 'heavy' in this family?"

"Look, Donnie, I spend much more time with the kids than you do, except on weekends. I'm not blaming you, it's your job schedule. The children have been very little trouble growing up, but now that they're all teenagers, or almost, I need to step up and take the upper hand when something comes up. They need to know how I feel about things they do or are going through, not just how you feel about things." Donnie, taken aback by Alice's new-found confidence, stared at her for a moment, then went to the living room to read the newspaper.

Alice had been raised in a patriarchal family and had never seen her mom stand up to her dad. She had followed the same model in her own marriage. But, at the urging of her liberal neighbor, Alice had recently accompanied her to a women's lunch group on Tuesdays at the community center. Most of the women there seemed confident and were outspoken, and she had begun to look at her way of life a little differently since joining the group. The women often discussed controversial issues in the community, as well as problems within their families. Even beyond that, they talked about dreams they had growing up, as well as dreams they still had. Some spoke of accomplishing things that Alice had never even thought of, like building a house or learning to fly an airplane. There were a couple of women there that she particularly admired, because they always seemed to make their own decisions. One was divorced, and one was still single. Alice thought about how much easier it would be to decide things if you didn't have to worry about what your husband would think. On the other hand, she wouldn't want to have sole responsibility for some of the decisions Donnie made. This was somewhat confusing to her, and she gave it serious consideration.

Thinking about the strong women she had been exposed to in the last few weeks, Alice decided she had done the right thing in speaking up to Donnie. She had been nervous about what his reaction might be, but so far there had been little reaction at all. She was glad, because in her heart, she knew that she needed to support Jaden more when Donnie went on a rant. Until now she had gone along with whatever Donnie said, but Jaden would be a thirteen in a few weeks, and the trials of being a teenager were hard enough, even with parental support, much less without. She and Jenny had always been close, but Jaden was going to need her, too. Thankfully, she thought, Brandon and Donnie were strictly on the same wavelength all the time. But that was about to change.

Brandon was having a tough time at baseball practice. All his life he had been used to being a star, and it was rather humbling to be on second string. Coach Cushing gave him plenty of practice at third base, but when it came time to scrimmage, he was always on the second team. With the first game coming up soon, he knew in his heart that he would not get to play. He had never let up on his hustle, but his hitting had not shown varsity caliber yet. He knew it, and Coach Cushing knew it. He tried not to show his disappointment in his attitude, but he couldn't help being resentful that his dad had encouraged him to play varsity, instead of JV. He knew he would be playing every game on JV, instead of sitting the bench.

When the first game came around, everyone, as they had done many times in the past, packed into the car to go see Brandon play. Since it was a family event, the twins were allowed to go, even though they were still grounded. Devon could walk to the high school baseball field, so he said he'd meet Jaden there. High school sports were so exciting to Devon that he decided he could forgive Brandon's words at the play unless he continued on in that vein, and he hoped Brandon would let bygones be bygones, as well. Plus, Jaden had said he and his brother were getting along pretty well now. So here they all were, lined up on the bleachers, Donnie, Alice, Jenny, Jaden, and Devon, ready to watch Brandon play. Only thing was, Brandon didn't get to play. Not one minute. Even though the Mustangs had a substantial lead by the fifth inning, Coach Cushing made no substitutions.

Chapter 15

When their two weeks of confinement were over, the twins burst out into the world again, like butterflies from cocoons. They immediately went to join the TEAM Club and were determined to be model citizens. They vowed to each other to help other students, instead of fighting them. Being grounded really had made them think.

Jenny had profusely apologized to Ms. Julia for having to miss play practices and had sworn it would never happen again. In a moment of uncharacteristic kindness, Ms. Julia had agreed to let Jenny keep her part.

"You have a lot of catching up to do, Jenny," she said. "The show must go on, and we've already finished Act One and are halfway through Act Two. You're going to have to spend extra time to learn all you've missed." Jenny's heart had dropped when Ms. Julia said extra time, thinking she wouldn't get to play softball after all, but cheered up immediately when Ms. Julia had added she could catch up on Saturdays.

Finally, it was February and time for softball tryouts. There were the perfunctory papers to take home and the usual pep talk about everyone doing her best but not being discouraged if she didn't make the team.

Coach Tenney said, "There are twenty of you trying out, but only fourteen will make it. If you have a good arm or a good bat, I need to see it during the tryouts. I noticed most of you are seventh graders, so there's always next year if you don't make it. But nobody has an automatic spot, even returning eighth graders." After reminding the girls to bring back their paperwork, she urged the girls to get in a huddle and do a team cheer. "Girls, there's no 'I' in team, so 'all for one and one for all!'" They yelled enthusiastically, ready to get down to business the next day.

"I like that coach a lot," Jenny remarked walking across the playground with her friend, Barb. "She seems like she'll be fair, and I really liked what she said about being a team. Jaden and I joined the TEAM Club a week ago, and I'm really down with being fair."

"I hope you're right, Jen. I probably won't make it, because I've never played on an organized team, but I'll try my best."

"You'll do great, Barb! See you tomorrow. Don't forget your glove."

The next day was a beautiful day for February, and all the would-be players charged into the softball complex like Roman gladiators into the ring. They knew that by the end of tryouts, if it was thumbs up, they had made the team, but if it was thumbs down, well, they didn't want to think about that. Most of the girls had gotten there very early and watched the high school team practice. All that did was fuel the excitement even more.

Finally, Coach Tenney called the group together and explained, in detail, how the day would go. First, they had to warm up their arms. Barb and Jenny paired up and began to throw. But, they couldn't help but notice that the "travel team" players, about eight of them, had set themselves distinctly apart.

"Look at that, Barb. You can almost see a line separating us from them." Those players were already whipping the ball back and forth as the other twelve slowly lined up and began throwing. Several of the newcomers looked intimidated. Jenny, who by chance, wound up near Erica, tried to look nonchalant. Erica was throwing with Liz, and they both had really good arms.

Even doing the best she could, Barb still wasn't very accurate with her throwing. Jenny was jumping and reaching for the ball, but inevitably, a few of the throws were too far out of reach and had to be chased down.

Returning for the third time after chasing down the ball, Jenny was shocked to hear Erica say in a low voice, "Give it up, bitch! You two will never make the team. You're wasting the coach's time even looking at you." The girl next to Erica giggled and then, high-fived her.

Oh, great, Jenny thought to herself. Is it going to be like this the whole time? Wondering how to respond, Jenny decided the best course of action was to ignore the nasty comment.

After warming up their arms, the girls lined up for stretches. Batting followed. A pitching machine would do the work of a live pitcher, so every girl would be given ten good pitches to swing at. Everyone would be fielding the balls as they were hit. When Liz and her groupies were batting, lots of chatter was heard around the field.

"You can do it! Drive it!"

"Good swing!"

"You're the one!"

It seemed to do the trick. They were all pounding the ball into the outfield. The field was noticeably quieter when the outsiders' turns came up. However, when Jenny stepped up to the plate, the chatter started up again, but it was of a different nature this time.

"Let's see what this one can do."

"Not much, I bet."

"She swings like a washerwoman ... " Coach Tenney shot them a warning look. Hearing their taunts just made Jenny that much more determined. On her third pitch, she knocked it way over the left fielder's head.

"Just a lucky swing, let's see you do it again." The rest of her pitches she hit soundly, but none as good as her third. She left the plate feeling satisfied, if not great.

The girls finished batting, and it was on to base running. Coach Tenney wanted to see who had speed and who knew how to run bases well. Finally, the first day's tryouts were finished, and everyone gathered around the coach for the wrap-up. After telling them all how much she appreciated the effort displayed, Coach Tenney's demeanor and voice subtly changed.

"I've seen a lot of talent out here this afternoon, but I've also seen and heard some things that I'm not pleased about. We should all be encouraging each other, not trying to cut each other down. I don't want to hear any more derogatory comments aimed at anyone on the team. Go home and think about that this evening, and come back with a positive attitude tomorrow. Okay, huddle up for our team cheer!"

Jenny breathed a sigh of relief, but leaving the field she heard Erica say to Liz, "If she thinks I'm going to bow down to anyone, she has another think coming."

Liz responded, "We'll just have to turn the volume down so Coach can't hear. Don't think I'm going to let that little low-life think she's all that. When you say something, keep it low."

Chapter 16

During morning announcements Jaden and Jenny found out that the first TEAM Club meeting was going to be before school the following day. They were excited and curious to see what the club was all about. The next day, yawning and sleepy, they trudged to school, feeling like no other kids would be out and about that early.

"Wow, Jenny, look how many people are here." The number of kids in the room was really surprising. Keeping a low profile, they went to seats in the back of the room. Although many kids looked familiar, they didn't really know anybody there and were feeling a little shy. Looking around they saw black kids, Hispanic kids, and a girl in a wheelchair. They also saw two or three kids sitting all by themselves.

Jenny whispered, "Maybe we aren't the only ones here who don't know anybody."

At exactly seven-fifteen a teacher walked through the door. They knew it was a teacher, but she didn't exactly look like a teacher. She had on crazy oversized glasses that had every color in the rainbow on the frames. She obviously had a bright red wig on, because her hair looked ridiculous. She limped in using a cane, and everyone noticed her blouse was buttoned all wrong. Giggles were heard all over the room, which were met with a toothless grin from the teacher. After a few moments when the giggles had turned into boisterous laughter, the teacher took out her mouthpiece to show a row of even, white teeth.

"Being different is not a bad thing," she began. "Everyone had a good laugh, *with* me, not *at* me. In fact, think how boring life would be if everyone looked the same, acted the same, or spoke the same. Everyone has individual strengths and characteristics that make him who he is. Some of us are black, and some are white, tan, or brown. Many have difficulty learning or doing things that others find easy. Some of us wear glasses," she said, pointing to her weird glasses. "I don't really need glasses, but I like to be different. I *celebrate* being different. When you see someone new, look for the attributes that make him different. I'm sure many of you have encountered people who made you feel that if you're different, you're not accepted. They don't know who they are missing." She looked around the room as she spoke, trying to make eye contact with everyone, especially those sitting by themselves. Then she encouraged each student to turn to someone in the room and ask them what makes them different from the crowd. This was the first time that someone had asked them to describe what set them apart from others, instead of what they had to do to fit in. This was kind of cool. The meeting went on and before they knew it, it was time to go to class. Several of the loners walked out of the room in conversation with someone they hadn't known before.

"I'm so glad Mr. Anthony told us to join the TEAM Club. This is going to be fun! I can't wait to see what projects we do." Jenny talked all the way to first period. "What did you say about being different, Jay?"

"I said I wasn't like the rest of my family, because I don't like sports, and I like to cook. Oh, and that I am left-handed. What did you say?"

"I told my partner that I'm a twin."

The first weekend that Jaden was allowed to go swim at the Y was Trevor's third weekend to work. When he walked out of the changing room, his eyes immediately went to Trevor up on the lifeguard stand. He looked sort of small up there, but amazing nevertheless. Trevor watched Jaden walk toward him and gave him a huge smile, starting with his eyes and going down to fill his whole face. Jaden basked in the fact that this beautiful person was smiling at him, and staring into Trevor's eyes, smiled right back.

This is it! Jaden thought. This is what I've waited all this time for. I just wish Trev could be down here swimming with me. He began to do the backstroke in one direction and breaststroke in the other. That way he could keep his eyes on Trevor the whole way.

The time to go home came all too quickly. Jaden's parents had told him he could only stay two hours. Drying off, he asked Trevor when he would be working the next weekend. Jaden thought it would be great to be there toward the end of his shift, so that he could spend some time alone with him. Hammering out the details, they made a plan for the next Saturday.

"How was your swim, honey?" his mother greeted him.

"It was great, Mom! I can't wait to go again. I swam twenty-five laps today."

"Why, that's wonderful, Jaden. I'm so glad Miss Bonnie got you interested in swimming. It's really good for you, too."

"I know, Mom. I want to go every Saturday."

———

Softball tryouts were over, and the names of those who made the team had been posted on Coach Tenney's classroom door. Barb and Jenny had made a pact to meet at the lunchroom and then go over together to see the list. They couldn't get there fast enough. Jenny saw her name right away, and they both pored over the list several times, looking for Barb's. Trying to hide her disappointment, Barb congratulated Jenny.

Jenny responded, feeling a little awkward, "Why don't you ask Coach if you can be a manager or something else for the team?"

Barb brightened considerably, "That's a great idea, and if I watch, I can learn more about the game."

That afternoon Jenny called her mom and told her the good news, then walked to the field early with Barb. Spotting Coach Tenney, Barb anxiously asked her about being the manager.

"Yes, you certainly can. I'm sure you'll do a good job, because I saw how hard you worked at tryouts. If you keep at it, there's no doubt that you'll make the team next year. You really did do well, but some of the others have way more experience." That's for sure, Barb thought.

Continuing, Coach Tenney said, "Your job will be to make sure all the equipment is ready at the field and accounted for after practice and games. Also, you'll hang out near me, so I can ask you to do whatever is needed, as things come up."

"That shouldn't be a hard job, Coach. Thanks so much for finding a place for me." Walking back to tell Jenny, she thought, I can also be around to have Jenny's back if she has trouble with those girls.

When practice started and everyone was warming up their arms, it was unusually quiet, and as it went on, Jenny began to notice a lot of dirty looks coming her way from Liz and her friends.

Thinking it was probably going to be that way every day, Jenny continued to throw and catch. But by the end of practice, she had finally realized that Andrea, one of Liz's friends, was not at the field. *Now I know why I was getting the "stinkeye". Andrea got cut, and I didn't,* she thought.

Walking away from the field with Barb, she said, "I guess all those snobs are out to get me, but maybe I'll learn something at TEAM Club to help me deal with it."

By the end of the first week of practice, positions had pretty well been decided. Jenny was playing first base, Andrea's old position. The rest of the infield was made up of girls from the traveling team, and the anger aimed at Jenny was almost palpable. As they scooped up grounders and threw to first base, the throws were fired with venom, or just wide enough that Jenny really had to reach and stretch out to get them. Whenever she missed, a look of satisfaction went around the infield. Actually, though, they were making Jenny look good, because she caught almost everything thrown. It could have been just normal throwing, but Jenny didn't really think so. Barb told Jenny later that Coach Tenney had told her how good Jenny looked at first base. Jenny grinned with pride, although a bit self-consciously.

By the week of the first game, Liz, Erica, Steph, and Kathy had made it perfectly clear what they thought of their new first baseman. Despite her fielding and catching ability, they wanted Jenny gone and Andrea back. They took every chance they had to make that known by saying things under their breath, making bad throws, and ignoring Jenny. She responded by being cheerful on the outside, while being in agony inside.

When they took the field for the first game, Jenny was dismayed to see Andrea sitting in the bleachers right by first base. Since her team was in the third base dugout, she was the only who could hear Andrea's remarks.

"Hey, slut. So you think you can play first base, huh!" That was her opening remark, and it went downhill from there.

"Hey, big-shot! You think you're so cool, but you're nothing but a big old dyke."

When she started getting louder, "Yo! First base! That was you I saw on the corner last night ... " the first base umpire stopped the game, went over to the bleachers, and warned Andrea about her mouth. Another suggestive statement by her, and she would be out of the stands. Andrea didn't care. She had made her point and could see the distress on Jenny's face. She was also noticing that Jenny was dropping a throw or two during the game that she normally would have caught, no problem. Gleefully she saw Jenny strike out her first time up. It was the fourth inning before Jenny finally settled down and played well.

At the end of the game when Coach Tenney was evaluating the team's performance, she commented, "You seemed to be off your game a little, Jenny. Was it first-game jitters?" As Jenny just hung her head and said nothing, Liz and Erica, standing out of the coach's direct line of sight, smiled slyly.

After dinner, Jenny quietly asked Jaden, "What's a dyke?"

"I'm not sure, Jen, but I can try to find out." Instead of waiting to ask Miss Bonnie, he texted Trevor to see if he knew.

His reply was, "A dyke is slang for a lesbian who's more like a man than a woman."

She asked, "You don't think I'm like a man, do you Jay?"

"Not at all, Jenny. That girl was just trying to say crude things to get to you."

Chapter 17

At the next TEAM Club meeting, Mrs. Cohen said, "Today we're going to talk about discrimination and lack of tolerance. Can somebody give me an example of either? And, I would prefer it to be from your own experience, not something you've read in a book." The small girl in the wheelchair, Hannah, raised her hand right away.

"Lots of times when I go places, people either stare at me, or ignore me. They act like I'm not really a person, because I'm in a wheelchair."

"I know that must be awful for you, Hannah. Good example. Who else wants to share something?"

Chris said, "People make f-fun of me because I s-stutter. I can't h-help it."

"And I'll bet the harder you try, the worse your stuttering gets," said Mrs. Cohen sympathetically. Chris just nodded, his face red. "Who else? We all want to know how each of you feels. When we realize that everyone else could be privately going through a personal struggle, it helps us to know we're not alone. We all have problems that most people don't know about. Even if you don't know what someone else is going through, you can almost always assume that they have problems, too, and you can be more empathetic. Do you all know what empathy is?" Nods all around. Jenny raised her hand next.

"I'm on the softball team, and there are girls on it that say ugly things to me every day."

"What do you do, then?" asked Mrs. Cohen.

"I haven't been doing anything except trying to ignore them, but I have to admit, it isn't easy."

"All right, then. We have several situations to think about. You know, a lot of the loudest, most obnoxious people really have low self-esteem. They try to hide it by picking on others. Other people learn to be cruel, because someone has been cruel to them. Between now and next meeting, I want you to study someone who is rude or nasty to you, and see if you can come up with a reason they might be picking on you."

Alice continued to feel more empowered by being a part of her women's group. The idea of meeting other women for lunch once a week, going somewhere without Donnie's knowing it, and associating with women who seemed so different from herself, gave her a rush. Just being around those women made her feel more confident. And the discussions were relevant to the community, as well as to her own situation. At the last meeting they had discussed a Muslim family that had moved to town recently. Alice had made no comments, but many of the others had voiced opinions.

"It just makes me nervous, having that kind of people in our little town. We're a Christian community, and we don't need people like that to upset the applecart." Grace had been forthcoming with her remark to start the discussion.

"Now, Gracie, we need to welcome and get to know all our newcomers," Dorothy said in opposition.

Judy, siding with Grace, commented, " Personally, I think they have something to hide, wearing that cloth over their face! I've just never been comfortable with that."

"That's called a yashmak, Judy, and it's a symbol of religious expression, although some people think, oppression. They're not trying to conceal anything from people."

"I don't like their being here, either," Nancy expressed with some emotion. "There's something unnerving about those people. Look what happened to the Twin Towers."

Carol was quick to respond. "Let's keep this down and real. You know that family had nothing to do with the Twin Towers. They are Americans just like we are. They love their children and try to do what's best for them, just like we do. There are bad Muslims, just like there are bad Christians. You can't judge a person by where they come from or what religion they are."

Joanna sided with Carol, saying, "We're a group of women trying to improve our lives. Why should we discriminate against others who are trying to improve their lives, just because they're not like us? Don't we all want to be accepted? We should always maintain and exhibit tolerance."

The spirited conversation continued for a while, but finally, most seemed to get the point of tolerance for others. Alice went home impressed with what she had heard. She had never been one to point a suspicious finger at those who were different, but she had also never spoken up for someone she felt had needed defending. She began to wonder if keeping silent was the same as agreeing.

———————

After agonizing for days about a birthday present, Jaden had finally ordered a poster online for Trevor. Miss Bonnie had used her credit card to buy it, and he had paid her back out of his allowance. He had thought it would have already arrived, but it hadn't. It was a copy of one of the original playbills of the Broadway production of *Peter Pan*, and he could hardly wait to give it to him. He really hoped it would get there in time.

When the Saturday following Trevor's birthday finally arrived, as had his present, Jaden rushed to the pool to give it to him. Trevor still had an hour of work left, so Jaden jumped in the pool and started swimming laps. He had to do something to work off his excitement. He was eager to give Trevor the gift, but he could hardly wait for Trevor's shift to be over for another reason. The night before when Jaden texted Trevor that he was going to give him his birthday present at the pool, Trevor had texted him back that he had a surprise for him, as well. Jaden had spent several sleepless hours wondering what it could be. Trevor wouldn't even give him a hint.

The time seemed to inch by, but finally he saw Trevor climb down from the lifeguard chair.

Drying off quickly, Jaden said, "I have your present in my locker."

Trevor replied, "Let's get dressed, and I'll show you your surprise first." Shyly glancing at each other's bodies, they got dressed, and Jaden tucked Trevor's present under his arm. Walking out the door the first thing Jaden saw was Trevor's mom's car. Jaden looked at Trevor confused. Trevor just smiled broadly, grabbed his arm, and led him to the empty car.

"Mom said I could take her car to work today! Now we can drive around for an hour and be together!" Jaden's heart soared! As soon as they got in the car, Jaden produced his present to Trevor. After opening the gift, Trevor grinned from ear to ear and seemed truly touched. He leaned over to give Jaden a kiss.

After getting ice cream, cruising both schools, and sitting at the park for a few minutes, Trevor said, "I guess I'd better get you home. You shouldn't be late."

When Jaden walked in the door, Alice raised her eyebrows and inquired, "I heard a car; who drove you home?"

"Just a friend, Mom. He's sixteen."

"Who is this friend?" Reluctantly, he told her it was Trevor.

"Please don't tell Dad. He doesn't like Trevor, for some reason."

"I suppose it doesn't matter, since it was only from the Y to here." Feeling guilty, Jaden nodded.

Nervous and exhilarated at the same time, Jaden went to his room. He wanted to think. In the park he and Trevor had engaged in fifteen minutes of holding hands, looking into each other's eyes, and shyly kissing a couple of times. Jaden couldn't think of when he had ever felt so alive, remembering the tingles all up and down his body. Thinking about their first kiss, and about kissing today, he decided he really must be gay. He wished he didn't have to deceive his mom or feel so guilty about something that seemed so natural and right.

Since the next day was Sunday, after church Jaden decided to walk over to see Miss Bonnie. It had been a few weeks since he had talked to her, and he wanted to fill her in on what had been happening. She hadn't even heard about the fight at school and being grounded. By the time he got her caught up in general, she was shaking her head.

"Lordy me, Jaden. You have been going through some stuff! And that Jenny! She sure showed some spirit, jumping right into it like that! What next?"

"Well, there is a next," Jaden began. "Yesterday I rode around with Trevor in his mom's car, and we went to the park and made out."

"Oh, my," said Miss Bonnie. "How do you feel about that?"

"It was perfect, Miss Bonnie. Except I feel so guilty..."

"Do you feel like what you did was wrong?"

"No...yes...maybe. I just don't really know. I know I didn't tell my mom everywhere we went or, for sure, everything we did. Only that Trevor brought me home from the Y. I do feel bad about that. I really don't like to be deceitful, but I don't think she'd approve, and I *know* my dad wouldn't."

"It's awful to have to hide things from our parents and friends, isn't it? It makes you feel you're all alone in the world. Maybe one of these days, you'll feel safe talking about it with your family. I hope so."

Chapter 18

As the softball season progressed, Jenny kept the insults and jibes from Liz's group to herself. Barb was aware of what was going on, but Jenny had made her promise not to tell Coach Tenney. The girls had gotten much slyer about their taunts, and they were flying completely under Coach Tenney's radar. She was oblivious. Barb knew Jenny was miserable and felt powerless to help her friend. She so wanted to get in the faces of those bitches, but knew Coach Tenney had an eagle eye for things like that and would be on to her. She also wanted Jenny to tell on those girls, but Jenny insisted she wasn't going to rat them out and give them more ammunition to use against her. Jenny was thirteen now, and felt she should be able to handle things on her own. She could tough it out.

In the meantime, she was asking people if anyone knew those girls or anything about them, as Mrs. Cohen had assigned. So far she had gotten nowhere, but at least she was trying. By the last game, things had not improved one bit. Jenny thought to herself that at least she had made it through the season with nothing serious happening. It had been hard, but she had not given in. The last game had been played against the best team in the district, and that team had beaten them unmercifully. After Coach Tenney had made her closing remarks to the team, Jenny said she was going to walk on home and not stay while Barb finished rounding up all the equipment. She was down about the loss and didn't feel like talking. As she walked out of the field gate, suddenly, there was Liz standing in front of her.

I'm not in the mood for this, she thought. After a moment she realized all the other girls were moving in close around her, even Andrea, who seemed to have come from nowhere. She tried to change her direction, but the ominous circle moved in closer, blocking her way.

"What do you want?" Jenny tried to sound unafraid as she glanced around looking for a way out.

At the next TEAM Club meeting, Mrs. Cohen started the meeting off by asking, "Did any of you find out anything meaningful about your tormentors?"

Hannah raised her hand and said, "I haven't found anything out, because I never know who will be next to ignore me. But, I talked to my mom about it, and she suggested I use a sense of humor. The next time it happened, I said, 'Hellooo. I'm down *here*. Can you see me?' The person smiled at me and apologized. I couldn't believe how easy it was to get someone's attention. I'm still not getting picked for groups in my classes, but at least people know I'm here. I've found my voice."

"That's wonderful, Hannah. What a great start! I know it will continue to get better. How about you, Chris? Have you made any headway with your stuttering?"

"No, ma'am," he lowered his eyes. "E-every time I t-t-try to say something, it g-gets w-w-worse."

"I know that must be very frustrating for you. There are ways to help stuttering, though. How would you feel if I referred you to the speech therapist who comes to our school?"

"Yeah, okay." He grimaced at the thought, but nodded.

"Jenny, how did things go for you?"

"Mrs. Cohen, I tried my best to find out stuff about those girls, but no one seemed to know anything. So I just kept ignoring them. But after the last game, they all stood around me in a menacing way, and wouldn't let me go home."

"Where was your coach?" Mrs. Cohen asked, with concern.

"She was still in the dugout and couldn't hear what they were saying. They started telling me it was all my fault we lost, that I did a horrible job at first base, that I'm a jerk, and then started calling me bad names. I was scared. It was six against one, and then Liz pushed me."

"What happened then?" By now the whole room wanted to know.

Jaden, alarmed, said, "Jenny, you never told me about that."

"I didn't want us to get in another fight." Continuing her story, Jenny said, "I was determined not to fight back, but I was really afraid they might all attack me. I said, 'Liz, it looks like you have a team surrounding me. Too bad we all couldn't have been a team on the field.' Liz looked at me funny. Then, I told her, 'I'm sorry Andrea didn't make the team, but I'm not the one who picked the team. The purpose of a team is to teach us all to get along. It seems that never happened this year, but I'm playing again next year, and maybe it will then.' Liz looked at the others and said, 'Let's get the hell out of here. We don't need to stay here and listen to her preach.' Then they left. I was really surprised they didn't fight me, but I guess Mr. Anthony was right that violence isn't the answer."

"What a great outcome!" exclaimed Mrs. Cohen. "I'm so proud of you. You took the high road, even though it was the hard road. I think we can all learn something from this."

As the baseball season progressed through the spring, game after game Brandon never took the field. He was miserable just watching, but didn't show it. Finally, in the last game of the season, he was put in at third base in the eighth inning. He only had one ball hit to him, which he scooped up and threw to first for the out. He didn't have to bat, so all in all, he did a good job. Instead of being glad that Brandon played two innings, Donnie was seething. By the time the last out was made, he was up and heading toward the dugout. He would tell this coach a thing or two. Walking in the gate leading to the field, Donnie got in the coach's face.

"What the hell kind of coach are you?" Startled, Coach Cushing took a step back. Aggressively, Donnie continued, "How do you expect the younger players to get any better if they don't get any playing time? You have a lot of seniors graduating this year, and now the second string has no experience. You could have at least put Brandon in a few innings throughout the season. He's a good player. He needs to face this kind of competition. But, no, you had to humiliate him by making him ride the pine all year and then, in the last game, put him in for two measly innings. You're a poor excuse for a coach." Brandon, who had walked up and heard most of the conversation, was mortified and wished he could disappear.

"Dad! Dad! What are you saying? You shouldn't talk to Coach like that!" Thoroughly embarrassed, he quickly turned to go sit in the dugout. Coach Cushing had patiently waited for Donnie's rampage to subside, and now he was speaking.

"Look, Mr. Hansen, I'm the coach, and you're the parent. I'm sorry you're so upset about your son's playing time, but he got plenty of practice every day for the job he'll do next year. I'm not going to take scholarship-potential seniors out of games when recruiters are watching. I'll do likewise for your son his senior year. He's learned a lot this year, including character and respect, which you don't seem to have. It's hard to be second string, but Brandon did it with dignity and good sportsmanship. Now, if you'll excuse me, I need to talk to the players." Red-faced, Donnie sputtered a second, then turned and stomped away.

On the way home from the game the ride was silent, and the tension could be cut with a knife. Alice wasn't sure what had transpired, but she didn't think it was good. Brandon and Donnie both looked very upset. Brandon was thinking that this season's fiasco was all his dad's fault. He had wanted to play JV, but was pushed to play varsity when he wasn't ready. The scowl on his face was enough to keep the younger ones quiet.

He did venture to say, in a surly tone of voice, "Dad, how could you have talked to Coach like that in front of everyone? Now I won't be able to face my teammates. Thanks a lot…"

"I was just trying to make a point, Brandon, to defend your playing abilities. I know you've been pretty unhappy all season." Brandon took the opening to voice what he had been thinking about.

"You're damn right I was unhappy! I would have been perfectly happy being on JV again this year. At least I would have been able to play!" He spoke harshly. So that's what the deal was about, thought Alice. Oh, brother.

Donnie didn't speak another word on the way home, still agitated about the incident. But now his feelings were compounded by the fact that he and Brandon had had their first major disagreement. His boy, his ballplayer, his first born, was mad at him. His and Brandon's interests had always been the same. His own major focus in school had been sports. They had always had that connection, almost like buddies, instead of father and son. Donnie wasn't quite sure how to handle this situation.

Chapter 19

The school year was quickly coming to a close, and everyone was excited about the summer. Jaden continued to see Trevor on Saturdays at the Y, and on the rare occasion that Trevor had his mom's car, they would ride around a little. He was sort of glad it wasn't every week, because he always felt guilty, which detracted from the excitement of being with Trevor.

Donnie had decided as soon as school was out to take the family on a week's camping trip in the mountains where it would be cool. They had never been camping, but Donnie had grown up camping with his family, so he knew the ins and outs. His announcement was met with mixed responses.

From the twins, "Oh, boy! That sounds like fun. Will we get to hike and cook out and see wild animals?"

From Brandon, sarcastically, "Oh, great. I get to spend a week stuck in a tent with my whole family. There had better be some electricity."

Alice was quiet for a minute, thinking that this might be another chance to experience something new, to grow and become more assertive in her own life.

"That's an interesting idea, Donnie. I think it'll be good for all of us."

"I just can't imagine a whole seven days in the wild, in a tent, with my family." Brandon was complaining later to his friend Chad. "A week is an eternity. I'll take my iPod, but I won't have anything else to do. A whole week..." he moaned.

"Hey, maybe you can stay at my house. I'm sure my parents wouldn't mind." Chad and Brandon had gotten pretty close after baseball season. He was one of the few kids like Brandon, both an athlete and a computer geek.

"Wow! That would rock! I'll ask my dad tonight."

"No, absolutely not!" said Donnie in response to Brandon's query. Donnie had been secretly thinking that the camping trip would be a chance for Brandon and him to bond again. He was still smarting after the baseball incident. Brandon's previously hopeful face immediately turned into a sulk.

"Fine. Just don't expect me to join in any stupid family activities or campfires. This really sucks!" The way he said the word campfires, would make one think they were pure torture. He went in his room and despondently texted Chad with the bad news. Donnie, in the living room, just shook his head.

"What happened to the boy I used to have who loved doing everything with me? Who is this monster who replaced him?" Donnie was upset again, even though he still had some hope that things would change once they were all in the wilderness together.

The next weekend Donnie went to the outdoor store to rent some camping equipment. Looking around, the first thing he saw were different size tents erected on the floor. Peering inside the first one, he saw sleeping bags that were royal blue, bright red, forest green, and camo. Wow, he thought, accessories have really changed since I was a kid. I'd love to buy some of this stuff. As high as his hopes were, though, there was still the reality of the fact that his family might hate camping, so he'd better rent instead. He figured if it turned out successfully, he could always purchase stuff later. He came out laden with a two-room tent, five sleeping bags, a lantern, a Coleman stove, and a cook kit. As he unloaded everything at home, at least the twins were excited.

"Can I have the blue sleeping bag?"

"I want the green one!"

"Look, a stove. Where's the refrigerator?"

"Are there any stores close by?"

"Are we going to see bears?" Donnie's spirits buoyed with their enthusiasm, and he explained they would use an ice chest for a refrigerator, and he hoped there would be no bears.

They would leave for the camping trip the next Friday after work, so there was still plenty of time to get things together and organized. Since Alice was a neophyte, like the kids, Donnie knew he would be left to attend to many of the details. Throughout the week when he got home from work, he would get plastic bins and assemble things like eating utensils, paper plates, spices, paper towels, and toilet paper. He wanted to leave nothing to chance, because he wanted this trip to be a good one. He went to the hardware store and bought a tarp and some rope. Rain, rain, stay away, but they were ready for it. The last thing he threw in were five bag chairs, so no one would have to sit on the ground.

Donnie took off from work at noon on Friday, because the campground was three and a half hours away, and he wanted to get everything set up before dark.

"Don't forget your pillows, a towel, and extra clothes," he reminded the family before they left. Stopping at a gas station when they were almost there, Donnie bought enough ice to fill one of the two coolers he had brought. They had plenty of dry food and canned food, but he stopped at a market to buy hamburger, hot dogs, and bacon. He put those supplies in the other cooler and covered them with ice. They should be ready for anything now.

Chapter 20

The campground was simple, but beautiful. All the sites were big and wooded with towering oaks, slender pines, and wild fern. Wildflowers peeked at them from behind patches of deer moss. Each site had a picnic table, and the campground had bathrooms and open-air showers. There was a wall around them, but at night a starlit sky illuminated late-night bathers. Although Alice was somewhat apprehensive about the whole experience, she was delighted with the surroundings. There were a few other campers at other sites, but it wasn't the least bit crowded.

"Oh, brother," was all Brandon could muster up, rolling his eyes. Jenny and Jaden could hardly wait to get out and explore. There were so many things to see.

"Don't anybody go anywhere yet," Donnie commanded. "We all have certain things to do to set up camp. Brandon, I want you to help me set up the tent." Brandon rolled his eyes again and sighed, but didn't say anything. "I want the rest of you to go look for firewood." He took time to explain what types of limbs, twigs, and logs to look for, and sent them off. "Brandon, this tent will be pretty easy, because it's mostly shock poles. But the second room can sometimes be a bear, so having two people for setup is helpful."

Brandon muttered, "Shock poles. Whatever." Donnie chose to overlook his statement and proceeded to show him how to put the corded poles together. Brandon stood there, barely paying attention, saying, "Yeah, yeah. I get it. Doesn't take a rocket scientist." Under his breath he said, "So this is my version of hell for a week…" After Donnie had un-bagged the tent and laid it out on the ground, Brandon was still standing there, doing nothing.

"Didn't I tell you to put the poles together? You should have had that done by the time I got the tent unrolled." Donnie was getting irritated. Brandon's next words didn't do anything to help the matter.

"I only came here because you made me. I hate it, and I don't want to put the freaking tent up." He turned his back and started to walk away. That did it for Donnie.

"You better stop right where you are, Brandon Alan Hansen! Everyone has a job, and yours is to help with the tent. I don't care if you like it or not. This is the way it is. And you better start straightening up your attitude if you expect to get your driver's license next month when you turn sixteen. No one in my house is going to drive with an attitude like that."

Brandon turned back and said, "Have it your way. You always do." But he did start putting the tent poles together.

When Alice and the younger kids returned with a wagon full of firewood (Jaden had seen a wagon and asked if they could borrow it for a while), Alice saw that the tent was up, but felt tension in the air. Donnie was hanging the tarp over the "kitchen" area, but Brandon was sitting in his chair with his arms crossed and his legs straight out, staring into the distance. He had ear-buds stuck in his ears. Even Jenny could read his posture and looked inquisitively at her mom. Alice walked over to Donnie with a questioning look, but he looked away and kept on with what he was doing. She helped the kids unload the wood, and Jaden offered to take the wagon back to its owner. Alice and Jenny were stacking wood near the fire pit when Jaden left.

When they were borrowing the wagon from the nice man at another campsite, Jaden had noticed another kid, about his age, doing something behind his tent with his parents. He thought he would give the wagon back and maybe make a friend. After all, they were going to be here a week! When he got back to the other campsite, the man was nowhere in sight, but there was a younger boy that Jaden hadn't seen earlier. When Jaden asked about the older boy, the younger boy, who said his name was Trent, yelled, "Taylor! Come over here. There's a guy who wants to meet you."

"Hi, I'm Jaden. Where are you from?"

Taylor said, "We live in Innis."

"Where the heck is that?"

"It's about two hours south of here, near the state line."

"Oh, yeah, yeah. I think I saw the sign on the way up here. We live farther away than that. What grade are you in?"

"I just got out of eighth. I go to high school next year," he said proudly.

Jaden replied, "Lucky you. I just got out of seventh. I can't wait until I get in high school!" Changing the subject, he asked, "Have you camped here before? Are there good hiking trails? What else do you do here?"

Taylor thought a minute and said, "You can swim in the lake if you like cold water. It's not for me. There are some cool trails, though. Want to go hiking tomorrow?"

"Sure, I'd love to, but for now, I'd better get back to camp to see if I need to do anything else to help set up."

"Okay, see ya."

Walking back to camp Jaden thought Taylor seemed pretty nice and might be fun to hang out with. He knew his dad had some activities planned, but surely they wouldn't take all day every day. When he got back to his own site, he saw Jenny carrying things from the SUV to put on the picnic table under the tarp. Donnie had found a place to hang the lantern and was standing back, admiring his handiwork.

"What do you need me to do, Dad?"

"We need to hang a garbage bag out of reach of all the critters, and then I'll show you kids how to build a campfire that we'll light after dinner. Honey, do you want to heat up the beanie-weenies on the camp stove? I thought we'd eat simple tonight since we just got here and dinner's off to a late start."

"Yay! We're going to build a fire!" The twins were excited. Brandon either didn't hear what Donnie said because of his ear-buds, or else he acted like he didn't hear. At any rate, he didn't move.

"Brandon, are you going to get over here?" Donnie spoke evenly.

"Wouldn't want to miss building a campfire," Brandon muttered. He knew he was pushing the limits with his dad, so he slowly ambled over. Donnie wadded up a piece of a paper grocery bag and threw it into the middle of the fire pit.

"We're going to use that for tinder. Tinder is something that will light and burn easily. Next we're going to build a small tee-pee over it with tiny, tiny twigs, like this one." He showed it to them, and Jenny was first to gather up a handful.

"Can I build the tee-pee, Dad?" Jenny found it difficult to get the twigs to stand up, but her technique improved after Donnie gave her some helpful tips. Finally, all were standing, if precariously.

"All right, good job!" Donnie praised her. "Now, we're going to build a bigger tee-pee around that one, and then, another bigger one around the next one. Jaden, you build the next one, and Brandon, I want you to build the last layer." Jaden gathered up some bigger pieces of wood and started his tee-pee, immediately knocking over the first one.

"Can't you do anything right, Dweeb?" said Brandon, still totally annoyed and ready for someone else to be criticized.

Donnie, irritated with Brandon all over again, said, "Don't you have anything nice to say to anyone?" Jenny jumped in nervously and began rebuilding her tee-pee.

"Don't worry, Jaden, I messed up the first few times, too. It's hard getting the limbs to stand up." Jaden smiled at Jenny, feeling better. But, he tried again and again, always knocking down Jenny's tee-pee. Finally, he just threw his sticks down and walked toward the tent.

As he passed Brandon, he heard him whisper, "Loser…" Jaden hesitated, and then kept on walking.

"When is that boy ever going to learn to do something useful?" Donnie was talking to no one in particular.

Jenny quickly defended Jaden saying, "That's not fair, Dad, Jaden can cook really good. That's useful."

Not responding, Donnie told Brandon, "Okay, I guess it's up to you to put on the kindling, as well as the fuel logs."

"Sure, Dad. Leave it to me do *everything.*"

"That's enough, Brandon. I warned you."

Alice, seeing what was happening, called out to Jaden before he went into the tent.

"I need you over here, Jaden. I want to show you how to light this stove, so you can help me cook."

When he was beside his mother, he said, "It's no use, Mom. Dad and Brandon will never like me. I can't do anything right. I'm just worthless." Nothing Alice could say could cheer him up, and he went back to the tent. Inside, he started crying, but at least the others couldn't see him. Suddenly, a thought popped into his head. He would text Trevor. Trevor could always raise his spirits. Getting out his phone, he was thwarted once again. No bars…no signal. Jaden lay there on his sleeping bag, upset and discouraged. *Why was I even born? What good am I? Sometimes…..I wish I was dead.*

The fire was finally finished, but not lit. Donnie explained they would start it after dinner. Alice went to get Jaden for dinner and found him sleeping on his sleeping bag, tears dried on his cheeks. She decided not to disturb him.

At the table, Donnie asked, "Why isn't Jaden eating?"

"He's already gone to sleep, and it's getting dark, so I just thought I would let him sleep through the night." Donnie frowned, but kept his feelings to himself. So far, this trip was a disaster.

There wasn't much talk around the table. Donnie was irritated, Alice was thoughtful, Jenny was nervous about the tension, and Brandon, well, Brandon was Brandon. He didn't talk much at the table, even at home. He was beyond all that "family stuff". He couldn't wait until this trip was over, but he knew he had to watch himself, because he wanted his driver's license!

After dinner, Donnie announced that Brandon would clear the table and wash up the bowls and forks, and of course, the beanie-weenie pan, because all he had done so far was put together some tent poles. When the others left the table to go to the fire pit, Brandon began slinging around silverware and swearing under his breath. He was beside himself! Couldn't his dad just leave him alone in this stinking place? It was enough that he even came. He would be sixteen soon, and the next two years couldn't come soon enough. He would be out of the house so fast that they wouldn't know what hit them.

Setting up the chairs around the fire pit, Donnie said, "If we've done a good job building the fire, one match will start it."

Tension forgotten, Jenny said, "Let's see, Dad, let's see." Poof! The paper lit and within seconds, the little twigs in the smallest tee-pee started to burn.

"Cool!" Jenny sat beside the fire and fed it more twigs until the kindling flared up. It was a done deal then. In ten minutes the fire was beginning to roar.

Donnie offered a suggestion, "You should always have two or three logs lying near the fire, so they'll already be warm when you throw them in." He had learned to be quite the woodsman growing up. As the temperature dropped, the fire grew.

After a short while, Alice gratefully said, "This fire feels wonderful. I was getting a little chilly. Wonder how cold it will get in the night?"

"Our sleeping bags go down to forty degrees. No way it'll get that cold in June, even in the mountains."

When Brandon finished cleaning up, he slouched down in his chair, but made sure it was not near the others. As the night wore on, though, he dragged his chair closer and closer to the fire for warmth. He would never admit it to anyone, but he thought the fire was all right as he stared into it. Conversation ceased as everyone got comfy, and each was lost in his own thoughts.

Temper calmed by the flames, Donnie took stock. He was extremely disappointed. He had hoped Brandon might enjoy being out and doing new things, and together, they could hike and build fires, and be close, just like it used to be. He had brought a football to toss and some games they could play in friendly competition. Maybe it would be better tomorrow, but it certainly hadn't been a good start.

Sitting next to her husband, Alice wondered when she might be able to talk to Donnie to find out what was going on between him and Brandon. She had heard some of Brandon's remarks, but wanted to know what started it. Usually, the two of them talked in bed, but that wouldn't happen here, with all the kids just a sheet of nylon away. She wanted to talk to him about Jaden, too. She knew her younger son always felt inadequate around the others, and now he was getting so down. He needed encouragement from Donnie, as well as from herself.

As the fire began to die down, the family started getting ready for bed. Except Brandon. He had stubbornly decided to sleep in his chair by the fire. He didn't want to get in that tent with four members of his family! That was for little kids. He retrieved his sleeping bag and wrapped up in it, throwing another log on the fire as his parents went inside. Donnie just shook his head and let out a deep breath.

Chapter 21

The next day dawned clear and chilly. It would stay that way until the sun rose above the trees. Emerging from the tent Donnie saw Brandon on the ground, curled in a tight ball, in his sleeping bag near the fire pit. He assumed it was Brandon because nothing was visible outside of the bag. The fire was dead, providing not one iota of warmth. Donnie stirred it around, found some hot coals deep down, and added more wood. By the time everyone else stumbled from the tent, the smell of coffee was wafting through the site, and he had bacon frying and pancake batter ready to go. Donnie was determined this would be a good day.

"How did everyone sleep?" asked Donnie. Brandon had stayed awake long into the night. He was tired and had not slept well, but the aroma of bacon sizzling couldn't be ignored, and he grudgingly got up and sat at the table. Donnie made pancake after pancake, and after consuming a hearty breakfast, the family was ready to meet the day.

"What are we going to do today?" said Jenny.

"First, you and Jaden are in charge of cleaning up, while Brandon and I throw the football. Then, you can explore, hike, or do whatever you want for a while. This afternoon we're going to have some friendly competition. I brought the cornhole game for us to play."

Thank goodness, Jaden thought. Even I can throw a beanbag. And Taylor and I will go on a great hike. He was rested and ready for a fresh start to camping.

Brandon got up reluctantly to throw the football, but deep down, he was ready for some action and glad to do it. He wouldn't let on to Donnie, though. No way was he going to let his dad know that he thought any of this camping crap was fun. When Jaden was through with his part of cleanup, he got his phone and headed over to Taylor and Trent's tent. Even if he had no signal, he could take some nice pictures to show Trevor. Taylor was ready, with a water bottle strapped to his waist.

"Oh, no," Jaden lamented. "I didn't think to bring anything to drink."

"No problem. I have another holster and water bottle you can use." After setting him up, he continued, "There's a great trail going up the mountain that starts over there," he said, pointing in the distance.

"Let's get going!"

"I want to go, too," was Trent's plaintive cry.

"You can go with us, tomorrow, when the hike won't be so rugged. I promise!"

Taylor and Jaden started out heading for the trail. When they got there, Jaden could see the first part went up gradually, but higher he could see rocks that they would have to maneuver over or around. This looked like fun, and he really hoped he could do it. When they had hiked up to the first set of rocks, Jaden found he was higher than he expected. He got his phone out to take a picture, and what do you know, he had a signal. He took a picture and then eagerly texted Trevor. He wanted to let him know why he hadn't texted him yet.

Taylor, watching, asked when Jaden was finished, "Who is that, your girlfriend?"

Taken aback momentarily, Jaden hesitantly said, "Yeah. Yeah, it is."

"I need to text my girlfriend, too. She really gets upset if she doesn't know where I am and what I'm doing every minute. I told her I only had bars when I was up high. I've been climbing up here every day. What's your girlfriend's name?"

Thinking quickly, Jaden said, "It's Tracy, but we call her T for short. What's your girlfriend's name?"

"Her name is Michelle." With that, he started climbing on the next rock. When they got to a plateau, looking out, the view was gorgeous. They could see several different colors of mountain wildflowers, gently sloping meadows, and the starkness above the tree line of the adjacent mountain.

I wish I had a way to carry a bunch of these flowers back to camp, Jaden thought. They would look so nice on the table. I know Mom would love them.

He took his phone out to take another picture and saw that Trevor had responded. The text read that Trevor was so glad to hear from him and that he missed him terribly.

Smiling to himself, Jaden offered, "She's already texted me back. She misses me." Taylor was busy texting Michelle.

When he finished texting, Taylor asked Jaden if he knew why the trees stopped part way up the mountain. He explained that at a certain altitude, trees couldn't grow because it was too cold, or they couldn't get enough water. In the west, the tree line falls around ten thousand to twelve thousand feet, but it's lower in the east.

"That mountain over there just doesn't get enough water to grow trees above five thousand feet.

"Awesome, man! How do you know all that?"

"My family spends a lot of time in the mountains, so I just find stuff out."

"How long have we been gone, Taylor?"

"Yikes, it's one-thirty. We better head back." Going down was easier than going up, but they still had to be careful, because one slippery rock could send them sliding down a rough path.

"Come over and meet my family," invited Jaden, when they got to the bottom.

"Sweet," said Taylor. "Just let me check in with my dad, and I'll walk over."

Taylor showed up just as the Hansen family sat down to eat sandwiches.

Jaden jumped up to introduce him, and Alice said, "Sit down with us, Taylor, and have a sandwich. Sounds like you and Jaden worked off some energy today."

"Thank you, Mrs. Hansen. I am pretty hungry." There was a choice of peanut butter and jelly or tuna. He opted for pb & j and began chowing down with the rest of the group.

"I'm glad you're here, Taylor," said Donnie. "After lunch we're going to have some friendly competition playing cornhole, and with you here, the teams will be even.

When lunch was over, Donnie walked off the distance between the cornhole boards and then started explaining the game to Taylor.

"It's a lot like horseshoes, but you try to get the bag in the hole. Each member of a team stands at opposite ends. You get some points even if it doesn't go in, if it's closer to the hole than the competition's. The first teams to compete will be Brandon and Jenny against Taylor and me. We'll play to twenty-one points then, Mom and Jaden will play the winner. The final winner doesn't have to cook or clean up tonight."

Getting in position beside Taylor, Brandon thought, I'm golden. Jenny will be good, and of course, I'm awesome! No chores tonight! Taylor and Brandon threw first, but all the bags slid off the slanted box. Then Donnie threw and got the first one in.

"Shit," said Brandon under his breath. "If Dad beats me, I'll never hear the end of it." Louder he said, "Come on, Jenny! You can do it!" Jenny managed to throw a bag that hung on to the top of the box for a point.

When it was Taylor and Brandon's turn again, Jenny encouraged, "Get it in the hole, Brandon."

Smirking, Brandon whispered to Taylor, "Watch this!" He tossed his first, and plop, into the hole. Fist pumping, Brandon was yelling, "Yeah!" Back and forth, it was a close battle, but in the end, Taylor and Donnie won. Sulking, Brandon sat in his chair.

When the next game started, unexpectedly Brandon cheered for Jaden, as he and Alice started their game.

"Come on, Jaden, buddy. You've got a good arm. Sink it." He didn't want his dad to win again! Jaden actually had a pretty good underhand toss and rallied to the task. He got both his beanbags to stay on the box. Flushed with success, seemingly for the first time ever, Jaden blossomed under Brandon's encouragement. He actually got several in the hole, and Alice was no slouch either. Brandon's encouraging remarks to Jaden seemed to goad Donnie who did worse and worse. Jaden and Alice tromped on Donnie and Taylor. While Jenny was congratulating Jaden after the match, Brandon and Taylor struck up a conversation. Taylor told him about their hike today, and Brandon expressed interest in going the next day.

Jaden was walking with his head high after the game. Not only had he won something but, his brother had spurred him on. His feet barely touched the ground. He gave his mom a big hug. Alice was so pleased to see this Jaden, one who didn't seem so downtrodden. Joining in the conversation with Brandon and Taylor, Jaden called Jenny to come over, too.

The three boys were making plans for tomorrow's hike, and Jaden said, "You should come along, too, Jenny. It's so beautiful when you get over the rocks. Look at this picture!" Never a slacker, Jenny didn't have to be persuaded, thinking the picture was gorgeous, spectacular even.

It was up to Donnie, Brandon, and Jenny to fix the dinner that night. Donnie and Jenny started preparing hamburgers good-naturedly, but Brandon wasn't too enthusiastic.

Buoyed up by his success and the fact that Brandon seemed to be on his side, Jaden volunteered, "Brandon, I'll do your part for dinner. I like to cook."

A little surprised, Brandon said, "Okay, sure, kid….thanks." Basically, Jaden just opened a can of beans and heated them up, while the burgers were cooking, but he felt like he was doing something special for Brandon. No matter what Brandon had done to him in the past, he still wanted to win Brandon's approval.

Brandon and Jenny built the fire after dinner, with Donnie looking on, and when it was lit, Brandon scooted his chair up a tiny bit closer to the others. The talk around the fire was mainly about Jaden's hike and how beautiful the mountain was.

Jenny said, "I'm excited about going tomorrow. Will we go to the same place you went?"

"I'm not sure because Taylor is bringing his little brother this time. He said it might be too rugged for him."

Brandon hooted, "We don't want any babies coming along."

"Well, it's up to Taylor. It's his idea."

At bedtime, Alice told them all, "We've been out here for two days and a night. I want everybody to shower before going to bed. That tent is not going to smell like a football huddle!" Grinning and acquiescing, they got their towels and ambled to the bathhouse. The girls headed one way and the guys, the other. At least the showers were warm, thankfully, because being open-air was a bit chilly. Making their way back to the tent, they were all glad for a warm sleeping bag. Brandon chose to stay outside again, but this time he grabbed his pillow before settling in.

Chapter 22

Donnie's mood was somewhat better the next morning. Brandon hadn't come around as he had hoped, but at least he was participating in some of the camping activities. Even Jaden had shown some spunk. Who knew he was such a good cornhole player? There were still a few more days left. Maybe the family would meld together yet, like they used to.

Alice got up to prepare oatmeal. As she put water on to boil, she thought maybe today she and Donnie would have a chance to talk, since all the kids were going on a hike. She had decided to speak firmly to him about Jaden. She could no longer tolerate what she felt was verbal abuse of her younger son.

Jaden and Jenny crawled out of the tent, shivering a little as they left the warmth of their sleeping bags. Even Brandon was up, anticipating a day that would not be total boredom.

As they wolfed down their oatmeal, Alice said, "You guys don't even have to do any breakfast cleanup today. I know you're anxious to begin your hike, so I'll take care of it."

"Gee, thanks, Mom."

"You're the best, Mom." Jenny and Jaden were grateful. Brandon, the typical entitled teen, just got up when he finished and went to brush his teeth.

When the Hansens got to the other tent site, Taylor and Trent were ready. Jaden had told everyone to bring water, so they were all prepared.

"Can we go the same way today, Taylor?" Jaden asked. "Jenny and I can help Trent when he needs it. He can do most of it by himself."

"Yeah, let's do that, Taylor," Brandon butted in. "You and I can hike to the top, and the others can go at their own pace." The plan was made, and they started their trek.

It wasn't long before Taylor and Brandon were out of sight. Brandon wasn't there to see the beauty. He wanted to see how high he could get. Jaden and Jenny didn't mind going slow with Trent. They explored tree cavities to see if anything was living in them and followed some deer footprints off the trail for a short way. Trent had spotted them, because he had seen deer prints before. Jaden and Jenny were thrilled. He told them if they were very quiet, they might see some deer browsing, because it was still early. Deer fed in the morning and at dusk. That did it! They crept along at a snail's pace without saying a word. Looking through the trees at every turn, they finally spotted the prize! A momma deer and two little spotted fawns were about twenty yards away, oblivious to the fact that they were being watched. Trent took a misstep on a rock, and his foot slid a little. A very little sound, but just enough that the deer sailed away, white tails in the air.

"That was so awesome!" exclaimed Jaden.

"Way cool," followed Jenny.

Ahead, Taylor and Brandon had already made it to the first plateau and stopped for a breather.

"This is where Jaden and I stopped yesterday to text our girlfriends. It's the first place you can get bars."

"Wait, what?" Brandon had an incredulous look on his face. "Jaden has a girlfriend?"

"Yeah….they texted back and forth a couple of times." Taylor seemed puzzled.

"Wonders never cease. I didn't know he had a girlfriend," responded Brandon. To himself, he thought maybe the little twerp wasn't a fag, after all. Just embarrassing and annoying. He continued pondering the situation, as they made their way to the top.

After resting for a brief period, Taylor and Brandon started back down. Sweaty, with faces red from exertion, they met the rest of their group just above the first set of rocks.

"We've been all the way to the top and back," bragged Brandon. "You guys are just to the first set of rocks," he said derisively.

"Brandon, we saw some deer eating breakfast!" Jenny was quick to point out.

"And we saw a hole in a tree where some animal lives," added Jaden.

"What is this, a sight-seeing tour, or a hike?" Brandon spoke brashly, but was secretly disappointed that he didn't get to see the deer. When Brandon and Taylor started back down, Jaden pulled out his cell phone and was relieved that he had time to text Trevor before they started back down the mountain.

As soon as the kids were out of sight on their hike, Alice turned to her husband.

"Donnie, we need to talk. What was going on with you and Brandon the day we arrived?"

"I just don't know what's up with him, honey. We used to be so close and do everything together, and now he acts like I'm the bad guy. When he talks at all, it's sarcastic. All I asked him to do was put the tent poles together. You would have thought I told him to dig a hole to China."

"Oh, Donnie, you know that teenagers go through a rebellious stage against their parents."

"Yes," he said exasperatedly, "but I don't feel like I'm the average parent. Haven't I taught him how to play ball? Haven't I supported him in everything he's ever done? Haven't I gone to every single game he's ever played in?"

"It's not that, Donnie. I'm sure he's appreciated everything you've done along the way. But didn't you go through something similar with your dad? I remember when we first started dating, your dad wouldn't let you use the car unless you did some major chore around the house first. That used to make you so mad! Remember that time when you came to my house all hot, sweaty, and ill-tempered, complaining about how your dad was a tyrant! You told me that as soon as you turned eighteen, you were leaving that house and never looking back."

"I guess I did say some rash things, too." Pausing, he continued, "But it just seems different with Brandon. If it is a phase, I hope he gets out of it soon."

"Honey, let's talk about Jaden." Alice, seeing the change in Donnie's face, almost lost her resolve to continue speaking up to Donnie.

"What about Jaden?" he said curtly.

"He so badly wants you to approve of him. He cried himself to sleep the other night."

"I don't disapprove of him, he's just such a baby. He can't seem to do anything right, and I'm so afraid he's going to grow up queer to boot. Maybe I am too hard on him. But no son of mine is going to be a fairy." He didn't speak again for several minutes, and Alice could see he was deep in thought. Breaking the silence, Alice spoke again.

"Well, you've got to find a way to deal with how you feel that's not so hurtful to Jaden. Every time you're harsh with him, a little more of his self-esteem is destroyed." Donnie didn't answer. It had been a long time since he had thought of Father Tom and his Catholic upbringing....

Alice felt relieved that she had spoken her mind to Donnie, but his silence made her wonder if it would make any difference.

———————

Taylor and Trent had stopped off at their campsite as they came off the mountain, and the Hansen kids were excitedly chattering when they returned to their own.

"Well! It looks like you all had a good time today," Alice smiled. Breaking in on each other, Jenny and Jaden recounted the story of the deer and the tree hole, and what a good kid Trent was. Brandon listened, but didn't contribute anything about his day. Rather exhausted, all three of them lay down on their sleeping bags for a few minutes before dinner.

Alice had opened some cans of vegetable beef soup, and then added in some fresh vegetables. Along with French bread, it would make a nice dinner for a chilly evening. Plus, it took almost no preparation and could be warmed up at a moment's notice. Donnie had gone for a walk, about an hour earlier, by himself, and when Alice saw him coming back, she started waking everyone up.

"Dinner's ready," she sang out. No sense taking a chance on Donnie's being irritated, because everyone was asleep and dinner wasn't ready.

As Alice was ladling out the soup, Brandon shocked everybody by saying, "Hey, guess what!" He looked around, settled his eyes on Jaden, and with a teasing grin said, "Jaden's got a girlfriend! He's been holding out on us. He's actually got a girlfriend. You go, bro!" Jaden squirmed in his seat and lowered his eyes. Not knowing where this might go, Jenny was uneasy, too. Shortly, though, she could tell Brandon was sincere, not being sarcastic as usual. He was teasing, but in a friendly way. Donnie had noticed the same thing and was amazed. He kept quiet as Brandon went on to say, "What's her name, Jaden? Did you get to first base yet? Why haven't you told any of us about her?" Jaden was tongue-tied, not knowing how to respond.

Jenny stepped in and said, "I'm sure he hasn't told us because you would tease him without mercy. Right, Jaden?" Thankful for the save, he nodded his head.

Later that night, lying in his sleeping bag, Jaden thought he might be able to use what Brandon had said to his advantage. It certainly seemed to make a difference with his brother. The past couple of days on the camping trip Brandon had treated him as he had always wished he would, cheering for him in a game and teasing him in a brotherly way.

Chapter 23

As the few days left raced by and the camping trip was almost over, Donnie wanted to plan one more family activity. He was hoping in this activity he and Brandon would have a last chance to make a connection. He had brought four big cardboard boxes that had been folded flat in the back of the SUV. Plastic garbage bags and lots of duct tape finished up the supplies. At breakfast he laid out his plan.

"We're going to build cardboard boats and have a race on the lake. The teams will be Mom and the twins, against Brandon and me. You'll have two cardboard boxes to use, as well as plastic bags and all the duct tape you want. We'll build the boats this morning and race after lunch. Someone has to be in the 'boat' during the race. Any questions?" Jenny had one.

"Can we use any trees or limbs?"

"If it is something from nature, you can use it."

"How far do we race?" was Jaden's question.

With a half-smile and a twinkle in his eye, Donnie said, "Until one of the boats sinks. The other will be the winner."

Brandon's face was neutral as he helped Donnie pick up their supplies. He had decided to participate without complaining and thought that his team would surely win. He needed to save face after losing at cornhole. As much as his dad irritated him these days, he was still good at stuff like this. The two of them decided they would put one box inside the other for extra strength and tape garbage bags over the bottom and sides to keep it dry. The next step was to take some more bags and capture air in them, so they could tape them to the bottom for buoyancy. It seemed like a good course of action, so they got started.

Jenny was directing the construction of the other "boat". She wanted the two boxes to be connected end to end so the rider could stretch his/her legs straight out, hoping the weight would be distributed outward, instead of compactly. They, too, covered the boxes with plastic bags to keep them waterproof. Jenny knew that limbs and logs float in water, so she thought it would be a good idea to find a couple and put them on the bottom like pontoons. Alice was letting her children make the decisions, but was pretty impressed with the concept. Her babies were growing up.

"Jenny, I have a great idea!" Then Jaden spoke in a low voice. "Why don't you be the rider, and I'll get in the water and push you, like a motor."

"That's an awesome idea, but do you know how cold that water is?"

"I don't care. I can take it for a little while, and at least I'll get to swim."

Getting into the conspiracy, Alice whispered, "Keep your idea quiet. It'll be our secret weapon."

It took most of the morning to make the boats, but by lunchtime, both were finished.

"Okay, I think we're ready," said Donnie. "After lunch why don't you get Taylor and Trent to come watch our race." Other campers who had strolled by had expressed interest in the goings-on. They, too, had been invited to watch. Despite himself, Brandon was gearing up to have some fun. Donnie had told him he would be in the boat, and he was looking for something to use as a paddle. He knew he could paddle faster than the little kids. He decided on a couple of palmetto leaves with their stalks attached. He took duct tape and fashioned them together into a paddle of sorts. He was ready; bring it on!

During lunch both teams could hardly keep their ideas to themselves, but neither wanted the other to know their secrets. Wolfing his lunch down, Jaden dashed off to get Taylor and Trent. When they got back, other curious campers started showing up, and by the time they walked down to the lake, there were about ten observers.

Jaden stuck his toe in the water, "Yowee, it's colder than I thought."

Donnie gave final instructions. On the count of three, boats will go in the water and captains will climb in and head straight out into the lake.

"One, two..., three!" They all started scrambling and laughing so hard that it was unclear to the spectators whether or not anything was going to happen. Brandon got in his boat, and it stood high - for a minute. He started paddling furiously. The other boat looked very seaworthy until Jenny actually got in. Jaden took off his shirt, jumped in the water, and began pushing Jenny for all he was worth. About five feet out, it was deep enough that he held the box and kicked with his legs.

Brandon looked over and shouted, "That's not fair. You're using two people!" But he didn't stop paddling. Every stroke he took, he sank a little more into the water. Jaden and Jenny weren't doing much better. Their boat had sunk to the point that only the top of the box was visible, but Jaden kept swimming and pushing all the while.

Only Jenny's shoulders and head could be seen, and she was laughing and screaming, "The water is freezing!"

On shore, everyone was laughing and shouting encouragement. By mutual agreement of all the on-lookers, it was decided that both boats sank about the same time. They had made it, by pure effort, about fourteen or fifteen feet out. All three Hansens were now swimming and towing their boats back in. Coming ashore, they received long and loud applause. If they had been disgruntled about being cold and wet, it quickly disappeared, and they all gave high-fives to each other. Trent was jumping up and down with excitement.

"That was the best thing I've ever seen on a camping trip!" He clapped his hands.

As the crowd dispersed, the Hansen kids got their towels and headed for warm showers. They were shivering, but exhilarated. Alice and Donnie hugged each other, happy about the way it had turned out.

"Maybe our family is coming together again," Donnie exulted.

The cardboard boat race was the highlight of the camping trip. The next day they started breaking down the kitchen area and the tent in preparation for heading home. When it was almost time to go, the three kids went down to Taylor and Trent's tent to say their goodbyes. They exchanged email addresses and promised to write. They had all become pretty good friends during the week.

On the ride home, everyone was talking about the fun they had, even Brandon. After about an hour, though, Brandon had his headset on, and the twins were dozing. Finally getting back, the family felt like they had been gone forever, and it seemed strange to be walking into a house instead of a tent. After they had unpacked the car and put away the things that belonged in the house, Donnie drove back to the rental store to return the equipment. After a sketchy start on the trip, he was extremely satisfied with the end. Donnie felt better than he had in a long time. The vacation had been good, Brandon was not as sullen as he had been, and maybe, just maybe, Jaden was going to be a normal boy. He felt as if a huge weight had been lifted from his shoulders.

Chapter 24

"I'm so glad ur back!" texted Trevor. "Will u be b able to come to the pool this Sat?"

"Nothing can keep me away," was the answer. Jaden decided to get there an hour before Trevor finished his shift. He felt he needed to swim a lot to make up for missing last Saturday. He really did want to be on the swim team in high school.

A few days earlier, Jaden had gone over to Miss Bonnie's house to swim and catch her up on how the camping trip went.

"It was really fun, Miss Bonnie. I met some new kids, and we hiked with them almost every day. Taylor was fourteen, and Trent was eight. Trent kept up with us really good for an eight-year-old. He knew a lot of stuff about the outdoors, too. Oh, and we had to shower in a place that didn't have a ceiling. It was like being outside." That really seemed to tickle Jaden. "There was only one little light on the wall, but the moon made it bright."

"That does sound like a lot of fun, Jay. How did you get along with your dad and brother?"

"It was great, Miss Bonnie! We all had a cardboard boat race, even Dad. Nobody won, because we all sank at the same time. It was so fun! And Brandon cheered for *me* in the cornhole game. Can you believe he cheered for me?"

It does my heart good to see him actually happy about how he got along with his family, thought Miss Bonnie. Jaden finally paused in his non-stop account of the week. With a sudden unsettled look on his face, he got serious.

"Miss Bonnie, something happened, and I'm not sure if it's good or bad. When we were hiking I texted Trevor, and Taylor thought I was texting a girlfriend. Taylor told Brandon, and Brandon told the whole family. I think that's why Brandon likes me better now, but it makes me feel dishonest."

"Unless you are ready to tell them about Trevor, let them think what they want, if it helps you. It's not like you told them you have a girlfriend. You do whatever makes you feel better about life."

"Thanks, Miss Bonnie. You always seem to have the right answer and know how to make me feel better."

One morning at breakfast, Alice declared to the family that on Labor Day, they were going to have a cookout and both sets of grandparents were coming for the weekend. The news was met with excitement from the twins, and indifference from Brandon.

Earlier, when she had discussed the plan with Donnie, he had said skeptically, "So, you're going to get everybody together again." The last time that had happened had been about four years before for an overnight visit on Christmas Eve, and it hadn't gone very well. Donnie's parents were loud and brash, while Alice's were conservative and soft-spoken. They knew each other, of course, but had never stayed in the same house together for more than a day except on that Christmas. Since both sets lived out of town, they would all be under one roof again, this time for three nights.

"Yes, honey," Alice had said. "I thought it was time to try again. The children are getting older, and I want them to be able to enjoy seeing both sets of grandparents at the same time." It was settled. Labor Day was only a couple of weeks away.

The Hansen house had four bedrooms, and Alice told Jaden and Brandon they would both have to give theirs up.

"Where are we going to sleep?" complained Brandon.

"You can have the couch, and Jaden can sleep in a sleeping bag on the floor in Jenny's room." That arrangement was fine with Jaden. He and Jenny had slept in the same room until they were five years old. He had been afraid of the dark for a long time and remembered those early years as comforting.

Thinking about the big screen TV in the living room, Brandon said, "Okay, that's tight."

Since school started back right after Labor Day, Jaden wanted to spend a little time with Devon before the end of summer. He had only seen him a couple of times during the break when they had gone to Miss Bonnie's to swim. When he called Devon to see what was going on, Devon invited him over to play Wii. The Hansens didn't have a Wii game, so it was always a treat to play somebody else's.

He had decided to ride his bike over to Devon's when Brandon shocked him by saying, "Hey, little bro, I'll drive you over if Mom will let me use the car." Jaden was beaming when his mom said it was okay. Brandon was still being nice to him. He couldn't believe it.

When he dropped Jaden off, Brandon stated, "I'll be back in a couple of hours to pick you up. I'm gonna go hang out with some friends at the club." After hearing that, Jaden felt a little deflated. Taking him to Devon's had been just an excuse to get the car.

He replied, "I thought you had to be eighteen to get in there … "

"Naw, you can get in at sixteen before six p.m. We're gonna play pool for a while," he said before he sped off. Devon met Jaden at the door.

"Hey, dude, 'sup?" They raced into the room where the Wii was and got started. He and Devon played bowling, baseball, and tennis. The more they played, the more ramped up they got. By the time they took out the Wii Fit, they were laughing wildly in hot competition.

"I love the downhill skiing, and you're killer on that, Devon!" Jaden yelled with enthusiasm. They were having a blast, and before they knew it, Brandon was honking at the curb.

"Thanks, Devon. That was awesome! I can't wait 'til school starts. Then we can hang every day again."

When they got home, Alice was irate.

"Where have you been, Brandon? I thought you must be lying in a ditch somewhere. I've been worried sick. I called Devon's mom to see if you were there, but she said you had dropped Jaden off and left!"

"Jeez, Mom. You'd think I committed a crime or something. I just hung out with some guys until it was time to pick up Jaden. Give me some slack!"

"Just because you're sixteen now doesn't mean you can decide to do whatever you want with the car. You didn't ask me about staying out with anyone, and you should have come straight back home! See if you get the car again anytime soon! Right now I want you to go clean your room. I'm not having it look like a pigsty when Grandma and Grandpa Hansen get here."

"What the hell, Mom, you don't have to be a Nazi. This sucks."

"That's enough street talk, Brandon!" He went grumbling to his room. Jaden was glad *he* hadn't done anything wrong.

Chapter 25

Part of each of the days preceding Labor Day was spent de-cluttering and cleaning the house. Everyone but Donnie, who was at work, had to help, because Alice wanted it to be spotless when the grandparents arrived the Friday before the holiday.

When the day finally came, Donnie's parents, in their young and active fifty's, arrived first, like a whirlwind. They had barely gotten to the door when Grandpa Hansen had Jenny by the waist and was spinning her around until they both were laughing so hard and were so dizzy that they fell in a heap on the grass. Grandma Hansen had grabbed Jaden in a bear hug.

"I just can't believe how big you kids have grown."

As soon as they got their luggage in the house, even before taking it to Brandon's room, Grandpa Hansen said in a loud voice, "Who wants to go for ice cream? I saw a Dairy Creme right before we got here and I wanted ice cream! Your grandma told me to get you kids first. So here we are!"

"Can we, Mom? Please, please?"

"All right, but don't spoil your dinner."

By the time they got back, the Reverend Brooks and his wife had arrived. Even though both sets of grandparents lived in Center City, there had never been a thought about driving down together. They certainly didn't want to be trapped in the same vehicle for two hours.

As everybody piled out of the car and went inside, Grandpa Hansen said, "Hey, Rev, how's it hanging?"

Always unsure of how to take him, he just replied, "Hello, Donald."

As the kids were hugging and getting reacquainted with their maternal grandparents, Donnie and Alice took the luggage to their respective rooms.

Donnie whispered to Alice, "I'm not sure if it's safe to leave them alone together, even for a few minutes."

"Don't be silly, Donnie. They're all adults."

When they returned to the living room, everything seemed normal. Alice's parents were sitting primly on the sofa, Donnie's mom was prowling around in the kitchen, and his dad was sprawled out in the recliner, asking Brandon for the TV guide.

When Alice went into the kitchen to check on how the roast and potatoes were doing in the crock-pot, Delores, Donnie's mother, said, "I guess you're not used to cooking for a crowd like this. When Donnie was growing up, we always had ten or more at the table. If it wasn't family, the kids in the neighborhood would show up. Our door was always open. I'm sure you must need some help in here." Alice wondered if her mother-in-law saw her as inept.

Delores, Dori for short, had already been in the refrigerator and was making a huge salad with lettuce, tomato, onion, cucumber, bell pepper, carrots, and broccoli. "I always say," she went on, " you can never get enough vegetables down a kid, unless you hide 'em in something. Of course, a good, hearty vegetable beef stew will always get eaten." Alice, who had planned to have broccoli as a side dish tonight, was a little taken aback, seeing her beautiful florets being sliced and diced. Hiding her consternation, she looked around in the pantry for a substitute. When she pulled out a couple of large cans of green beans, Dori said, "Don't tell me you're gonna serve that canned stuff?"

Luckily, Donnie stuck his head in and asked, "When's dinner ready?" That broke the awkward moment when Alice didn't exactly know what to say.

What she did say was, "Have the kids set the table and bring up extra chairs. There are a couple of folding chairs in the garage, and get another off the porch."

When they all sat down at the table, Alice suggested that her dad, who was a retired pastor, ask the blessing.

After asking that the food be blessed, the troops be blessed, the indigent be blessed, the sick be blessed, and the educational system be blessed, the Reverend finally said, "Amen."

As the dishes were being passed around, Donald said, "I guess that kind of praying took some getting used to, Donnie, but I can understand why you left the Catholic faith, being as your father-in-law was a Baptist preacher. But," he said scratching his five o'clock shadow, "if I recall, there was also some incident at the church that upset you. It's been so long ago, I can't remember exactly what it was about."

Donnie looked hard at his father and said, "Not a big deal, Dad. Forget about it." When the conversation turned to the upcoming school year, Donnie was relieved.

The next morning the Hansen clan, eager to get out and do something, made plans to go to the zoo where there was also an amusement park with rides. Alice said she would stay at home with her parents, who weren't the least bit interested in going to see animals or riding on rides. When the others left, Reverend Brooks took the opportunity to make some phone calls in the sudden peace. Alice and her mom sat down in the family room with coffee.

"Mama, it's so good to see you! I can't believe you're only two hours away and we see each other so seldom."

"I know, dear, but between your schedule and your father's, it sometimes seems difficult to get together. Since he retired, he seems busier than ever. He's still on the board of the church, and now other churches call him all the time to be a guest pastor or to lead a revival."

"It might be nice if just you could come visit sometimes, when Papa is busy," Alice said plaintively.

"Now you know, honey, that a pastor's wife has the duty to be at her husband's side wherever he is."

Alice replied in a small voice, "I just thought maybe once he retired, it might be different. But, I know he's always been your first priority."

"Surely you realize every wife's first priority is her husband, then kids and church. Don't you stand by Donnie in everything?"

"Of course I stand by him, Mama, but I can voice my own opinions, discuss things, and come to a mutual decision with him about how to handle situations." Alice could barely believe her own words. Not too terribly long ago, she had been just like her mother, standing back, and letting her husband make the calls. The women's group had taken her a long way, and she had begun to feel empowered to speak up to Donnie about her thoughts. Uncomfortable with such talk, Maxine Brooks steered her daughter in another direction.

"How are the kids doing, in general? Are they still doing well in school?"

"Yes, Mama, I have no problems with their keeping their grades up. Brandon is on the Hi-Q team, and the twins have been making honor roll almost every grading period. We have been having a slight problem with Brandon, because he's beginning to have a smart mouth. Donnie and I have been staying on top of that, though."

"What's wrong with the kids of today?" The Reverend had finished his calls and walked into the room. "You were never like that, Alice, when you were growing up. You knew when to speak and when to keep your mouth shut. I think the nation is in a downward spiral, starting with the high-schoolers of today. Don't they know they'll have to take over and run the country some day?"

"Papa, there were kids just like today's kids when I grew up. You were too busy in the church to see. Most of them grew up fine and have productive jobs."

The conversation was going in the wrong direction, and Alice was not in the mood to listen to the same things she repeatedly had heard growing up in the Brooks family. She walked to the bookcase and picked up the framed picture on top. It was Jenny's Sunday school class. Earlier in the year they had won the attendance competition. She showed it to her mother and explained the accomplishment.

"Oh, look, there's our Jenny. She looks lovely in that dress," said Maxine, who seemed to love her grandchildren even more when their appearance was to her satisfaction.

"She was instrumental in their win. Mama, she would call her whole class on Saturday and remind them of the importance of being there."

"That's a habit she should maintain her whole life," stated her father, who had gotten a cup of coffee and sat down with them in the family room. "It's a good way to witness to others."

Vividly remembering her childhood, Alice thought, it never changes. When you do something out of the ordinary, he never notices. He just thinks of it as something expected. However, if I forgot to bring my Bible to church or dawdled outside the sanctuary talking to someone and didn't go in until the music started, I had been reprimanded. He *always* noticed that.

She loved her father, but felt as if she had never really gotten to know him. She thought of herself as one of his flock, not his daughter. Her mother seemed oblivious to the lack of paternal attachment. And, although she had always seen that her daughter had what she needed physically, she had never really been "motherly." Alice had been determined that her kids would be raised differently.

Alice had previously thought of sharing some of Jaden's problems with her mother, but the conversation had not been at all conducive to revealing her inner thoughts about anything, much less the conflicts of her sensitive younger son. After seeming to race toward disaster at first, the rest of the day dragged by until, at last, everyone else returned home. She had never been so glad to get back into the noise and cyclonic pace of her in-laws.

The next day everyone except Donnie's parents got ready to go to Holmes Baptist Church. The elder Hansens had gotten up for early Mass and were already back, relaxing with coffee.

Donald, with his usual lack of tact, complained, "Now that we have the whole day ahead of us, you guys won't get back until after noon, or even later, if the preacher is as long-winded as most Baptists."

Reverend Brooks turned toward him, and said, "Sunday should be a day of God and reflection. You people are go, go, go. Don't you know there are more important things in life than finding the next adventure?"

Seeing that his dad was about to flare up, Donnie said, "Come on, everybody. Let's load up and get going before we're late." Donnie didn't want anything to get started between his parents and Alice's.

Once everyone left and they had the house to themselves, Donald remarked to Dori, "He sure is a jerk, to be a man of God."

After church, the Brookses abruptly decided to end their visit. They said they needed to get back for the evening service at their own church. Alice didn't actually believe that was the reason, but she didn't really protest, even though they would miss the cookout. As glad as she had been to see her parents arrive, she was equally relieved to see them go. She had always hoped that, with time, they might mellow a bit, but it had never happened. She wasn't sure she wanted her kids to really know how narrow-minded their grandparents were.

As they were backing down the driveway, there seemed to be a collective sigh of relief. Even the kids had felt the tension, without totally understanding it.

Donnie said, "Well, now, what should we do with the rest of the day?"

Alice reminded him, "You don't actually have the whole afternoon, because we're going to cook out around four." It was decided they would all go for a short canoe ride down a tributary of the river that fed the town lake. Donald and Brandon paired up, and Alice and Jenny went together, while Donnie and his mom got a canoe with Jaden in the middle. The more experienced canoeists, Donald, Alice, and Donnie, sat in the back to do the steering. They had all paddled a canoe before, but Jaden had never been very interested. You paddle downstream, then, you turn around and paddle back. Bor-ing. He would much rather swim.

As it turned out, it wasn't boring at all. Because of recent rain raising the height of the river, the flow of the tributary was faster than usual. It became more of a thrill ride, as they turned and twisted and ducked under branches. There were even some small rapids. It was probably only a couple of miles long, as the crow flies, but with all the turns, it wound up taking over an hour. Hitting tree limbs that had fallen in the water, and trying to dodge the occasional tree that suddenly appeared out of nowhere, they were almost dumped in the chilly water several times. There was no paddling back upstream in that torrent, but, thankfully, the canoe vendor had a trailer to haul them back to their car. Riding home, everyone was enthused about the trip, interrupting each other with laughing renditions. Most of all, though, they were glad they didn't spill.

As soon as they got back home, Donnie fired up the grill. Alice had marinated chicken the day before, and he was going to cook that along with hamburgers and brats. When Alice brought the meat out on a tray, Jaden was standing around the grill, hoping Donnie would invite him to help. Donnie, busy putting the chicken on, didn't seem to notice him. Summoning up some nerve, Jaden spoke up.

"Dad, I can help you grill. Remember Miss Bonnie taught me how?"

Reluctantly, Donnie said, "I suppose you can cook the hot dogs. They'll cook the fastest, so they'll go on last, after the burgers. You know when to turn them, don't you?"

"Sure I do, Dad!" Jaden reacted with such pleasure that Donnie almost felt ashamed.

When the dogs and burgers were almost finished, Donnie was taking the last of the chicken off the grill.

Jaden suggested, "Hey, Dad! Want me to get the buns and put a little butter on them? Then we can put them on the grill for a little while and toast them. They're delicious like that!"

"That sounds like a good idea, buddy. Go do that." As Jaden ran in to get the buns and butter, Donnie thought maybe there's a chance for the kid, after all. He was pretty good on the camping trip, and now this.

As the Hansens were enjoying the cookout, Jaden was basking in the compliments about his cooking. Donnie had made it known that the toasted buns were his idea.

Grandpa Hansen said, "Hey, Jaden, you can cook for me anytime! These burgers are fantastic!"

Jenny added, "I've never had a bun that tasted so good. Where did you learn that?"

"Miss Bonnie has shown me a lot of good cooking tips. She can grill anything."

The talk gradually turned to how abruptly Alice's parents had left earlier.

"There sure was a bee under the Reverend's bonnet," said Donald. "No offense, Alice, but he thinks things have to be 'just so' on Sunday. Does he think the rest of us are heathens just because we want to have fun on Sundays? Catholics are as reverent as any Baptist! First we worship God with others in church, and then we worship God by enjoying what He has provided for us - lakes and rivers and mountains, and family."

"Well, Donald," commented Dori, with a smile, "when did you become so philosophical? But, you're absolutely right. No offense to Baptists, Alice."

Donnie's dad kept on, "Come to think of it, Donnie, exactly why did you leave the Catholic Church? I know you left well before you got married, so that wasn't the reason." Donnie was suddenly very uncomfortable.

"I just got tired of all the trappings of the Church." He tried to let it go at that but, his dad was persistent.

"You were there day and night, you were a member of CYO, and then, bam. You quit going. I remember at the time, your mom and I thought you were old enough to make your own decision about going to church, but thinking back, it did seem sudden."

Memories of being in that room with Father Tom had been dammed up for years.

Now Donnie's thoughts raced. I couldn't deal with it then; I certainly can't think about it now. Looking at Donnie, Alice was alarmed to see a profoundly disturbed look cross his face. At that moment she was afraid he might do something totally foreign to his nature; she thought he was about to cry. Determined not to let that happen, Alice hurriedly instructed the kids to clean up the table and put away the food.

Then she said to Donnie, "Why don't you open that bottle of sparkling wine that we've been saving for a special occasion? Having your parents here is as special a time as I can think of." Donnie went into the house to find the bottle of wine, relieved to have something else to do besides think.

With the wine uncorked and the glasses filled, the previous subject seemed to be forgotten. The wine was good, the mood was lifted, and the family decided to play charades. But the unsettling incident was still very present in Alice's mind.

When everybody was finally tired and had gone to bed, Alice approached Donnie with what was troubling her.

She put her arms around him, snuggled up, and asked, "What *was* your father talking about? I saw your face, and I know that whatever it was, it had a big impact on you. Something happened back then. What was it? Nothing you could tell me would change my feelings for you, honey. You know I'll always love you and stand by you." Donnie really was fighting back tears this time. As Alice continued to hug him and caress his face, he broke down. "It's okay, baby. Let it out." He cried for a good five minutes, non-stop, totally out of character for the macho jock he had always portrayed himself to be. When his sobs quieted, he began to talk.

"It started when I was around twelve. The parish priest, Father Tom, was interested in all of us altar boys, you know, asking us about school, sports, home. He was so fun to be around. He talked to us like we were people, not just kids. He took us to ball games and movies on free days. All of us. Then one day we were all doing a project at church, and when we were done, he asked me to stay after and help him move some folding chairs in one of the rooms in the back." Donnie paused and almost couldn't continue. "I can't talk about this with you, Alice. Not you or anyone."

Still in a soothing voice, she said, "You have to. It will haunt you until you've faced whatever it is. He took a breath and stumbling to find the right words, he continued.

"When we got to that back room, there weren't any folding chairs there, just a couch and a big recliner. I realized this must have been part of his living quarters. It was kind of sparse, but then I noticed a TV and figured it was his living room. Father Tom said, 'If you don't have to go right home, let's sit down and watch the college football game.' I asked him about the chairs were that we were supposed to move. He told me someone must have come and moved them while we were in the other part of the church. Seemed a little strange that someone would do that without his knowing, but I figured that must be what happened. This was Father Tom, after all.

He turned the TV on, but instead of watching the game, he started talking to me about playing sports and how you have to be in great shape. Remember, I was twelve and was all into sports, so, of course, I listened to everything he had to say. When he told me all my muscles should be limber, that made sense. Then he told me to take off my shirt and let him see my muscles. I was proud of them and whipped my shirt up to show off. He acted impressed and asked to feel my biceps. I flexed them, and he rubbed his hand along them. Then he just sort of shifted around to my back and commented that those muscles seemed sort of tight. He said, 'Let me loosen them up for you, Donnie. You can get a lot more power throwing a ball if your back is loose.' Made sense again, so the next thing I knew, he was massaging my back.

After a little while, I told him I'd better get home, so my mom wouldn't worry about where I was. He said, 'Sure, see you tomorrow in church.' As time went by, it got so that my folks expected me to stay after church to help Father Tom do this or that. Whatever we did, it always ended with a massage to keep me loose and in shape. He talked me into letting him rub my quads and hamstrings for the same reason. He told me that nothing is as crippling to an athlete as hurting a hammy. By the time I was thirteen, I personally knew that to be true, because I had strained mine once, by not warming up on a cool day.

The massages became a ritual of all my visits to the church. One day when I had turned fourteen, he was rubbing my quads and his hand drifted to the crease in my hip. That being a sensitive area, I jumped and told him it tickled. He laughed and said sorry. It didn't happen again, but another time I was lying flat on my stomach, and he was leaning over my back, rubbing it. I felt something poking my butt. As he rubbed up and down my back, whatever it was, rubbed up and down my butt. In a flash, I realized Father Tom was hard. I was mortified, and it made me want to hurl. I jumped up and ran home. I pretended to be sick the next day and didn't go to Mass.

Dad wouldn't let me miss two Sundays in a row, so I tried to avoid Father Tom the next week. I was about to escape with my parents when my dad saw him beckoning to me to come over where he was. I had no choice but to go to him.

He told me we really needed to talk. I said talk to me right here. He said of course. We sat down in a pew and he told me how sorry he was about that 'unexpected thing' happening. He said, 'You're a young man, and you should know by now that sometimes even a random thought can make that happen, right? Surely, you have had it happen to you from time to time. Remember, I'm a priest, so I'm celibate. But that doesn't mean my mind doesn't wander from time to time. That little event had nothing to do with you.' He actually convinced me, for a time, that it was purely accidental. I knew that it had sometimes happened to me when I had least expected." Once Donnie had started talking, the floodgates opened.

"I continued going over there for most of the next year, but probably not as often. The clincher was when I went over one day around dinner time. I was supposed to have been there right after school, but making up a test I had missed took me way longer than I had thought it would. It was almost dark, and I went through the living area calling for Father Tom. I couldn't find him at first, and I was starting to feel spooked. Suddenly, he came out from the shadows of the hallway right next to me, and he only had on boxers. He was very obviously aroused, and he embraced me. During that embrace his hand brushed my privates and lingered. I shoved him away and ran home as fast as I could."

"Did you tell your parents?"

"No, I couldn't. I was *so* embarrassed. I never, ever wanted to talk about it or even think about it again."

"Oh, sweetie, I can't believe you've held that inside you for all these years. It wasn't your fault."

"I felt so ashamed and so guilty. I shouldn't have kept going over there. It was my fault."

"Donnie, you did nothing to bring on that priest's attentions. You were a twelve-year-old boy when it started, and you innocently believed that a man of God, a priest, wouldn't do anything to hurt you."

"But I let him rub my back and my legs over and over, for three damn years. He must have felt I was leading him on."

"Donnie! You were twelve! You couldn't have known." Pausing for a beat, Alice had a thought. "Honey, do you think anything about being molested has influenced your feelings about Jaden? That you may feel that if he's gay, he'll be just like that priest? Nothing could be farther from the truth."

"I wasn't molested! He didn't try to have sex with me. It was just gross that he touched me. And Jaden is not going to be gay!" Donnie was through being vulnerable and back to his old bravado.

"Honey, do you think counseling might help you?" Alice asked gently.

"No!' he said vehemently. "Counseling is for the weak. Talking doesn't help anyone. It's nothing but a pacifier for people who aren't man enough to handle their own problems." Alice let it go, for the time being. Once Donnie had an idea in his head, there was no changing it, but she didn't intend to give up.

Chapter 26

Mid-morning the next day, Donald and Dori Hansen packed their car for the ride back to Center City. After lots of hugs and promises to visit, everyone watched them pull out of the driveway, waving and blowing kisses.

Alice told the kids, "After lunch we're going to the mall to buy school clothes. Make sure you wear something decent that's easy to get in and out of."

"But Mom, we don't have anything decent! That's why we have to go shopping," Jaden teased.

After lunch they all left Donnie sitting in front of the big screen, watching a baseball game. The mall was on the other side of town, but still only fifteen minutes away. Jaden and Jenny were excited at the prospect of buying school clothes. They couldn't wait until the next day when school would start. Brandon made a show of indifference, but he, too, was ready for summer to draw to a close. This was his junior year, he had passed his driver's test, and he would be playing varsity football.

He said, "Mom, I'm going down to American Eagle to look around. I'll catch up with you when you get down that way." He was not going to be seen in tow with his mom and younger siblings.

"Okay, but don't make me look for you. I don't want to spend the whole day here," she warned.

Jaden and Jenny were pulling her into Old Navy, their eyes trained on jeans and tops.

"Dude!" Devon appeared from a fitting room as they walked by. He and Jaden shook hands the way Devon had shown him a couple of weeks before, touch palms, draw thumbs back, bump fists. This was followed by a one-armed hug, barely close enough for chests to brush. This was the "cool" greeting.

Grinning self-consciously, Jaden said, "What's up, bro?"

"Come on, man. Let's check this place out together," Devon said. They separated from Jenny and Alice, who were already heading toward another part of the store, anyway.

In another section, unbeknownst to Jaden, Trevor, who had watched them come in, was wondering who the cute, light-skinned kid with the braids was, and why he and Jaden had hugged. With his heart beginning to beat faster, Trevor headed for the door before he was seen. He quickly made his way down to the opposite end of the mall, where he could get his thoughts together before possibly running into Jaden again. *I can't believe he was hugging that other kid. He looks like he knows him really good, too. I'm sure that wasn't their first hug. I don't know what I would do if Jaden.......* He couldn't even finish the thought. That hug had upset him more than he could have imagined.

After picking out a few things at Old Navy, the Hansen crew headed for Target. Devon had dropped away from them a little while back when he had seen his mother looking for him. Alice liked to get essentials such as socks and underwear at Target, because they always had good back-to-school sales. In addition, she could buy the notebooks, pens, pencils, and backpacks that were needed. She sent the twins to look for Brandon while she shopped for those items. On the way out of the store, Jaden spotted Trevor over at the jewelry counter, trying to look inconspicuous.

Jaden said, "You go ahead, Jenny. I'll catch you in a minute, or else you can just bring Brandon back to Mom. Trevor's over there, and I want to talk to him."

"Where?" she said, looking around.

"By the jewelry counter. Don't look! Just act like you don't see him. He looks like he doesn't want to be seen."

When Jenny was out the door, Jaden rushed over toward Trevor, with a happy smile on his face.

"Hey! I didn't expect to get to see you here. I sent Jenny on, 'cause you looked like you didn't want to be seen." When Jaden was close enough to get a good look at his friend's face, he paused and said, "Wait, is something wrong?"

"I'm okay."

"Well, you don't look okay. You look sad or maybe upset. Did something happen?"

Flustered, but thinking quickly, Trevor lied, "Yeah, my dad slapped me for talking back to my mom, so I just came to the mall." Quickly he added, "He's never slapped me before." He was sort of stalling, because he wasn't sure if he wanted to address that hug he had seen. At least, not here. Or now.

Trevor's conflicting thoughts almost made him forget the good news that he'd been anxious to tell Jaden all weekend. He hadn't been in touch because he knew Jaden wouldn't have any privacy while his grandparents were there. His mood took a dramatic upturn.

"You'll never guess what!" he said excitedly.

"What? Tell me what!"

"My dad told me Saturday that I don't have to go to private school any more. He's enrolling me in Lake Griffin High tomorrow, and if I make good grades the first quarter, he's going to take me car shopping. Not only will I have the money I've saved up, he and my mom are going to throw in some extra money so I can get a better car. Isn't that great?" Jaden was so excited he almost hugged Trevor right there in the mall.

Chapter 27

The next morning everyone had a tough time getting up early. The twins were so excited that they hadn't slept well. Plus, they had been used to sleeping in all summer, and morning had come far too soon. Brandon had to leave before the twins, because high school started a little earlier than middle school. In addition, he was eager to hook up with his computer club friends. Jaden and Jenny weren't far behind because even with a restless night, they could hardly wait to see their friends and find out who had done what over the summer. Jenny saw Barb right away, while Jaden was scanning the area for Devon. When they saw each other, they were both sporting new Old Navy clothes. They grinned at the sight of each other.

"What's your schedule, Dev?" Jaden wanted to know how many classes they had together.

"I forgot to check it online last night. I guess I'll have to wait for home-room to get mine."

"Meet me at the water fountain after homeroom then."

As they went their separate ways, Jaden thought he would stop by Mrs. Cohen's room to say hello and ask when the first TEAM Club meeting would be. When he looked in the door, there was a strange teacher at Mrs. Cohen's desk.

"Did Mrs. Cohen change rooms over the summer?" Jaden asked.

"Oh, no," replied the lady. "I'm only going to be here for a couple of weeks. She's out having surgery. Are you in her home room?"

"No … . no, I'm in her third period history class, but I was actually stopping to see when the first TEAM Club meeting will be. Is she all right?"

"I'm sure she'll be fine. She wouldn't want you to worry."

When he sat down in homeroom, he could hardly wait to tell Jenny.

"Mrs. Cohen is out for two weeks having surgery!"

"Surgery! What for?"

"I didn't ask. The substitute said it was nothing to worry about, though."

"Well, I'm still going to worry until she gets back. Surgery is surgery."

After homeroom, when the two boys met at the water fountain, they discovered they had the same math, English, history, and PE classes. Life was good.

After school Alice wanted to know all about how their day had gone.

Listening to their chatter, she commented, "I'm glad you have math and history together. Jenny is very good in math and can help you if you have trouble, Jaden." Nothing was very exciting to report, other than neither of them liked their math teacher, and Jaden was a little unhappy because he and Devon had separate lunches, but the big news was about Mrs. Cohen's surgery.

"I sure do hope she'll be okay." During the last year, they had grown to love Mrs. Cohen's funny personality and her genuine caring for each student. Jaden especially, felt safe in her room, because he believed she wouldn't turn against him if she knew about his secret. They both wanted her to come back soon!

The school year was off to a busy start for the Hansens. Brandon was occupied with football, and Jaden and Jenny were feeling the pinch of homework for the first time. It seemed the eighth grade teachers felt it was their duty to prepare their students for high school work, and they were pouring on the reading, projects, and other assignments. Except for Jaden in math, neither twin was having any specific problems, just lots of work.

Mrs. Cohen hadn't come back in the expected two weeks, but was promised to return in a few more days. The substitute was nice, but she wasn't Mrs. Cohen, and the TEAM Club hadn't met yet. Jaden and Jenny both were eager to get it going, especially since Jenny was going to run for club president. They didn't think Mrs. Cohen would *ever* get back.

Finally, the day arrived when they went to history class, and there she was. All the students were gathered around her desk, where she remained seated.

"Mrs. Cohen, I'm so glad you're back."

"We missed you so much!"

"Please don't be absent ever again."

"That other lady didn't teach us anything."

"Why did you have surgery?"

"Are you okay?" It was abundantly clear that Mrs. Cohen was popular and missed. It was also very clear that she looked thinner and pale, perhaps even drawn. But eighth graders are typically not so quick to pick up on subtle clues.

She finally spoke in a quiet voice, "I have missed you all terribly, too. Hopefully, I won't have to be absent any more. I had surgery to remove of a tumor, and the doctor says it's all gone. It just took a while to recover. Let's try to get back to normal now. Okay, everyone, in your seats. Let's get started."

Walking home that day, Jenny remarked to Jaden, "Mrs. Cohen didn't look that great. She seemed very weak. I wonder where the tumor was." Jenny was worried.

Jaden said, "Oh, don't worry Jenny. She said the doctor got it all. She'll be fine. I wonder when she'll start up the club again." Jenny was irritated at Jaden's lack of concern.

"She didn't act like she felt well at all, Jaden. There's more to worry about than when the club starts. What if she has cancer or something?"

"That's crazy, Jenny. People who have cancer don't go back to work." Jenny hoped he was right.

Chapter 28

Brandon was definitely going to be a starter on the varsity football team. He was a junior now, and he had bulked up a little over the summer. Not that he was big, but his muscles had started to stand out a bit. He had his driver's license, he was going to be a star on the team, and lots of girls had started noticing him - even the cheerleaders. He was beginning to feel his own importance. He thought that once he had earned his letterman's jacket, he could have his pick of all the girls.

When Brandon got home from practice on Thursday before the first game, girls were on his mind more than the upcoming game. Kristin, one of the most sought-after girls in the junior class, had watched his practice and waited for him to come out of the locker room.

With eyes and a smile that could make him melt, she said, "Brandon, you looked really good out there. I can't wait to see you play tomorrow." She was hot! She had filled out in all the right places, and Brandon could do little more than gawk.

He finally found his voice enough to say, "I know. I can't wait for the game either." How lame can I get, went through his mind. She didn't seem to notice. She put her arm around his waist and was walking him toward the street.

When they got to the student parking lot, she asked, "Want a ride home?"

"Uh ... yeah. That'd be great." It wasn't far to his house, and Brandon didn't know whether to look out the window or stare at her. He stared. So much for being cool, he thought. When they arrived at his house, she leaned over and gave him a peck on the cheek.

"See you tomorrow," she said, with a smile. His feet didn't touch the ground all the way up the drive.

At dinner all Donnie wanted to talk about was the next day's game. He knew Brandon would be starting on varsity, and he felt like he, himself, was re-living his first game on varsity. Donnie had been well known all over Lytle County when he was playing football. His name was still sometimes mentioned in Center City. He felt his son's athletic career was going to be just as exciting, even though he had been much bigger than Brandon in high school. But Brandon had hardly reacted to anything Donnie said at the table. He just sat there with a goofy look on his face.

"Son! What are you thinking about? I don't think you've heard a word I've been saying."

"Uh, nothing, Dad. I was, uh, zoning on the game."

"If you can't concentrate on the game any better than you can on this conversation, Coach will yank you out in a heartbeat."

Pulled out of his daydream, Brandon responded in his usual sarcastic manner, "Don't you worry, big daddy. When I get on the field, everyone better watch out! Clear the way! Brandon Hansen, coming through!" Alice didn't like what she was hearing and glanced at Donnie.

He merely told Brandon, "Show us, don't tell us."

The next day at lunch, Kristin saw him and went over to put her arm through his. Brandon just couldn't believe it! The most he had hoped for was that she'd go to the game, but showing the whole lunchroom that she liked him was more than he could have dreamed of. When she wanted him to walk over to another table to see some other friends, Brandon was thrilled to do it and to get the attention of the whole lunchroom. When they passed by Kristin's old boyfriend, she glanced at him, and then snugged in tighter to Brandon. The look on Eric's face was hard to read. Was it surprise, consternation, shock? Or was it just plain hurt? Brandon didn't know, all he was concentrating on was Kristin.

While the team was warming up that night for the game, Brandon couldn't keep his eyes from straying to the crowd, searching for Kristin. He hoped he would see her before the game started, or he could be in some serious trouble, not paying attention to his position. Finally, he saw her walk up to the fence to give a little wave of encouragement. That's all he needed to get his mind on what he was doing. He was really going to impress her with his fantastic playing tonight.

It was the first game of the season for both teams, and there were jitters, a few fumbles, and some failed plays. Brandon was aggressive on defense and managed to get a quarterback sack. A quick glance to the sidelines told him she was no longer there. She's up sitting in the stands, he thought. She had to have seen it, though. Most of the rest of the game was a yawner, other than brief excitement when two touchdowns were made. Lake Griffin made theirs by picking off a pass, deep in the other team's territory and scampering to the end zone, a total of about ten yards. The other team made theirs on the kickoff return. Their fastest guy caught the ball and kept running. Kickoff return is one of the most vulnerable times for defense, and the Mustangs weren't prepared for it. They did, however, have a great kicker, and when they had moved the ball down to the Panthers' twenty-yard line, he was able to kick a twenty-eight yard field goal in the last minute of the game. The game ended Mustangs, nine, Panthers, six. Not too terribly bad for a first game.

The whole time Coach had them in their post-game huddle, Brandon was looking for Kristin in the stands. He hardly heard the words of wisdom from Coach. He finally spotted her, down by the gate, deep in conversation with Eric. After the team huddle broke up, Brandon walked toward the gate, but stopped short and kept watching them. They weren't paying attention to anything but each other. It looked like Kristin's gestures were angry and from Eric's miserable face, he assumed they were arguing. After about five minutes of this, Eric put his hands on her arms. Kristin stopped gesturing, and her face softened. Then they embraced and kissed. As they walked off together, holding hands, Brandon felt like he had been kicked in the gut. If Eric's face had been miserable, Brandon's was now wretched. He quickly walked away, out of the stadium lights, so no one would see him upset.

It was all around school the next week that Kristin had used Brandon to get to Eric. Everyone knew that if she didn't get her way, things could get ugly. She had chosen Brandon because he was becoming a name in the school, and he was cute with his dark hair and blue eyes. Rumor had it that she was a controlling bitch, albeit a gorgeous one, and that she had broken up with Eric to make a point. All day Friday, Eric had walked around with his head down, looking like he had lost his only friend. However, she never had intended to stay broken up, and Eric, who was so whipped, gladly took her back Friday night after only a day and a half of being without her.

Brandon had never before encountered anyone who would use someone else's emotions to get what she wanted. He was angry, but he was also hurt. He tried to act nonchalant to his friends.

"I was just trying to see if I could get past second base with her. I'd heard she puts out. You know how it is. I don't have time to have a real girlfriend with football and gaming in computer club." He didn't know exactly how to handle his rejection, but he guessed he would figure it out eventually. In the meantime, he was trying to save face. Dan, Brandon's computer friend, couldn't leave it alone.

He said, "Hey, dude, how far did you actually get with the ice princess? Did she melt at all with you?"

Brandon replied, "We made out for a while in her car. She's not that good of a kisser, though."

Dan said, "Oh, come on now, you can tell me. Did you get a little feel of what's under that stacked sweater? You must have. Last year when she used me to get to her boyfriend, I was all over under there. Pretty nice."

"I didn't know you...."

"What? You didn't know I had a fling with her, too? Mine lasted a week, and we got pretty hot and heavy." Hearing everything that Dan had to say made Brandon even more upset and angry than he had been.

"Just shut the hell up!" Brandon stalked away. What a fool I've been, he thought. I was used and barely got a kiss. Dan practically had sex with her. And the whole cafeteria knows I've been dumped with nothing. I wonder who else she's used?

Chapter 29

Mrs. Cohen's health had seemed to improve in the month after she returned to school, but not enough to start up the TEAM Club. It seemed as if even that little extra would have been too much for her to manage. Then, starting on Halloween, she began being missing a half-day every other Friday. All the kids were getting really worried. Jenny got permission to go around the cafeteria during both lunches to try to organize an informal meeting of the club. She succeeded in getting about twenty kids to agree to stay after school the following Monday. When the afternoon arrived, there were about thirty-five kids there. Jenny clapped her hands to get everyone's attention.

"All right. I asked you all to come here because I think we should do something special for Mrs. Cohen."

"Yeah, you're right."

"What can we do?" Heads nodding, all were in agreement.

Jenny continued, "She must be really sick. I know a person has a right to privacy, but we love Mrs. Cohen like family. If we knew what was wrong with her, maybe we could help."

"But who's going to ask her?" Everyone seemed nervous about being the one.

Jaden spoke up, "Why don't you ask Mr. Anthony to find out for us?"

"That's a great idea. Let's go find him now."

The large group crowding outside of his office got Mr. Anthony's attention right away.

"Where's the fight?" Whenever there was a fight on campus, a large group always gathered around to help stop it, or in many instances, to egg it on.

"There wasn't a fight, Mr. Anthony. Our TEAM Club is wondering if you would tell us what's going on with Mrs. Cohen. We're really worried."

"Although I'm aware of Mrs. Cohen's situation, ethically, I can't talk to you about it. I *will*, though, go to her and express your concerns. I'm sure she'll appreciate knowing that you all care about her."

"Okay, guys, I guess that's all we can do for now," said Jenny, their acting leader, and they went their separate ways.

Mrs. Cohen didn't say anything on Tuesday, but on Wednesday she put the word out that she wanted to meet briefly with last year's club members on Friday. During class changes, kids talked in low voices wondering what she would have to say to them. Friday she met them looking pale, but with a smile on her face.

"I know you're all wondering what to think about my being sick. I appreciate it, but I don't want you to worry. I was diagnosed with breast cancer over the summer, and I had surgery right before school started. That's why I wasn't here the first few weeks of classes. Now I'm having chemotherapy every two weeks, and following that, I'll have radiation." Seeing their upset faces, a few with tears in their eyes, she said, "I told you not to worry. There have been so many advances in cancer treatments lately that my prognosis is very good, and they told me they got it all in the surgery, too. The treatments I'm having now are just to make sure any stray cancer cells are destroyed."

"But, you seem so tired all the time," someone ventured.

"That's part of what the treatment does to me. It makes me nauseated and tired. But I'll be fine. Just wait and see. I haven't wanted to talk about it for just that reason. I didn't want you to worry." Seeing a few faces begin to lighten up, she gave them a mischievous smile and told them she had to go home and take a nap.

Chapter 30

Brandon came home a few days later saying, "Hey, Jay and Jen. I saw your *Peter Pan* friend at school today. I've never seen him there before; he must have transferred from somewhere."

"Where did you see him?" Jaden quickly asked.

"I told you, dumb-shit, I saw him at school."

"No, I mean where in school did you see him?"

"He was flitting around the lunchroom, going table to table, just like the host of a party. Is he still doing that theater crap?"

Defensive, Jaden said, "His parents are in the theater and have been for years. It's a family thing."

"Can't you just see our family in the theater? Boy, wouldn't Dad love that!" Brandon laughed and walked on, then suddenly stopped. "So, Jaden, you still have that girlfriend from the summer?"

Nervous that Brandon may have put two and two together, Jaden said, "Uh, no. We broke up when school started." He was afraid to look at his brother. Never in a million years would he have expected what Brandon did next.

He went over and lightly punched Jaden in the shoulder and said, "Oh, well, buddy. You'll get over it. There're plenty of fish in the sea." With that he went in his room and started strumming his guitar.

Texting Trevor later that evening, Jaden told him what had transpired.

Trevor texted back, "What wld possibly make u think the idea of u having a gf wld b linked to me?"

"Idk, Trev. It makes me paranoid, I guess."

"Well, get over it. There's nothing to feel guilty about!" Feeling that now might be a good time to bring up the hug he had witnessed before school started, Trevor texted, "Can u call me? I want to ask u abt something." When Jaden called, Trevor started the conversation with, "Who was that cute guy you were shopping with before school started?"

"I didn't go shopping with any cute guy," Jaden denied.

"Don't even try. I saw you and him hugging in Old Navy. Light skin, braids? Come on, Jaden!"

Jaden cut him off, "Oh, you mean Devon. I've told you about him. He's my best friend at school. We weren't shopping together anyway. We just ran into each other."

"Looked like a little more than 'running into each other.'"

"Trevor! Are you jealous?"

"Hell, no, I just wanted to know who he was," Trevor tried to play it off. "I thought he was pretty cute."

"Don't worry about Devon. I've known him since fifth grade. We're just friends. You're the only one I care about that way." Hearing himself say those words made Jaden feel kind of funny. It was one thing to feel it, another to talk about it. After noting Jaden's sincerity, Trevor felt relieved, but still a little unsettled.

———

The first quarter at the high school ended with homecoming. There were going to be activities all week and a dance after the football game. Everybody who was anybody planned to go to the dance, including Brandon. And Trevor. Ever since the fiasco with Kristin, Brandon had been scouting around for a possible date and had his eye on Emily, a cute girl from his government class. He had gotten over the hurt of Kristin after a few weeks, but he still carried the anger and betrayal, deep down. His friend Dan, the one who had been impressed with Jenny at the play, had actually asked her to go, and Alice had given a provisional okay. Brandon had to attend the dance, and he had to double date with Dan.

Gathering up his nerve one day at lunch, Brandon said, "Hey, Emily, how ya doing?" When she gave him a wide smile, he felt a little better and proceeded. "Do you want to go to the homecoming dance with me?"

"Sure! I'd love to!" He saw a genuine look of happiness on her face as she answered him. That was excellent, because he wasn't about to be used again.

The dance was going to be in the gym, and there was going to be a live band. Everyone had to be dressed up. Jenny felt so mature as she and Alice were shopping for her dress. After discarding dress after dress, one really caught Jenny's eye. It was stunning! It was simple, but accentuated Jenny's long legs, and it was her favorite color, hunter green. A little pattern of rhinestones arranged right where the dress went up over the left shoulder completed it. Even Alice was amazed at how Jenny was transformed from a girl, almost fourteen, to a young lady. My little girl is growing up, and she's beautiful, Alice thought. Wait until Donnie sees her in this dress. While they were shopping, she picked out a new dress shirt and tie for Brandon.

"Who are you taking to the dance, Brandon?" Alice wanted him to ask his date what color her dress was, so that he could pick out the right corsage.

"I'm taking a girl named Emily, but you don't know her. I'll text her about her dress now." After a few minutes of texting, he reported to Alice, "She says she's going to wear a medium blue dress, and she'll need a wrist corsage, whatever that is." Alice just smiled at her elder son.

It was arranged that Brandon would use Alice's car. He would pick up Dan first, then Emily, after which he would go back home to get Jenny. Both Donnie and Alice wanted to meet Dan before letting their little girl go off with him.

When Brandon knocked on Emily's door, she greeted him, and his eyes almost popped out of his head! Her strawberry blond hair was done up on top of her head, like a princess. Her hair color set off her blue dress and made her look like she was a model or something. But it was her blue eyes that captured him. Her dress and her eyes were the same color of blue, and he was astounded that he hadn't noticed her eyes before now. He could look into those eyes forever.

He handed her the corsage and told her, "You have the prettiest eyes I have ever seen."

He could tell she was pleased with the compliment, but she only said, "Come in and meet my parents."

After the introductions were over, Brandon and Emily walked back to the car where Dan was waiting.

"Wow, Emily! You look terrific!" said Dan. He wondered what he would see when they got back to Brandon's. Jenny was still an eighth grader, but she was blossoming into a striking girl.

When Dan knocked on the door, Donnie answered and invited him in. Jenny was nowhere to be seen, so he nervously engaged in small talk with her parents. When Jenny walked through the door into the living room, it was Dan's turn to be struck with awe.

"Jenny, you look amazing!" Her dress emphasized the parts of her that had been steadily filling out since she had turned thirteen, but not in an immodest way. "I believe I'll have the prettiest girl at the dance, excluding no one! I can't wait to get there." Jenny lowered her eyes in embarrassment.

Donnie seemed to be showing no emotion about the fact that his baby girl was going to her first big dance. Not so much for Alice. Tears filled her eyes as she saw Jenny walk out the door. Jaden, who had come out of his room, looked at his mom like she was crazy.

"She's just going to a dance, Mom. She's not getting married."

When Brandon got his first look at Jenny he thought, she cleans up pretty well for a sister.

Aloud, he said, "You look nice, Jen." Praise from her big brother was worth more than almost anything. He had been her hero for so long, even though he had sometimes been mean to her.

She thought she must really look nice for Brandon to say so. She held that praise in a special place in her heart all the way to the school. When they arrived at the gym, they saw streamers and balloons all over the place and a big banner that read "Welcome to Homecoming." They went straight to the refreshment table, got a Coke, and began to mingle, hoping to find someone to hang out with. Looking around, Jenny suddenly felt very uncomfortable, because she knew very few high school kids, and no one looked familiar. Then she saw Devon, who saw her at the same time. He was walking with some girl she had never seen.

"Hey, Jenny. I didn't know you were going to be here. This is Teletha. She's in the ninth grade and invited me. Is Jaden here?"

"No, he's home." Remembering her manners, she added, "This is Dan, my date." Devon sized him up and remembered seeing him before, but couldn't remember where or when.

Devon shook his hand, turned and said, "How's it going, Brandon?"

"It's going good, can't you tell?" he said turning to smile at Emily. He was proud to show her off. After introducing her, they saw someone they knew and wandered off.

Devon said, "Do people actually dance at these things? I haven't seen anybody dancing yet."

"Oh, yeah," Dan said. "In about fifteen minutes, they'll turn off some of the lights, and then everybody will get out there."

"Good, I'm down with that. I like dancing, and I know Teletha does. How 'bout you, Jen?"

"I've never really danced before, but I have done 'Dance, Dance, Revolution' on the Wii."

"No problem, then. I wish they'd hurry up and turn off the lights; I'm ready to boogie."

Just before the lights went down, Jenny was startled to see, of all people, Trevor. He was with some girl she had never seen. Of course, she had never seen most of the people there.

She wondered what Jaden would think. Trevor just better not break her brother's heart! She was still staring at him when the lights dimmed, and Dan dragged her out on the floor. They danced almost every dance, until a mosh pit formed near the band. The chaperones put a stop to it right away. They tried to explain that they didn't want anybody to get hurt, and they should save their moshing for the "club." Grumbling, the students broke it up and started free dancing again.

Dan and Jenny went over to get something else to drink, and Jenny started looking around for Brandon, and especially for Trevor. Trevor was easy to spot. He was in the middle of the dance floor, all tall and good-looking, dancing with that girl. He kept dancing with her, even cheek to cheek, when the band played the occasional slow song. He looked like he was really into her. Jenny was more concerned than ever. She really felt like talking to someone about it, but there was no one who could know. It's just not fair, she thought. I can talk to Mom, Dad, or even Brandon about my problems, but Jaden has to keep everything a secret, except with me. I really need to be there for him if Trevor dumps him.

Jenny finally saw Brandon right before the lights came back up at the end of the dance. He and Emily were huddled in a secluded corner of the gym, making out. It didn't look like the chaperones had seen them at all. They separated quickly as the lights began to brighten. A high school dance is a real eye-opener, Jenny thought. It's certainly not just for dancing. She was glad that Dan wanted to dance and not make out. Dan was cute, and he obviously liked her, but she wasn't ready for an all-night make-out. I wonder if I'll feel the same way next year.

When the dance was over Brandon reversed the order of the pickup. He dropped Jenny off first, and Dan walked her to the door. She felt awkward, as he just stood there looking at her. Then he reached over and kissed her briefly on the lips. Jenny had an unexpected thrill. Maybe there really is something to kissing. Dan picked up on her reaction, and kissed her once again, a little longer and slower. As Dan walked back to the car, she stood there stunned. Wow! My first kiss, and with an older guy to boot, she thought dreamily as she went in the house.

"How was the dance?" asked Jaden, as she came in. "Was it fun or boring?"

"It was lots of fun! And Dan is really cute, and he kissed me good night! Jaden, it was a real kiss, sort of drawn out. It made me feel really good. I guess you know what that's like," said Jenny remembering Jaden's confession to her a while back. Jaden just grinned, glad that his sister had enjoyed her first real kiss. Jenny continued, still pumped, "I can't believe Mom and Dad let me go on a car date, even if my brother was the driver."

"What did you do?"

"We drank soda and ate chips, and mostly, we danced. I saw Devon there."

"Devon was there?" Jaden asked incredulously. "How did he get to go?"

"Some ninth-grade girl asked him. I guess she lives in his neighborhood. And you'll never believe who else I saw there."

"Who?" Jaden said a little crestfallen. It seemed like everyone got to go but him.

"Trevor was there!"

"Trevor?" said Jaden, and now his heart really sank. "Was anybody with him?" he asked anxiously.

"You don't have to worry. It was a girl, not a boy. And all they did was dance." Seeing Jaden's reaction to the news, she changed the subject and told him about the mosh pit and followed with, "Jaden! You wouldn't believe it. Your brother sat in a corner all night and made out with the girl he took, Emily. She really seems to like him and vice-versa. Actually, though, I thought it was pretty disgusting, and I was a little embarrassed that people might know he was my brother. But, after Dan kissed me, I felt a little different about it." Jaden sat and listened while Jenny was unwinding and wished he could have gone, too.

Somewhat relieved that Trevor had been with a girl, but still shaken, Jaden went to his room. He couldn't believe Trevor hadn't told him that he was going. Who was the girl he was with? As he lay on the bed, he was trying to decide if he should text Trevor or not. Now he understood why Trev had not answered any of his texts throughout the evening. He was dancing and having fun with someone else! Feeling left out he decided he would let Trevor text him first. No text came, though, all weekend.

Chapter 31

When Jaden saw Devon on Monday, he asked him, with a dismal look, how the dance was.

"Hey, dude, what's up? You don't look so good," Devon said.

Jaden answered a little petulantly, "It's just hard, because it seemed like everybody got to go to the dance, but me. You and everybody else were out having fun, and I was home by myself."

"Hey, bro, don't let it get you down. My neighbor didn't want to go by herself. It was just a dance. You and me will be going to all of them together next year." They did their special handshake. Looking at his friend with sudden clarity, he realized he shouldn't blame his feeling left out on Devon. He was still his best friend. Devon always knew how to cheer him up.

Trevor had taken off Saturday the day after the dance, so Jaden didn't see him at the Y. When Monday evening arrived, and still no text, Jaden decided to break the ice.

"Hey, Trevor," he texted. "What's doing?" Jaden felt sort of hesitant to even text him, because his texts on Friday had been ignored, but he couldn't stand to wait any longer. Trevor answered right away with a text asking Jaden to call, if he could.

"How are you?" answered Trevor on the first ring. Trevor sounded normal. Whatever was going on with him couldn't be that bad.

"I've really missed texting and talking to you - *all* weekend." Jaden couldn't help sounding dejected.

"I've missed you, too, Jaden. I've just been, well, really busy."

"I know. I heard you went to the dance with some girl." Jaden tried to keep his jealousy hidden.

"That was just a girl I've known forever, sort of like how you've known Devon forever." Jaden wasn't sure, but he thought Trevor sounded a little smug, which didn't help the situation at all. Then, as if nothing had happened, Trevor said, "The dance let out late Friday, and then Saturday, my dad took me shopping all day for, guess what? My car! We went to all the used car dealers in town and couldn't find what I wanted, so Sunday we went twenty miles away to Brownsburg. At the second lot, there it was! I held off texting, because I knew I wouldn't be able to keep it a secret if I talked to you. I was gonna try to surprise you next weekend. See what I mean? I already told you!" Trevor laughed.

Negative emotions forgotten, Jaden excitedly asked, "Did you buy it? What kind is it? What color is it?"

"It's a ten-year-old Mustang, blue with gray interior. It only has a small dent in the back fender on the driver's side, and everything works. We bought it for $3250. Dad chipped in like he said he would. Mustang, Jaden! We're gonna be stylin'."

"That's way cool, Trev. I can't wait to see it."

"Dad said I can start driving it to work, so you can see it Saturday."

"You rock, Trevor." Gone were the feelings of possible betrayal and anxiety, replaced with the exhilarating thought of riding around town with Trevor, in a Mustang.

The days until Saturday seemed to drag by for Jaden. He couldn't wait to see the new car! When Saturday finally punched the clock, he rushed over to the YMCA. There it was, in the parking lot, in all its glory. He didn't really want to look at it by himself, because he knew Trevor would want to show it to him. But, it was all he could do not to peer in the windows. He went to the pool area with a huge grin on his face.

"You saw it, didn't you?" Trevor said, disappointed that he had missed seeing Jaden's expression.

"I couldn't help but see it, Trev, but I didn't look inside or even go close."

The hour until Trevor's shift was over went slowly, but Jaden made the time pass by swimming all the competition strokes, three hundred yards each. (That was quite an accomplishment with the butterfly, if he did say so himself.)

At last, climbing down from the lifeguard chair, Trevor said, "Let's go!" Jaden had never dried off nor dressed so fast in his whole life.

The car was indeed as beautiful inside as it was out. The upholstery was in excellent shape, and the interior was clean as a whistle.

"This car will take us where we want to go, Jaden! Hop in."

Riding in the Mustang was incredible. Just being able to ride with your boyfriend, instead of your parents or brother would have been enough, but a sports car! Once again they drove to all the places where they might see or be seen, and then stopped at Sonic to get a slushie. When the carhop brought their beverages, they put their seats back a notch, held hands, and had the keen pleasure of car ownership and of being together in it.

"I guess I better get you home, so you don't get in trouble," Trevor finally said with regret. "What's your curfew on Saturdays, anyway?"

"I don't know. I guess I don't have a curfew yet. Mom just tells me what time I have to be home depending on where I go."

Jaden gave Trevor a kiss on the cheek before his house could be seen, and when they pulled up, Jaden jumped out quickly hoping no one would see him arrive. He wanted everyone to see Trevor's beautiful car, but didn't want to answer the questions that would surely follow.

Saturdays riding around in the car were awesome, but the time was just so short.

After a month of Saturdays, Trevor asked, "Do you think your parents would let you go out on a school night, say, if you told them you were going to the library?"

With a troubled look, Jaden responded, "I don't have a clue. I'm pretty sure my Dad wouldn't let me, but if I could ask my mom without him being around, maybe. Would your parents let you?"

"Oh, sure. They'll let me do anything if it's school-related."

After contemplating the idea, Monday after school, Jaden said, "Mom, do you think I could go to the library tonight? We have an English project due in a few days."

"What's your project about, hon?" Caught off guard and flustered, Jaden couldn't think fast enough. He didn't expect his mom would ask him what the project was about.

All he could get out was, "It's a hard project that takes time." Jaden was not a good liar, nor did he really want to be, but he really wanted to go out with Trevor.

"Is it a poster, or a report, or what?" He decided he had better backtrack.

"I guess I should find out more about the project before I go to work on it, Mom." Perplexed, Alice knew he was lying, but she had no idea why.

Jaden went to his room and texted Trevor about how royally he had screwed up.

"I just couldn't think, Trev. I'm not used to lying."

"I have another idea then. When u go to bed tonite, go out ur side window, and I'll pick u up abt 9." Jaden's eyes grew wide as he read the text.

"Crap. I really don't think I can do that. I've never done anything that bad bfr. What if I get caught?"

"Sure u can! It's not bad, ur not gonna do anything wrong. Just going to ride around. I'll have u back by 10. They'll never know the difference." As scared as Jaden was about doing something behind his parents' backs, he hesitantly agreed to meet Trevor at nine.

That evening Jenny went to Jaden's room to see if he understood the math homework. He had seemed to have trouble with it in class and didn't really get inequalities and absolute value inequalities. With a quiz tomorrow, she wanted to help him. She found him sitting at his desk, just staring at his book.

"What are you doing, Jaden? You know we have a quiz in math tomorrow. Have you done your homework?"

"I'll never get it, Jen, at least not in time for the quiz. Why bother?"

"That's no way to think! Don't be so negative," she said with a little irritation. Then, changing her tone, she cajoled him, "Come on, Jaden, I'll help you learn it." He lowered his head on his folded arms on the desk.

"I don't know what to do. I'm really upset, Jen. I'll never learn that math, and I'm sneaking out the window tonight to meet Trevor." Jenny gasped and stared at him.

"You will get in sooo much trouble. Are you nuts? Where will you meet him?"

"He has a car now, a Mustang. He's going to pick me up. I won't get in trouble if Mom and Dad don't find out. You won't tell, will you?"

"You know I would never tell on you, but don't you think Mom and Dad will see the car?"

"He won't stop right in front of the house."

"I think it's a crazy idea any time, but especially the night before a big math quiz. How do you think you're going to pass it if you don't study?"

"It's only eight now; maybe you could help me for an hour."

Jaden didn't think he would be able to concentrate, but he managed to for about forty-five minutes, enough that he would probably pass the quiz. At around eight forty-five, though, he had to stop, because his stomach was churning with nerves. Jenny left the room. She didn't want to see him climb out the window. Trevor was nice and cute, but she didn't want to be a witness to her twin doing something so sneaky. When she left, Jaden sat and stared at the clock, watching each minute go by. It was dark, but he was still afraid someone might look out the front window and see him get into the car. It was a Mustang, after all, and sure to be noticed.

He heard the car coming before he saw it. Holding his breath, he eased out the window and made it to the car before Trevor actually got to the house. The two boys rode around for about an hour, not really going anywhere in particular. Even with Jaden's sense of dread, it still was exhilarating. Being with Trevor really helped. He made it all worthwhile. A little before ten, Trevor pulled into the shadows near Jaden's house. Jaden hopped out and carefully made his way back to his window. He slid into bed, put the covers over his head and hoped to goodness his absence hadn't been detected. He breathed a sigh of relief that he was back home.

Chapter 32

Brandon and Emily had really hit it off and had become an item around school. Football had been over for a while, and there were still a couple of months before baseball started, so they spent almost every afternoon together. Whenever he saw Kristin, though, it aggravated him. He certainly didn't want to date her, but he was still angry about being used. He didn't even like passing her in the hall. That episode was over, but not done. The few spats that he and Emily had experienced were when Emily occasionally tried to get Brandon to talk about Kristin and what was eating at him. She could see with her own eyes the subtle change that came over him whenever Kristin was mentioned or encountered. He reminded her of a dog, ears flattened back, growling a warning. The animosity was obvious.

Brandon had told Emily when they first got together that he had a very short "thing" with Kristin, but found out she was a "bi-atch." Emily was well aware of what had happened, just like most of the other kids, but she didn't understand the continued antagonism he felt. She thought that if he just talked it out and let it go, he would feel a lot better and realize no one was making fun of him behind his back. But, he would have no part of a discussion about it. In fact, by the holidays, Brandon had escalated into verbally jabbing Eric, despite the fact that Eric had done nothing to him. Eric wasn't a hothead, so he didn't respond, but he was getting tired of being call a "wuss" or "whipped." Rather than have a confrontation, he just tried to avoid him.

Dan and Jenny's relationship coasted along for a few weeks, as teen relationships do. They called each other and texted some, but Dan ultimately decided that maybe Jenny was a little too young for him. It was not so much her age, but the fact that they had little in common to talk about. Jenny wanted to talk about middle school happenings and Young People's Theater, while Dan really was past that period of his life. They parted on good terms, because Jenny wasn't ready, nor did she have time to have a relationship yet. Dan thought he might try to start it back up when Jenny was in high school next year. She really was cute.

Chapter 33

Jaden and Trevor had made it a habit to see each other on Saturdays and again, at night, once or twice a week. Their relationship had progressed to a new level and was becoming a lot more intimate. There was a lot of touching and long embraces. Jaden was still very nervous every time he snuck out, but it seemed to get easier each time. Trevor's arms around him made him feel so safe, something he hadn't felt at home. It was a feeling he had never known before. He felt he could tell him anything, and it would be okay. Devon was his best friend, but he could never talk to him about emotions and feelings. When he was with Trevor, he felt like they could take on the world together. It wouldn't matter what anyone else thought. Jaden couldn't think of anything that had ever made him happier.

The only part that bothered Jaden was facing his parents the mornings after he had snuck out. Knowing how his parents would feel about it made him conscience-stricken. He made eye contact with them as little as possible, and his guilt grew, but being with Trevor was something he couldn't sacrifice.

"Donnie, do you think Jaden is acting a little strangely?" Alice wanted her husband's take on the situation.

"No, why do you ask?"

"He just doesn't seem to be himself. He's always been so open about what's going on at school, who his friends are, and how he's feeling. But now, he just stares at his plate when he's eating and spends a whole lot of time in his room."

"Oh, I don't think that's anything to worry about, Alice. He's just being a typical teenager. You know how Brandon is."

"I hope you're right, but somehow I think he's lying to me."

"If he's not talking much, what could he be lying about?" said Donnie, being practical.

"Something just doesn't feel right."

At the next women's group meeting, Alice decided she would speak up about her family for the first time, instead of just listening. Actually, she wanted some advice. Surely, at least one of these women had experienced what she was going through. After everyone admired the table setup, poured coffee or tea and helped themselves to sandwiches and cookies, the meeting got started.

Alice bravely spoke up and said, "I know I haven't had much to say since I've joined this group, but I've learned a lot by listening. And I've discovered that so many of you are strong, positive women and yet, still run into the same hurdles in life that I do. I'm hoping someone can shed some light on my current one. I'm worried about my younger son. He's almost fourteen and has always been a cheerful, outgoing kid. Lately, he's become withdrawn, reticent. I don't know what's going on with him."

Grace spoke first, negative, as usual, and said, "He's probably experimenting with drugs. They all do."

"That's not one bit fair, Gracie," retaliated Debbie. "Just because a kid becomes withdrawn doesn't mean he's on drugs. Maybe he's having trouble in school or his girlfriend dumped him."

"I think that's a more likely explanation, too, Deb," said Carol. "I know when my son was in school, his whole world fell apart when he was fighting with his girlfriend. Sometimes, it seemed like every day."

Alice said, "I don't think he has a girlfriend yet, and his grades seem okay."

"Then it's drugs, like I said to begin with," repeated Grace. Groans sounded around the room. Carol had a good idea.

"Why don't you have a parent/teacher meeting to see if his behavior has changed in school? I used to have to go to those once a quarter, but it was the teachers who called them," she said wryly. Her son hadn't been the best of students. Alice offered up one more piece of information.

"I don't know why, but I think he's lying to me. He's never lied before."

"I know how unnerving that can be," consoled Joanna.

"Well, you may not all agree that it's probably drugs, but when kids stop talking except to lie to their parents, it's a sure sign that they're doing something they don't want their parents to know about, something they feel they need to hide," said Grace, speaking again.

"Well, what are other signs that I should look for?" asked Alice.

Sally spoke up saying, "The classic signs of hiding things, like drug use, are personality change, as you mentioned, as well as a new group of friends, loss of interest in old activities, truancy, tardiness, behavior problems in school, mood shifts - the list goes on, but those are some of the more obvious signs."

"Where did you learn so much, Sally?" asked Carol.

Sally laughed and said, "My sister is one of those guidance counselors in high school that had to call parents like us for conferences." Carol smiled ruefully.

Sally continued, "Alice, maybe you should just pay attention to your son for more changes. It's not a given that it is a drug problem, either. He might be going through something that he doesn't want to talk about. Have you thought about talking to *him* about your concerns?"

Alice was still worried, but at the same time encouraged. She told them he would be her number one priority until she got to the bottom of this, and that the first thing she would do was talk to him.

Chapter 34

Miss Bonnie

*I*t had been a while since Jaden and I had talked, other than a few words in passing. He was growing up and getting busier, and I had expected that he would branch out from me. But he came to see me after school today, very upset.

"Miss Bonnie, I've been messing up. I've been sneaking out my window at night to meet Trevor."

Seeing the look on his face, I responded, "It's not easy to deceive your parents, is it?"

"It's awful, I feel so guilty, but I can't stop," he said sorrowfully.

"What do you do when you sneak out?"

"We don't do much of anything. We drive around in his Mustang and make out and stuff."

"Have you asked your parents if you could go out with him?"

"No, I'm sure my dad wouldn't let me."

"Jaden, I know you're feeling guilty, and while it's wrong to deceive your parents, you may be being too hard on yourself."

"But, I'm scared. I know how my dad is, and we've sort of been getting along since this summer. But if he found out about Trevor and told me I couldn't see him anymore, I would die."

"Have you considered that even if he knew about Trevor, that it wouldn't necessarily mean he would know about your relationship?"

"Well, no, I hadn't thought of that. I do know that he thinks Trevor is a fag, though."

"Jaden, that was over a year ago. He hasn't called you a fag lately, has he? Could it be possible that he's calmed down about that?"

"Man, that would be great! I hope you're right, Miss Bonnie. Maybe I'll talk to my mom about all this."

Alice had been watching for Jaden to come home from school. When he finally came around the corner, she watched him stop at Miss Bonnie's house first and go inside. She had hoped he would come straight home, so she could talk to him before the others got there. She was relieved when he only stayed a few minutes, then headed home.

"Hi, Sweetheart, how was school?"

"It was fine, Mom. We have a history test tomorrow." Alice was somewhat encouraged. For weeks his comments had been little more than one word. At least this was a start.

"Jaden, let's sit down and talk a little." He looked at her quickly, wondering if she knew what he was thinking. He had wanted to start the conversation himself, and he was a bit nervous about where this was going. He decided to let her go ahead without saying anything. "How is your history class going, honey?"

"It's going okay. It's so much better than at the beginning of the year when Mrs. Cohen was out."

"How is Mrs. Cohen doing?"

"She's still tired a lot, but she said she finishes her chemo right before the holidays, so she can rest up then. When she gets back, she starts radiation treatments. Who knows how that will make her feel."

"Are you doing okay with your grades?"

"Mom, you know I made three As and three Bs on my report card!"

"That was almost six weeks ago. It's almost time for another report card. Are you keeping up in math?"

"It's kind of hard. I might make a C this time. Jenny helps me, but sometimes I just don't understand what's going on." Jaden thought, maybe Mom is just worried about my grades. But, then she changed the subject.

"Why did you decide not to be in Young People's Theater this year?" she asked. "I thought you loved it." He couldn't tell her that the real reason was that Trevor wasn't in it.

"Oh, I don't know, just decided not to. I know Dad's happier that I'm not." Alice was at a loss for a response, because she knew it was true. She changed her tack.

"Have you made any new friends in school this year?"

"I have friends in all my classes, but mostly Devon and I hang out. But he has basketball practice after school, so we can't then."

Feeling as if she were getting nowhere, Alice finally asked, "Is something troubling you, Jaden? You haven't seemed to be yourself lately." Jaden sighed and thought she was finally getting to the point. This would probably be a good time to bring up Trevor.

"Actually, Mom, something is bothering me. I've been scared to talk to you about it, because I was afraid you would tell Dad."

"My goodness! What is it?"

"Do you remember Trevor, from the play last year? He's one of my best friends, and I know Dad doesn't like him. I hardly ever get to see him, and I want to do stuff with him, like go to the mall or the movies. I'm afraid Dad will say no."

"Honey, your dad isn't an ogre. I can't believe he wouldn't let you be friends with Trevor." Inside, she felt a little less confident than she sounded.

"Would you ask him, Mom? I'm scared to." When she said yes, the look of relief on his face made her feel awful. Poor kid, afraid of his dad.

When the usual commotion of evening was over, and the kids were in their rooms, Alice said to Donnie, "I talked to Jaden today."

"Did you get anywhere?"

"Donnie, he wants to be friends with Trevor, the boy in the play. He's afraid you won't let him."

"You're damn right I won't let him! Didn't you see how well he did this summer when he was away from that freak? I'm not going to let him get his hands on Jaden."

"Really?" she said with a little sarcasm. Then more to the point she said, "Donnie, please. Jaden is the same way he has always been. He's not into sports, so you think there's something wrong with him."

"You don't understand, Alice. If you hang with a fag, you'll become a fag. I won't have that happen to my son."

"There are lots of people who have friends who are homosexuals, and they don't *turn* gay. Plus, we don't even know that Trevor is that way. You just think he is. Do you think you might be overreacting because of what happened with that priest?"

"I'm not overreacting, and Jaden's not going to be friends with that boy. End of story." Then he said somewhat bitterly, "I knew I shouldn't have confided in you."

"I really think you need some counseling, Donnie. You need to make peace with your past."

"End of that story, too! I'm not going to go bellyaching to some kook and have him tell me all that psycho-babble." Alice knew she was making no headway, so she stopped trying.

When Jaden searched his mom's face in the morning, she just shook her head with a pained look. Back to plan B, Jaden thought. I guess I'll have to keep sneaking out the window, 'cause no one is stopping me from seeing Trevor.

Chapter 35

Christmas holidays came and went, and Mrs. Cohen returned to school, looking like a new person. The two weeks off with no chemo had made her feel much better. Jaden was still sneaking out, and softball and baseball had started for Jenny and Brandon. Alice wasn't as worried as she had been about Jaden, because she believed he was just upset because he couldn't see his friend.

Softball tryouts went smoothly this year, not at all like the year before. Barb had practiced enough since then that she actually made the team this time. Jenny was thrilled because now she had a friend who was actually a player. The "travel team" girls seemed to be doing little more than ignoring her. She and Barb warmed up together daily, and practice was going like clockwork.

"I wonder what caused the change in those girls this year?" marveled Barb. "I can't say they're nice, but at least they leave you alone."

"I don't care what caused it," Jenny said. "I'm just glad that maybe we can be a team this year." What the two friends didn't know was that Mrs. Cohen had gone to Mr. Anthony last year. This year before the season started he had called in that whole clique and had a little heart-to-heart with them. They seemed to have gotten the message.

———

Brandon knew he had a starting position at third base this year. Jason, last year, had been a senior, and no one else was close to beating him out. His glove was as good as ever, and his hitting seemed to be improving. He just wished he had a little more power. As pre-season wore on, he became good friends with the left fielder, Derek.

"Derek, what gym do you work out in?"

"I go to Hard Body Fitness, over there near the Y. I went all summer and in the off-season. I'm really trying to get a community college scholarship."

"Did you work out every day? Look at the size of your muscles! You've got some guns!"

"Actually, I did work out every day, one day legs, the next, upper body, but even though I've always worked out off-season, that was my first time to work out in the summer, too."

"How did you get so big, then?"

"This guy that comes in the gym has some protein pills that help build muscles. I bought some from him, and they work. But you still have to bust ass for them to be effective. Nothing happens automatically. No pain, no gain," grinned Derek.

"How much are they?"

"My trial pack was ten dollars for twenty-eight pills, but now I buy the hundred-twenty pack for thirty-five bucks.

"Do you think you could get me some? I have a membership at the Y. Maybe some days you could meet me there and show me your workout. Then, some of the time I could probably go to Hard Body with you."

"Sounds like a plan, Brandon. It's much more fun to work out with somebody, than alone."

Two days later, after practice, Derek gave Brandon the high sign to meet up with him.

"I have your trial pack. Do you have your money? I had to pay the guy out of my own pocket."

"Yeah, I've got the cash. I can't wait to get started. How do I do it?"

"You take two five mg pills in the morning, and then two more in the afternoon. You should notice a difference in a week. You'll gain some weight, too."

"Sweet! I'll go work out with you tomorrow after practice if that's good with you."

"That's cool. On the days we have practice, I only work out an hour, but on weekends, I do two hours. By the way, don't tell anyone about the pills. I'm pretty sure they're legal, but I'd rather not broadcast it." They fist-bumped in agreement.

Chapter 36

Except when he was with Devon, Jaden had started hanging out with Jenny and her friends in school. He didn't seem to have many guy friends, except the ones who had been in TEAM Club, and since the club wasn't meeting, he rarely saw them. Jenny's friends liked him and thought he was cute. That striking blond hair, blue eyes, and the fact that he was quite a bit shorter than Jenny all made him adorable to them. He liked them, too. They would ruffle his hair, smack his butt in passing, and had started confiding in him when they had boy problems. Since he and Devon didn't have lunch together this year, he became the only boy to sit with the girls at their table. He fit right in, and there were lots of spirited discussions, as well as lots of laughter at that table.

Other kids at second lunch had begun to notice Jaden at the girls' table. Usually, the tables were either a good mix of the sexes, or all boys, or all girls. A single girl at a boys' table was not unusual, because typically several of the boys had invited her. However, a double standard existed when there was a single boy at a girls' table. He must be a fairy. Everyone knew that girls just talked about boys, and this kid was joining right in. Murmurs started at one table, moved to another, and soon, the whole lunch group was aware that the name of the boy sitting with the girls was Jaden. Middle school kids can be cruel, and some of the boys started calling Jaden names, when they passed in the halls.

At first it was under their breath, but as they got bolder, they would say it to his face.

"Fag!"

"Queer!"

"Gay Jay!" That was their favorite. Jaden didn't know what to think. He had never done anything to any of those people. He let it go as long as he could, then spoke to Jenny about it.

"I don't know why they're calling me names, Jen. I don't even know most of them, and I've haven't said anything mean to them."

"Who's calling you names? You tell me right now!" He told her the ones he knew, but there were a lot he didn't know.

The next day at lunch Jenny was on a mission. She made her way over to a table of boys, several of whom Jaden had mentioned by name.

Indignantly, she asked, "Jeremy, how do you get off calling my brother names? And, Alberto, I always thought better of you. You used to be nice. Kendrick, I remember back in fourth grade when people made fun of you because you had nappy hair and ashy skin. How can you call people names when you know it feels? I can't believe that boys who are almost in high school can be so stupid."

"Come on, Jenny, don't get your panties in a wad. We're just teasing him. Plus, you know he really does like boys."

"That's bull! I don't know it, and neither do you!" Jenny was mad.

Jeremy said, "Then why do I see him every Saturday, riding around with a boy in a Mustang, sitting real close?"

"You're just jealous because you don't have a Mustang to ride around in. I don't want to hear any more name-calling or I'll go to Mr. Anthony - with *your* names!"

As Jenny returned to her own table, she saw panic on Jaden's face.

He called her away from the table and asked, "What did you say to them, Jenny? I didn't want you to talk to them about it. Now it'll only get worse."

"It's not going to get worse. I told them if they kept it up, I'd tell Mr. Anthony."

Jaden grimaced and thought, now I'll be a fag that has to have his sister and the assistant principal stand up for him. Could things get any worse?

Then he told Jenny, "Please don't say anything to anyone else. I'll find a way to deal with it."

Jenny continued the conversation by accusingly saying, "By the way, Jay, I thought you went swimming at the Y every Saturday. Jeremy said he sees you riding around in a Mustang every Saturday."

"I do swim, Jenny. I really want to be on the swim team next year. But after Trevor gets off from lifeguarding, we ride around for a while. I hate being sneaky, but Dad won't let me be friends with him."

Jenny heart softened, and she sighed deeply and thought, it's so unfair; I wish there was something I could do to help him.

At least those boys at lunch don't bother me anymore, Jaden gratefully thought after a few days, but it's really hard to ignore the ones who still do. He had been getting pretty down about it. Summing things up, Jaden felt his dad thought he was a fag, just like the kids at school did. He wasn't allowed to cheer, he wouldn't let him see Trevor, he couldn't seem to do anything right, and he was beginning to think he was worthless. His posture had begun to slump, and he walked around with a hangdog look. He lived for Saturdays and the nights he sneaked out. There was one bright spot on the horizon, though. Cheerleading tryouts for high school were coming up, and he was looking forward to that. He knew he couldn't try out, but he had offered to help the girls at his lunch table with the stunts and cheers he knew. The enthusiasm they had displayed when he made his offer made him feel good. It was nice to know he was valued by at least someone, for something he loved.

Chapter 37

Right around the time of cheerleading tryouts, the swim coaches at the high school called a meeting at the middle school for potential swimmers. They had the meeting in one of the classrooms, and it was crowded, standing room only. Devon went with Jaden, but he was debating whether to swim or play football.

"Devon, I'll be so disappointed if you don't swim," Jaden said wistfully. "But, I can see why you'd want to play football. You're so good! I know the high school coaches were watching you play last fall. I've gotten used to practicing by myself, so I guess I can stand it if you don't swim. I don't want you to feel guilty if you decide to play football instead."

"My mind's not completely made up yet, Jay. We did make a pact to swim together in ninth grade. I could play football from tenth on, if I wanted to. I'm going to think about it over the summer."

"Oh! That'd be so great!" Jaden finally felt like one thing might go right in his life.

Glancing around the room, Jaden noticed a lot of kids he had seen in the halls, a few he knew, and thank goodness, no one that had tormented him. There was this one kid, though, a boy, that he had never seen. Something about the way he looked made Jaden feel he'd like to get to know him.

After all the endless paperwork had been handed out and the meeting was over, Jaden walked up to him and said, "Are you new here? I don't think I've ever seen you before." The kid had dark hair and eyes, and a soft, almost effeminate body.

"I just move here from Brownsville, Texas." Jaden noticed that he spoke with a Spanish accent.

"What's your name? Mine's Jaden."

"I am Ricardo." He spoke slowly, as if he had to think through his words.

"Have you been on a swim team before, Ricardo?"

"Oh, si, I swam very much in Texas. Then my parents had to move us here to find work."

"Was today your first day here?"

"Yesterday. I know no one."

"What lunch do you have?"

"I have second, but I don't go to cafeteria."

Jaden exclaimed, "Why not?" Then he felt embarrassed as he realized that maybe Ricardo didn't have money for lunch. Ricardo dropped his eyes and didn't answer. Jaden thought he would do something about that. "Where do you go when it's lunch time?"

"I go to library. There are several in there at lunch."

"Well, tomorrow I want you to sit at our table in the cafeteria. I want you to meet my sister and some of my friends."

"Okay. I go to there tomorrow."

When Jaden arrived home, he found Alice in the kitchen.

"Mom, can I take my lunch to school tomorrow? And, can I take an extra sandwich?"

"Sure, honey, what's up?"

"I met a new friend today, and I don't think he has money for lunch."

"Sweetie, that is so good of you." She hugged him then, said, "You've always been my sensitive and caring child. I love that in you." Jaden hugged her back with a big bear hug. He loved pleasing his mom.

The next day at lunch, Jaden scoured the room looking for Ricardo. He had almost given up when Ricardo shyly came in and stood by the door, eyes searching the room. Jaden bounded from his seat and rushed over to him. He grabbed him by the arm and practically dragged him back to the table.

"Here, sit here," Jaden said excitedly. "This is my sister, Jenny, and this is Ellen, Katie, and Bev." Slightly overwhelmed with all the attention, Ricardo didn't say anything.

"Take this sandwich, Ricardo. My mom made an extra for you."

"You can share my grapes, too, Ricardo," said Bev.

"I can't take your food," Ricardo finally said.

"No, please eat this. Mom made it especially for you."

"My family is not poor," Ricardo said defensively.

Jenny, always the wise one, said, "Just because you share someone's food doesn't mean you're poor. It just means you are willing to consider that person a friend. I hope you consider all of us your friends." Giving in, Ricardo took the sandwich and ate it with relish.

"So, why haven't you come to the cafeteria before?" asked Ellen, naively.

Jaden jumped quickly into the conversation saying, "He probably just didn't know where it was before. This is just his third day." Satisfied, the girls went back to their conversation about cheerleading tryouts.

When lunch was over, the two boys walked out and down the hall together.

Ricardo shyly told Jaden, "The office told me I could eat for less money. I just have to have my parents sign the paperwork. But, that is not why I don't come to cafeteria."

"Then, what is the reason?" They walked a few paces with no conversation.

Stopping at a classroom door, Ricardo at last said, "This is my class. I tell you tomorrow." As Jaden walked to his own class, he wondered what the reason could be. Maybe it's just because he didn't know anyone. That was as good a reason as any, and the only one he could think of.

"How did your friend like his lunch?" Alice asked when the twins walked in.

"He seemed to love the sandwich. He scarfed it down!" said Jaden.

Jenny added, "It must be true that he didn't have any money for lunch. He seemed really hungry."

Alice told them, "You know, the school has a program that will help kids like that get lunch if they don't have money. Should I call the school and let them know there's a needy student?"

"No," Jaden said. "He already has the paperwork for it." Jaden thought, but there's another reason. Maybe I'll find out tomorrow.

The next day, like every other day at lunch, the girls chattered about the cheerleading tryouts that were starting Monday. Even though Jenny didn't plan to try out, she was still excited for her friends. Softball season had finished uneventfully the week before. No tears, no blowups, and they had actually had a decent season, going six-four. Mr. Anthony had seemed to be the biggest faculty supporter of the team, going to every home game. It had made Jenny and Barb feel good that a faculty member cared enough about the team to show up at the games. No one knew that he was doing double-duty - enjoying the games but also keeping an eye on the "travel team." The boys' teams always had good crowds, but except for basketball, the girls' teams were usually only cheered on by parents and a few friends. Maybe it would be different in high school.

Jaden was in the middle of every cheerleading conversation at the lunch table, suggesting different moves he could teach the girls to get the judges to notice them. Even Ricardo started to liven up a bit.

"I can do that one," he would say. "Maybe I can help, too."

"Awesome, dude," said Jaden. "That would rock!" It was arranged at the table that Jaden and Ricardo would show up for thirty minutes after school each day prior to the formal tryout practice. They would work with their friends during that time, and then watch them do the other required moves during the rest of the practice.

The next day leaving lunch, Jaden was impatient to hear what Ricardo might say.

"So, what's the deal, Ricardo? What was your reason for avoiding the cafeteria?"

"It's kind of hard to say, mi amigo, but I trust you. At my other school people would make fun of me. They would say I walk like a girl and call me a *maricon*, a faggot. I find it's easier to stay away from people." Jaden couldn't believe his ears. Here was someone else, in his own school, who had the same problem he had. I wonder if he's gay, too, thought Jaden. I know Miss Bonnie told me that lots of kids are, but I didn't expect to find anyone in my own middle school. Jaden decided not to press the issue right now. It really didn't matter that much if he was gay or not. All that mattered was that he had a friend who needed help, and he was there to give it. Maybe there would be strength in numbers.

When cheerleading practice actually started, Jaden and Ricardo had a blast. Ricardo could already do a lot of the moves that Devon had taught Jaden, and those that he couldn't, he picked up quickly. It was so much fun for Jaden to teach Ricardo. Then they would demonstrate together for the girls. Each boy would take one of the girls through the steps and critique their efforts. Ellen and Bev caught on fairly well, but Katie really struggled.

"I don't think I'm cut out for this," she said mournfully. "My body doesn't want to move that way."

Jaden quickly encouraged her saying, "You don't have to do everything we can do. Just make sure you can do the required things. These are just extra." Katie kept trying, but it was clear that she was not very agile, nor suited for stunts. Ricardo seemed to blossom as he helped Ellen. Apparently, his self-esteem had been rock bottom, and no wonder with the cruelty at his other school. But, it was being buoyed up by being able to help someone. A lot of the other girls trying out noticed right away the extra help those girls were getting. They started coming early, too, hanging out around the boys, watching them as they taught. Unfortunately, boys who were playing spring sports began to notice the boys also.

"Set your feet like this when you get ready to do your handspring, Bev." Jaden was a good teacher, pointing out tips that would help shorten the learning curve. He did a round-off, then, stopped in exactly the right position to follow with a back handspring.

"You make it look so easy, Jaden," she replied. "I'll never get it that good."

"Don't forget I've been doing this for a couple of years, Bev. You can do it with a little practice." As she rewarded him with a big smile, a couple of unfriendly onlookers moved closer.

"Hey, queer-boy. You trying out this year? You'll look pretty cute in the short skirts they wear." Snickering, two or three other boys joined the little group.

"Yeah, you gonna wear tights under your skirt, too?" That must have been the funniest thing said in years, because all five of the outsiders began hooting and hollering.

"Woo-hoo! Can you picture his package in tights?"

"That's nasty! That's something I'd rather not picture." That set off another round of laughter.

"Hey, look over there. There's another faggot. Where did he come from?"

"Who knew there were Mexican faggots?" Enraged, Jenny flew out of her seat, ready to do damage to at least one of those boys.

"You're nothing but a dick, you and all your idiot friends. You make fun of people doing stuff that you probably couldn't come close to doing." As

Jenny was about to raise her knee to the crotch of a kid who had grabbed her shoulders, the cheerleading coach rushed over to see what was going on. Ricardo was trying to disappear into the ground, while Jaden was trying not to look as humiliated as he felt.

The cheerleading coach said, "You boys get out of here and go wherever you're supposed to be. I don't want to see you around here again! Is that understood?"

"Yes, ma'am, Mrs. Spencer. We weren't trying to cause trouble. We were just having a little fun."

She said, in a voice that was not to be reckoned with, "Having fun at someone else's expense is not fun. It's just plain bullying. Do it again, and I'll write you all up."

Put in their place, the boys left. While Mrs. Spencer was talking to the group, Jaden and Ricardo took advantage of the opportunity to "get the hell out of Dodge." When they were well out of sight of the cheerleading practice, Jaden's emotion turned from impotence to anger. He could see how upset Ricardo was and thought how unfair the attack on them had been.

"Ricardo, I know how you feel! We were trying to do a good thing by helping our friends. Those guys had no reason, no business at all coming over and messing with us. Who do they think they are?" Ricardo was silent. Jaden ranted on, "Can't people just leave us alone? We haven't done anything to anybody. Why do they always have to ruin everything?" Ricardo was still silent. In another moment, Jaden's face fell. His anger had fizzled out, and his old feelings of worthlessness took over. He thought, why do I even try? It never works. Finally, Ricardo sorrowfully spoke up.

"It's not your fault. It's me. That is what happened at my old school. You are my good amigo, but you shouldn't be with me. There is always trouble."

"No, no, Ricardo. It happens to me, too, almost every day in the hall. Those guys are just bullies. We'll just try to finish up school this year, and next year we'll be on the swim team! Then they'll give us some respect." Ricardo seemed doubtful, but didn't comment.

Chapter 38

Ricardo and Jaden had become fast friends. Their similar plight drew them closer and closer, and they tried to meet up after every class, so they could walk to their next class together. They walked down the hall staring straight ahead and trying not to listen to the derogatory remarks that never seemed to end, at least from one faction of the student body. Boys, especially rednecks and jocks, couldn't seem to live-and-let live and keep their mouths shut.

When Jaden first told Trevor about Ricardo, he said, "Oh, is he cute? Take a picture with your phone, and send it to me."

Jaden said, " You don't have anything to worry about. I'm only interested in you."

When Jaden sent Trevor the picture, Trevor texted back, "Holy shit! I didn't know he'd b that cute!"

"I told u, we're just friends," Jaden texted back.

However, when they met up that Saturday and were finally alone, Trevor grabbed both of Jaden's hands, seriously looked in his eyes, and said, "Are you positive we're okay? I can't help but be a little nervous about the fact that you and Ricardo get to see each other every day." Jaden pulled Trevor to him, kissed him on the neck, and held him in a long embrace.

"It's all you, Trevor, it's all you."

Trevor sighed deeply and said, "You mean so much to me, Jay. You make me want to get up in the morning, and I think of you all day long. You're the best thing that's ever happened to me." Jaden felt so warm and secure in Trevor's arms. It was incomprehensible to him that Trevor would ever have doubts about his feelings.

———

Brandon was very happy with the progress his muscles were making. At home in the bathroom, he would flex in front of the mirror, turning this way and that. On the baseball field, he was hitting harder than he ever had.

He was thrilled when his coach noticed and told him, "Your body is finally maturing, Brandon. I told you to have patience. You're hitting harder than anyone else, and I know some recruiters are already looking at you."

In school, Brandon was becoming more and more rowdy. He couldn't keep his hands to himself; he would jab and punch everyone, in a kidding way, but people were tiring of his annoying behavior. He had a lot of energy that he couldn't seem to find an outlet for. Outside of the classroom, if someone disagreed with him, he was ready to scrap. Now, he even looked for Eric, so he could make coarse insults to him. If he walked up behind him, he would intentionally bump into him, then sarcastically say, sorry man, I didn't see you there. Eric was at a loss as what to think of Brandon's unpredictable behavior. How long was this going to go on?

At home, Brandon was argumentative. After having had a brief respite over the summer, he and Donnie were at each other's throats again.

"What in the hell is wrong with you, Brandon? You don't run this household, and I'm tired of you picking fights with your brother and sister."

"There's nothing wrong with me! Those kids are annoying. Just leave me alone!"

Even Emily was getting tired of the way he was acting. She knew his encounters with Eric were escalating, but she didn't know how to stop it. One day after school as they were walking to their lockers, some kid brushed against Brandon's shoulder. Brandon turned around with fire in his eyes and his fist cocked. Astonished at the reaction, the kid told Brandon to chill and tried to move on. Brandon blocked his way.

"You wait a minute, jerk. Don't think you're gonna knock me around and get away with it."

"I accidentally brushed your shoulder, man. Just chill!"

"You want 'chill'? Well, here's some 'chill' for you!" With that, he hauled off and punched him in the face.

The guy, with his hand on his bleeding mouth and looking like he wanted to tear Brandon's head off, said, "You've just made a big mistake, dickhead. You'll live to regret it." He turned on his heel and stomped off.

"Now you've done it, Brandon. Who knows who that kid will get to gang up on you. I'm sick of the way you act, I'm sick of your attitude, and I've had it. We had a great thing going, but I'm done. You're not the same person you used to be." As she spoke, it was Brandon's turn to be shocked.

He just stared at her a minute, then said, "Fine, I'm tired of you, anyway. You're always trying to run my life, telling me what to do and when to do it. You're history!" Emily was so hurt at that accusation that she couldn't say a word. Crying, she walked out to her car.

The next day Mrs. Mackey, the principal, called Brandon into her office.

"You want to tell me what happened yesterday, Brandon?" He tried to play it off cool.

"What are you talking about?"

Mrs. Mackey replied, "You know exactly what I'm talking about!"

"You mean the little snitch told on me?" He couldn't believe it! Nobody ever told on anybody else.

"A custodian witnessed the event and told me that you hit James Blair, and he didn't hit back. What I want to know is, why did you hit him?"

"Because he's just a dumbass."

"Really? You're sure that's the story you want to stick with?" Brandon shrugged, as if he couldn't be bothered. "I'm calling your father right now. You're suspended for five days." Suddenly, his demeanor shifted drastically. This might turn out badly for him.

"Wait a minute, Mrs. Mackey. You can't suspend me during baseball season! We're about to go into the district tournament."

"I can, and I will."

As she reached for the phone, she said, "I'm calling your father while you're here. Do you want to tell him what you've done, or do you want me to?" She paused expectantly.

What she didn't expect was Brandon's standing up in anger, pushing his chair back so abruptly that it crashed to the floor, and shouting, "Screw this shit! I'm outta here!" Mrs. Mackey raised her eyebrows in shock and alarm. Here was a student that neither she, nor any other administrator, had ever seen in their offices for discipline.

Brandon stormed out of the office and headed for the door, not sure where he was headed, not caring. He was royally pissed, and he knew his dad would hit the ceiling. His dad had been on him for months now, and when he heard about this, he would be grounded the rest of his life. He decided not to go home for a while. He just didn't want to hear it.

When Mrs. Mackey got Donnie on the phone and began to explain the nature of her call, he thought there must be some mistake. There must be another Hansen in the school. As she continued, the blood drained from his face, his legs got shaky and he sat down. When she repeated Brandon's exiting remarks, Donnie expelled his remaining breath and felt a cold sweat beading on his forehead.

After a moment, Mrs. Mackey said, "Mr. Hansen, are you there?"

He managed to summon enough composure to reply, "Yes, yes, I'm here. I'm just dumbfounded. What happens next?"

"I was stunned myself, Mr. Hansen. You son has never been in trouble. Procedure dictates that he be suspended five days for fighting, and another five for insubordination to a school official. Since this is his first disciplinary incident, I don't want to hit him with that much time. If you'll sign him up for our district anger management class, I'll drop five of the days."

Donnie thought for a bit, and said, "I'd like talk it over with my wife, if I may."

"Of course, Mr. Hansen. Just let me know, and keep him home starting tomorrow."

Chapter 39

After talking to Mrs. Mackey, Donnie left work early and went home with a heavy heart. Alice was just pulling in after grocery shopping. He started explaining what had happened with Brandon, barely able to believe he was talking about his own son. He felt as if it were surreal, as if he were talking about some kid he had read about in the newspaper.

"What are we going to do, Donnie?" Alice asked anxiously.

"I just don't know. We've always thought he was a good kid, just going through typical adolescence. I never, ever thought he would fight at school or be disrespectful to the principal, of all people. There's got to be something going on with him that we don't know about."

"What could it possibly be?" Alice was painfully perplexed, wringing her hands. "I think we should definitely enroll him in that class Mrs. Mackey mentioned."

"To tell you the truth, hon, I'm at my wits end about what to do. I really thought he was just going through a phase, because at times, he reverts back to being almost human. But, fighting at school, and talking back to an administrator! I just don't know what to think now." Alice decided to take a chance and mention that maybe they should call the school guidance counselor to schedule a meeting with all of Brandon's teachers. Although the idea had been suggested for Jaden, it now seemed to be even more pressing for Brandon. Alice wasn't too sure about what Donnie would think about her taking the initiative to suggest it. But she had decided it didn't really matter if he liked it or not. They had to do something to get their son back on track. Donnie felt so deflated and helpless that he eagerly listened to his wife's advice.

"You're right, Alice. I think we do need to have a meeting with his teachers. Plus, we probably do need to enroll him in that class. It will take away five days of suspension at the very least."

Alice replied, "It might give him some insight about his anger, too."

Brandon walked aimlessly, avoiding going home as long as he could. As he walked, he tried to figure out how he had gotten to the point of being suspended. It was crazy. True, he had hit that kid in the hall, but it didn't seem that big of a deal. Talking back to the principal was pretty bad, though. He didn't exactly know how he had so completely lost it in her office. Come to think of it, he seemed to be on edge a lot lately, even to the point of losing Emily. He hadn't wanted that to happen, but when she had confronted him about his temper, he couldn't seem to control what he said to her. So he had lost her, his first real love. Now he was in big trouble with the school and his dad, and he was sure that his coach would be equally pissed. He was getting nowhere in his thinking. All thoughts seemed to lead to a dead-end. He decided he couldn't walk forever, so he headed home to face the music.

When he got home, looking through the front window, he saw his parents sitting in the living room, waiting for him. He took a deep breath and went in. Expecting his dad to explode, he wasn't prepared for what happened next.

In a quiet voice, his dad said, "Sit down, son, we need to talk. You haven't been yourself for a very long time, months even. We want to know what's going on in your head. Are you in some kind of trouble? Are you having girlfriend problems?"

Alice softly asked, "Are you experimenting with drugs?"

"No, no, Mom! I would never do drugs. I'm an athlete. Athletes have to be in top form. I just seem to lose my temper a lot lately." Adding plaintively, "I really don't know why."

"We obviously know about what happened at school. Do you have any explanation as to why it happened?" Donnie was easing the conversation back on track. Since his dad seemed to be in control of his feelings, Brandon took a breath and tried to let his tight shoulders relax. He knew the worst was yet to come, but maybe it wouldn't be as bad as he had imagined.

"I don't know what made me hit that kid, Dad. He was suddenly just so annoying. It was like I couldn't stop myself."

Trying not to show irritation, Donnie replied, "Could you not stop yourself from acting like an idiot in the principal's office either?" Brandon immediately jumped back on guard, sensing Donnie's mood shift.

"I know I shouldn't have done that. But Dad, Mrs. Mackey is keeping me from playing in the district tournament. That's not fair." He sort of hoped his dad would agree with him.

"Is that your complete explanation of what happened? That's it?"

Oh, brother. This was totally going the wrong way. Brandon felt doomed. All he was trying to do was explain, but every word he said dropped him into an intractable pit, further away from his father's understanding.

"Well, here's a reality check for you, Brandon. Because of your actions, you've been suspended for ten days."

"Ten days! You've got to be kidding. Mrs. Mackey said five days!"

"I'm not kidding one bit. It was five days until you made that scene in her office. You have a chance to reduce that number back to five days, if you attend your school district's anger management class."

Brandon spoke brashly, "What the hell does that mean? Do I have to talk to some counselor or something? You're fulla shit if you think I'm gonna do that!"

Brandon was astonished when his dad smacked him. His face showed raw pain before it clouded over, hiding his true feelings. He clenched both fists, but didn't make a move.

"I don't know what it means, but whatever it is, you're going to do it! This is not negotiable. And don't you ever speak to me like that again!" Donnie shouted.

"Both of you, stop it! That's not the way to handle this," Alice spoke sharply. "Let's try to summon up some reason and deal with this in a mature manner. I think we should continue this conversation after dinner, when everyone has had a chance to get back under control." Brandon stomped to his room. Donnie shakily went to read the paper, and Alice finished dinner preparations.

Dinner crept endlessly by. There was little to no conversation. The younger ones knew something big was up and excused themselves right after finishing.

After they left, Brandon started the conversation by saying, "Okay, I surrender. I'll go to the anger class. I have no choice, anyway." But he was thinking that he would just go through the motions and serve his time. Maybe there would be a chance to finish baseball this season.

"I'm glad you see reason, son," Donnie felt relieved, but still was in turmoil about the whole situation.

Alice spoke up to say, "I'm sure the class will be beneficial, Brandon. You even said you don't know why you respond the way you do in certain circumstances. Give it a chance to help." Brandon knew one thing that would be beneficial, and that was that this conversation would be over soon. After a couple of minutes of silence, Brandon said he was going to his room.

The next morning Donnie woke Brandon up to let him know that while he was suspended, he would be expected to get up at the normal time and attend to a list of chores he would receive each day. Brandon didn't even argue, just got dressed and went to have breakfast. Today's chores included mowing the grass and weeding an impossibly big garden. He rolled his eyes when he saw the list, but maintained his silence. He did a good job, and that night Donnie ached to praise him, but felt it wasn't appropriate under the circumstances. He did tell Brandon that he had registered him in the anger class, and it would be two full days, Friday and Saturday. Since this was only Wednesday, Brandon knew he had another day ahead of hard labor.

The next day Brandon was still at it when Jaden got home from school. This was a night he was going to sneak out to meet Trevor, so he began doing his homework right away. He had a lot of math to do, so he started on that first. After a few minutes he broke his pencil and looked in his backpack for another. No such luck, and Jenny wasn't home yet. Not to worry. He went into Brandon's room and looked in his backpack. When he reached in the little zipper pocket, there was no pencil, but there was a bottle of pills!

"What are you doing going through my backpack, you little weasel?" Brandon suddenly appeared.

"I'm just looking for a pencil. Mine broke. What are these pills? Are you sick?"

"No, stupid. I'm not sick and they aren't really pills. They're supplements that make me stronger and play baseball better. Not that it's any of your business."

"Did Dad get them for you?"

"No, I got them from a friend, if you must know."

"Maybe I could take some to help me get stronger for swimming."

"You stay away from them. You're just a little kid. They could be really dangerous for you. And, don't you dare say anything to Dad about them!"

"I wouldn't, Brandon. I'm on your side."

"Here, take this and beat it," Brandon said gruffly, handing him a pencil.

When Jaden met Trevor that evening, Trevor was somewhat subdued. He definitely was not his usual happy self.

"What's the matter, Trev? Is something wrong? Did your Dad hit you again?"

"No, he only did that the one time. I keep thinking about you and Ricardo. You get to see him every day, and you only see me two or three times a week. You're going to start liking him better."

"I would never like him better, Trevor. I love you. You mean everything to me."

"I just wish we could see each other more often, Jay."

"You know my dad would go ballistic if he found out I was seeing you at all."

"You could sneak out more nights. It'd be easy enough. No one ever even knows you're gone." Jaden started feeling stressed. His stomach was queasy, and he started breathing harder. He didn't know what to say for a few beats. Trevor just didn't know how nervous he got every night he sneaked out, and what relief he felt when he was safely back in his bed.

"Come on, Jaden," Trevor encouraged. "You could do it. You'll never get caught, and we can spend lots more time together."

"I don't know, Trevor," he started apprehensively, but Trevor butted in and said, "If you really care about me, you'll do it." Jaden finally agreed, but with fear in his heart. Trevor was so hard to say no to.

Jaden sneaked out three nights in a row! He was so scared that he got sick to his stomach the first night and could barely enjoy being with Trevor. Trevor tried to calm him down by rubbing his shoulders and massaging his back. The first night met with little success, but by the third night, Jaden was calming down and really enjoying the rubbing, which led to more intimacy. He decided being afraid was well worth it.

Chapter 40

Jaden hadn't been to see Miss Bonnie for a few weeks. He had been so busy and had only been focused on Trevor. After sneaking out those three nights in a row, he decided it might be a good time to talk to her again. Her garage door was open, and he saw her standing on a ladder reaching up on a shelf for a suitcase.

"Hey, Miss Bonnie, whatcha doing?"

As she climbed down the ladder she said, "I'm just puttering around trying to get things in order. How have you been?"

Without answering her question, Jaden asked, "What are you doing with that suitcase? Are you going somewhere?"

"I need to go to Kentucky to see my sister. Her daughter and her grandson were in a serious car accident."

Jaden butted in, "How did it happen?"

Miss Bonnie replied, "There were on a curvy road, and someone swerved across the center line and hit them head-on. My niece is still in the hospital, and my sister needs me to help take care of her grandson. He's banged up pretty bad."

"That's terrible!" Jaden cried. "How old is he?"

"He's fifteen and was driving with a learner's permit. I'm not sure how soon his mom will be out of the hospital. She broke her arm, her collarbone, and hit her head on the windshield. She may have a head injury."

Jaden went to Miss Bonnie and gave her a big hug.

"When will you be back?" he asked with concern in his voice.

"I'm not sure, Jaden. It will depend on how quickly my niece recovers and is able to take care of herself and her son again."

Putting aside the reason he had gone to see Miss Bonnie, Jaden wished her well and returned home.

The anger management class was just about what Brandon had thought it would be. One or two "suits" from the school district stood up and talked for hours about behavior that was "appropriate." The whole session was a yawner, except when one guy, probably about nineteen or twenty, talked about how he had majorly screwed up in school and messed up his whole future. He wouldn't elaborate on what he did, but he admitted it was a felony and that he would be on probation for ten years.

True, he was speaking because he had to for community service, but he was sincere when he said, "Most kids don't really recognize the life-changing consequences that happen when they're just going along with what everyone else is doing, or when they get mad and take things into their own hands. For the next ten years I have a curfew. I have to be in my parents' house from eleven p.m. until six a.m. every single night. I have to have a job to pay for the probation officer that I'm forced to see every month, and I can't even leave the county without asking my PO for permission. You think you have it bad because your parents tell you what to do? Think again!" Brandon had hoped he would go into it more, but he had concluded with that statement.

When Brandon's suspension and class were over, he went back to school and tried to maintain a low profile. The baseball team had lost out in the district tournament, so the season was over. He hadn't talked to the coach yet, but figured what did it matter? The season was over and he couldn't play anyway. He failed to realize that a talk with his coach now would go a long way toward getting him back in good graces for the next year. He didn't have time to think about all that. Even though it seemed he was controlling his anger, he was expending all his energy keeping it inside, and he was about to blow.

Chapter 41

The last month of school, the students in Mrs. Cohen's class had another upset. She started being frequently absent again, and after two weeks felt she needed to share the situation with her students. They had been through a lot together.

"Class, the cancer has hit again, but this time in a different spot. No, don't look so stricken, and don't worry. It'll be fine, just like it was before. I'll need to have treatments again, and they'll start next week. I want to tell you good-bye, and not leave you hanging like last time. I'm going to miss the last two weeks of school, so I'm encouraging you all to do your best on your final exams. I know you'll be in high school next year, but you can stop by to see me any time." The students tried their best to look upbeat for Mrs. Cohen's sake, but most did a poor job.

When Jaden and Trevor hooked up that night, Jaden was down in the dumps. Trevor tried to reassure him by saying that Mrs. Cohen beat it before, and she would do it again. It didn't help much. There was a feeling of doom hanging over Jaden, and he finally told Trevor that he might as well take him home.

The feeling persisted over the next few days. By Friday, in the midst of his gloom, Jaden realized Devon hadn't had much to say lately. He guessed Devon was tired of hanging around someone depressed all the time, so after school, he decided he would try to shake it off a little, and see if he could engage Devon in a conversation. Strangely, Devon didn't seem to want to talk to him. He wouldn't make eye contact and said he'd catch him later.

"Wait! Where do you have to go?" Jaden said anxiously. He sensed something wasn't right.

"All right, bro," Devon said, seeming cool and detached. "Let's get it out. Some of the guys kept telling me you were gay, but I kept telling them they were nuts. Then I see you and this dude all cuddly in a car in the park one night, so I guess it must be true." He asked him straight out, "Are you gay?" Jaden was overwhelmed with emotion. As he fought and failed to keep back the tears, his face distorted, and he couldn't get a breath. He certainly couldn't speak. Devon looked at him and said, "Ok, I get it, but I can't deal with it. See you around."

Jaden couldn't see for the tears, he couldn't breathe, and he couldn't think. Devon had been his best friend, his anchor, his confidant for four years. In some ways, he felt even closer to Devon than he did to Trevor. They had swam and played and planned and dreamed of high school. They had lived so much life together. He was crushed and felt he couldn't manage without Devon.

When he got home, Alice said with concern in his voice, "Honey, what's wrong? Are you sick? You're so pale." Feeling his forehead, she said, "You're hot, and I bet you have a fever." He went straight to his room and lay down, while Alice got the thermometer. She couldn't believe it when his temperature was normal, but was convinced that he was sick, nevertheless. She sat there a while, rubbing his chest, until he turned away from her. He just lay there and tried not to think. He couldn't bear it. His mom brought soup in at dinnertime, but he had no appetite.

"You need to eat something, honey. You have to keep up your strength. I'll leave the soup here on your night stand." Jenny stuck her head in hurriedly, because she was getting ready to spend the night with Sarah.

"What's wrong, Jay? Are you really sick, or did something happen with Trevor?" He just shook his head sorrowfully. There was nothing to say. "I'll be back tomorrow night, and we'll talk it out, okay? Whatever it is, it'll be all right." She gave him a hug and left.

Chapter 42

At the high school that same Friday, as he was leaving to go home, Brandon saw a familiar figure striding toward him. His body tensed a little, but he was ready for anything. The pent-up anger of the past few weeks was volcanic. The figure was James, the kid who had gotten him in trouble. What the hell does he want? This time, though, James was prepared.

Before anything could start, James said, "School's almost out, and payback is hell. Unless you're a chicken-shit, you'll meet me tomorrow behind the deserted gas station on Poplar Street. Then we'll have a fair fight, not a sucker-punch like you did before."

"I'll show you who's a chicken-shit. You want to go there now? Bring it on."

"We're not doing this when you say, dickhead. We're doing it when I say. Just be there tomorrow at noon."

"I wouldn't miss it."

Brandon was still fired up when he got home, but took a jog before dinner and had settled down enough that it didn't show. That was one thing he had learned at that stupid class. When you're feeling really wired, do some exercise, and it will take the edge off. After dinner he asked Donnie if he could take the car to the mall and hang out with some friends.

Anxious to be generous with his elder son for a change, he said, "Sure, just don't be out past eleven." Brandon muttered a thanks as he picked up the keys and went out the door.

On his bed, Jaden turned left, then right, trying to concentrate on his poster of the Grateful Dead, but to no avail. Trevor had given him the poster for his birthday a few months ago, and it was his favorite possession. Images of dancing bears turned into Devon dancing in his mind. He had the light on then, he turned it off. As much as he tried to block out the mental pictures, every way he turned he would see a picture of Devon and him. Devon teaching him stunts, Devon racing him in the pool, Devon sticking up for him with his brother; these poignant scenes in his head were inescapable. Jaden had finally dozed off for a troubled interlude, but soon his eyes snapped wide open as he realized he was supposed to meet Trevor. He looked at the clock and saw it was only eight forty-five, although it seemed like the middle of the night. He didn't even feel like meeting Trevor tonight. It wouldn't be any fun with the way he felt. He didn't feel like doing anything at all. He debated with himself for a few minutes and decided he couldn't just stand Trevor up. At least he had to go out there to tell him he didn't feel like doing anything.

At nine, he halfheartedly climbed out the window and dragged his unwilling feet around the corner to the Mustang. Trevor knew right away something was wrong.

"What is it, Jay? You look like somebody died."

"I don't feel like talking. I just came out to tell you I'm not going out with you tonight." As he turned zombie-like back toward the house, Trevor's anxiety began to build.

"Wait, please wait! You can't just leave me like this. You've got to tell me what's wrong!"

"I told you I didn't want to talk. I don't even care anymore. I don't care about anything anymore." Trevor couldn't believe what he was hearing. I'll bet this has something to do with that Ricardo. How could Jaden do this? Starting to freak, Trevor tried again to get Jaden to respond.

"I love you, Jaden. Whatever it is, we can work it out together." Jaden didn't even pause as he continued his trudge back to the house. Nearing hysteria, Trevor tried another tack. "If you leave me like this, we're through!" Jaden barely heard what he said. As he saw that Jaden wasn't going to turn around, Trevor was devastated and started up the Mustang, flooring it. Suddenly, Trevor's world was as upside-down as Jaden's, and he was without a clue as to why.

With his eyes clouded with pain, the likes of which he had never experienced, Jaden took a minute to realize his window didn't look right. It was closed! Tentatively reaching out to open it, Jaden stumbled backward when the window was abruptly opened by the imposing presence of his father.

"Where the hell have you been? How long have you been gone? I heard the commotion of a car roaring off. Who was that?" Donnie added sarcastically, "I just stepped in to see how you were feeling. Looks like you've had a dramatic recovery."

"I haven't been anywhere, Dad. I just went out to talk to my friend for a minute." His voice was so low that Donnie barely heard him.

"And who might this friend be?" There didn't seem to be any letup or mercy from his dad. Jaden didn't want to tell him. "I said, who is this friend?" Donnie spoke louder than before. He was fed up with being patient. Brandon had drained him with his crazy behavior. He wanted answers, and he wanted them *now*. Jaden felt cold and dead. It was as if he were detached from the situation and was watching and listening to his father from outside of himself. He couldn't speak.

Donnie spoke again, this time quieter, but very forcefully.

"If it was that fairy boy from the play that you went to talk to, it had better be the last time you ever do that. I've told you not to be friends with him, and if you disobey me, you will never leave this house again, at least not until you're eighteen. I will not have you purposely disregard what I feel is best for you. Not as long as you live in this house!" Donnie stormed from the room, seething. He had been totally frustrated when Brandon had pulled *his* stunt, and now there was no way he was going to let his other son get away with things that could destroy his life.

Jaden hadn't said anything beyond his initial statement. He crawled back in the now open window. He was stunned. His world had fallen apart in less than a week. Mrs. Cohen, the most understanding teacher in the whole school, was sick again, and he was disconsolate, afraid that she might not recover. Plus, he had lost his very best friend and his boyfriend in the same day. His father would never understand him, and he wouldn't be allowed to have the chance to make things right with Trevor. How much could he take? He lay back down on his bed and just stared at the ceiling. His eyes were dry and painful, unrelieved by his usual free-flowing tears. What's the use? Things will never be right again. What was the point of living? There's no sense in trying. He continued staring at the ceiling until sometime very late in the night, when the blessed solace of sleep overcame him.

Chapter 43

Brandon was up early Saturday morning, calling Dan to come get him, under the auspices of going to the public library to do research together. He wanted to be away from the house well before his appointed rendezvous with James. He wanted no one to foil his plan. They cruised over to Sonic and had a breakfast sandwich and a shake. He had filled Dan in on the particulars, and Dan had wanted to be at the fight in case Brandon needed another set of fists, but Brandon had said no. He felt like he'd lose face with James if he didn't come alone.

"Are you nervous at all?" Dan had wondered aloud, still wishing Brandon would let him stand by.

"Hell, no!" bragged Brandon. "I'm ready to scrap. I have something inside me that needs letting loose! Just drop me off, and I'll text you when I get through with the little asshole."

At the Hansen house, Jaden was late getting up. After tossing and turning half the night, he had slept a scant few hours and dragged out of bed around nine. Lying there in the relentless dark of his emotions had practically immobilized him. No one seemed to be home, and he almost lay back down. Almost. Instead, something seemed to direct his steps to his brother's room, where, with no problem at all, he found Brandon's backpack with its illicit solution to all his problems.

Brandon and Dan had wasted all the time they could before the noon hour and headed to the deserted station a few minutes early. They saw nobody close by, so Brandon hopped out, reminding Dan to check for a text in a little while. Dan was out of sight by the time Brandon had walked around to the back of the station. He certainly wasn't expecting what he saw when he got there.

"Oh, shit! How could I have been so stupid?"

As if in a fog, Jaden saw the pills and stuffed them in his pocket. Not even wanting his phone, stopping by the fridge, he grabbed a soda and stepped out into the overcast day. With no destination in mind, he started walking. A while later, he looked up and realized he was near the park where he and Trevor had kissed passionately for the first time.

"Now," an inner voice said. He wasn't sure if he had thought the word or said it aloud. It didn't matter. He fumbled in his pocket for the pills and started downing them with his soda. When all the pills were gone, he thought, at first, it had been a waste of time. But as he continued his trek toward the park, his stomach began to feel funny, and he suddenly felt light-headed.

Is this it? Is this how it will end? Has there been no meaning to my life? Why does it have to be like this? As his vision began to blur and his thoughts began to jumble, Jaden collapsed to the ground.

What Brandon saw behind the station was James, flanked by four burly guys who looked like they meant business.

"Wait a minute," Brandon protested. "You said this would be a fair fight."

"Sucker! Since when did *you* fight fair?" Somewhat nonplussed, but still determined, Brandon's adrenalin soared. He powered forward into James and drove his right fist into his face. This was his only shot. Two of the guys grabbed his arms and restrained him while the others began swinging. They hit him in the face and the mid-section over and over, until the pain became intolerable and his legs gave out. He tried to curl up in a ball before they began kicking him, kicking him, in the arms, the legs, in any unprotected part of his body.

Finally, James said, "Enough." Not sure if Brandon was even still conscious, James leaned over to say, "Next time you better know who you're messing with, smartass."

Dan was getting worried. He had dropped Brandon off over thirty minutes before, and he hadn't heard a peep. I don't care if he did say to stay out of sight until he texted, Dan thought, I'm going to check on him. This doesn't seem right.

He drove to the station and saw no one. With trepidation, he drove around back and found his friend lying in his own blood, his face beaten to a pulp. He also noticed his right arm seemed to be at a funny angle.

"Oh, my God! What happened?" He looked nervously in all directions to see if anyone was still lurking. Satisfied that they were alone, he tried to pull Brandon to a sitting position. He was conscious, but barely. His right eye was swollen shut, and he could barely discern Dan out of his left.

He managed to mumble, "Five guys."

"You need to go to the hospital!" Dan was panicky, but did have enough presence of mind to know his friend needed medical attention. The blood had been enough, but looking again at the funny angle of Brandon's arm made him want to hurl.

Dan called 911 on Brandon's cell phone without giving his name and took off as soon as he heard a siren in the distance. He didn't have any answers, and he didn't want to be identified or questioned, that was for sure.

When the ambulance arrived, Brandon was very groggy and slightly incoherent. He was able to give his name, but that was about it. It may have sifted through his subconscious that he didn't want his parents notified, but if so, he wasn't fully aware of it. When he got to the emergency room he couldn't give his parents' telephone number at first, he was so confused, and when he did, it was a couple of numbers off. The triage nurses went to work and stabilized his condition. He was given a CT scan, sewn up, and his arm was temporarily casted until his parents could be contacted and give consent for surgery.

Chapter 44

Lying there in the low light, Brandon was very groggy. He was dozing off and on, finally out of pain. He wasn't sure what roused him, but when he opened his eyes he was surprised to see his parents there. In spite of all his previous bravado, he felt like a small child who had been lost and then found.

"Dad, Mom," he whispered hoarsely, tears in his eyes. "How long have you been here? I can't seem to keep track of time."

"Brandon? Brandon, honey? Oh my God, is that you?" Alice couldn't make sense of what she was seeing. She and Donnie hurried to his bedside. "Baby, what on earth happened to you?"

"Were you and Jaden together? What happened?" Donnie felt completely confused.

"Me and Jaden?" Brandon couldn't think straight. Jaden? "What do you mean, Dad?"

"You're both in the hospital. You look horribly beat up, and we've been told he overdosed. Was it a drug deal gone bad?" Donnie was desperately grasping for an explanation.

"Drugs? What? I don't know anything about Jaden, Dad."

Conversation was interrupted when Alice's cell phone rang. She handed the phone to Donnie who spoke briefly before turning back to Brandon.

"We've got to leave your room and find Jaden. Are you okay for a little while, son?" When Brandon nodded, Donnie said, " Come on, Alice, let's go find him."

Hurrying once again to the ER information desk, the Hansens asked specifically where their son, Jaden, was.

"Did I send you to the wrong room?" she asked concerned. Donnie's frustration was building astronomically, and he was in no mood for niceties.

"Just tell us where the damn ICU is!"

Just around the corner from Brandon's room, they found a large, softly lit area with a central nursing station surrounded by small glass-walled rooms. There was a patient in each one. The quiet beeping of monitors gave a small, but steady sense of security. A stern-looking nurse questioned whom they were there to see. When she heard "Jaden Hansen", she pursed her lips, wondering what took them so long.

All she said was, "Only one of you can go in at a time. She gestured toward one of the cubicles. He's been stirring, but has not quite come to full consciousness. His vitals are steadily improving."

"I'm going in first," Alice said softly, but emphatically. "That's my baby."

With no protest from Donnie, she stepped in quietly and stood by Jaden's bed. She caressed his hand and kissed his cheek.

With tears sliding down her face, she whispered, "My baby, my baby. What happened? What did we do wrong? You don't deserve anything like this. If you'll just get well, I promise things will change. I know I haven't done enough for you. This is all my fault." Then she closed her eyes, praying. Jaden's eyes flickered, and he took a gasp of air.

"Not your fault, Mom," he spoke weakly. Then his eyes shut, and he drifted back to nothingness.

While Alice was in the room, Donnie had gone back to the desk to see if he could learn any details that would help him make better sense of the situation. All he was able to find out, though, was that apparently some passerby in a car had seen Jaden lying in a heap and stopped to help. After getting no response, he had called 911.

When Alice saw Donnie return, she left the room so that he could have a minute with their son.

All too soon the nurse said, "That's enough excitement for him for now. You folks can come back for a few minutes later this evening or have a little longer with him in the morning, if he's doing better. We'll call you if there's any change."

After speaking to the charge nurse about Brandon, they went back to his room and sat with him for a while, but he slept steadily. Finally, they woke him to say they would be back in the morning to take him home. Donnie and Alice spoke little on the ride home. The shock of Jaden had rendered them unable to fully consider what might have happened to Brandon, or even to think clearly. When they walked into the house, Alice called Jenny, telling her to come straight home. Something in her mother's voice sounded urgent. Rushing home with fear in her heart, Jenny found her parents sitting in the living room, with dazed looks and tears in their eyes.

"Mom! Dad! What's happened? Did somebody die? Where's Jaden?" Pausing, and then, almost tearfully, "Where's Brandon?" And again, with increasing panic in her voice, "Where's Jaden?" Alice spoke first.

"Your brothers are both in the hospital."

"What? Mom, why? What happened? Are they going to be okay? Were they in an accident?" Jenny had been scared before, but now a chill ran down her back. "Is it...is it serious? Are they going to make it?" She couldn't say the word, *dead*.

Donnie said, "Don't worry, princess. They will both be fine eventually. We don't fully understand what happened to either one of them. Brandon looks like he was in a bad fight, but we don't know any details yet."

"And Jaden?" she asked, her voice getting louder.

"Honey, the hospital told us he tried to commit suicide."

"Suicide?" she screamed. "What are you talking about? He couldn't have. I know he was upset, but he couldn't have." She sank to the floor sobbing. Sitting down beside her daughter, Alice circled her in her arms, rocking her back and forth, murmuring soothing words. They sat like that, with Donnie watching, for a long time.

When Jenny finally cried herself out, Donnie told her, "There's nothing more we can do or find out now. We'll sort it all out in the morning. Meanwhile, we need to eat. It will make us feel better. How about we order in a pizza?"

After picking at the pizza, all the Hansens decided to go to bed and try to rest. Tomorrow would be a full day. Before turning out her light, Jenny texted Devon what was going on. Devon only texted back "OMG!" She didn't hear any more from him.

Chapter 45

The next day dawned bright, the antithesis of the day before; however, the Hansens' gloom belied the cheery morning. As they loaded into the car, each was wondering how they would find the brothers, and what the day would bring.

As he parked, Donnie said, "We'll see how Jaden is first, and then go check Brandon out of here, if they'll let us." Alice and Jenny were both grateful that Donnie had made the decision to see Jaden first. Jenny had tossed and turned all night worrying about her twin. She felt she had failed him. He needed her, and she had blithely traipsed over to Sarah's house, ignoring, she realized now, Jaden's devastated appearance. How could she ever forgive herself? Please let him be all right!

They were surprised to find Devon sitting on the floor outside the ICU. He looked disheveled and exhausted.

"How did you know Jaden was here?" Donnie asked him.

"Jenny texted me last night, and I asked my mom to bring me here. I've been here all night, but they wouldn't let me in to see him. I'm not family." He couldn't bring himself to confess to the Hansens that he felt his actions had driven Jaden to this unthinkable act.

"You *will* see him today," Donnie said firmly.

Jaden had been drifting in and out of consciousness most of the night. He didn't know where he was or why he wasn't in his own bed. When Alice walked in his eyes were open, but looked swollen and heavy.

"Oh, Jaden, my baby. You're finally awake. How are you feeling?"

"Not so good, Mom. Why am I here?"

"Don't you remember, honey?" Jaden was confused and shook his head. "Oh, sweetie, do you remember an ambulance bringing you here?" There was a tiny stirring of a memory, but it had an unpleasant undertone so Jaden pushed it back, not wanting to think. "Don't worry about it now, hon. We'll talk about it later. Your dad and sister want to see you. Oh, and Devon is here wanting to see you, too." Hearing Devon's name opened the memory floodgate that now he could no longer push back. Achingly, he wished he could just shut his eyes and go back where he had been moments before, blissfully unaware. Seeing the pain appear on Jaden's face, Alice knew he was remembering.

Outside the window Donnie caught Alice's attention and motioned for her to come out. He had cajoled his way past the nurse on duty by promising not to go into the room.

Not wanting to leave the room, Alice just stuck her head out. Donnie said, "Stay with Jaden. I'm going to see what needs to be done to get Brandon released." With that, he strode off in the direction of the nurses' station around the corner.

"I want to check my son out of here," he offered to the nurse's inquiring look.

"Name, please?"

"Brandon Hansen, right down there," he indicated with a small movement of his head.

"The doctor is with him now. Go on in." As he walked in, the doctor was unwrapping the bandage on Brandon's head.

"I'm Don Hansen, Brandon's father," he said by way of introduction.

"Ah, yes, Mr. Hansen. I'm glad you're here. Brandon needs a procedure to fix that arm of his. We couldn't continue without your signature. Seems your son took quite a beating."

"How did this happen, Brandon?" Donnie spoke without emotion, as he seemed beyond shock.

"Dad, I was attacked by five guys. I didn't have much chance to fight back."

Barely comprehending Donnie replied, "Okay, we'll talk about it when the doctor finishes up, son."

"I'm about through here, Mr. Hansen. What do you want to do about his arm? We can get him on the surgical schedule here, or if you have an orthopedist, you can take him to your own."

Donnie considered a moment, then, said, "We don't have one, but I want the best for my son. Do you recommend the doctor on staff?"

"Absolutely! Dr. Edwards came to us a few months ago, highly recommended. We're lucky to have her. We'll set him up as quickly as possible on the schedule. In the meantime, you can check him out by going to the Admissions Office. Keep that arm secure and still, Brandon. Stay here in your room until you've been officially released. You'll have to be taken downstairs in a wheelchair, hospital policy.

As he headed toward Admissions, Donnie received a text from Alice saying that he should come back to the ICU immediately, because the doctor there wanted to talk to them both. Donnie quickly returned to Brandon's room with a wheelchair he had seen at the end of the hall. Brandon's discharge would have to wait. Pushing Brandon down the hall, he saw Dr. Hernandez at Jaden's door. He motioned Donnie into the room and spoke to both parents near Jaden's bed.

He said, "Your son is out of the woods now, but you need to know that yesterday his system was full of anabolic steroids. He was lucky to be found when he was."

"Steroids? Jaden, where did you get steroids?" Donnie was perplexed.

"I don't know what steroids are, Dad. I just took some pills I found in Brandon's backpack." He looked down and continued, "I can't do anything right, and I'm not what you want in a son. I'm not like Brandon. Besides all that, the best teacher ever is dying, and I've lost my best friend." And the boyfriend I love, he thought to himself. Tears that had begun slowly while he talked turned into a steady stream. "I thought I might as well die and get it over with." He turned over and buried his face in his pillow.

Alice tried to comfort him, and Donnie abruptly turned and said, "I'm going to get Brandon."

A moment later Brandon was pushed into the room. In the hall, Jenny, who had been very gently hugging Brandon, was left wondering what was going on. First, Brandon's face was a mess and his arm looked painful. Now, they were scooting Brandon into Jaden's room. She hadn't been able to question Brandon or even see Jaden yet.

"Where did you get steroids, Brandon?" Some of Donnie's fire had returned, and he spoke grimly.

"I don't have any steroids!" Brandon denied.

"Don't even try that with me, Brandon." Donnie said harshly. "Your brother took them out of your backpack and nearly killed himself with them. What would you have done if he had died?" Horror washed over Brandon's face. He looked at his brother face down on the pillow. His brother had almost died? All, because of him? The seriousness of the situation made him feel slightly nauseated.

Then, "Are you kidding me? I've been taking steroids?"

"Where did you get them, Brandon?"

"A kid on the baseball team, Derek, told me they were supplements that make you strong and build your muscles. He told me they wouldn't hurt anything."

Dr. Hernandez broke in saying, "Anabolic steroids should never be taken unless under doctor's orders. As you can see, they can cause extreme damage, but that's not the half of it. There are lots of side effects including acne, heart problems, deceleration of the natural steroids your body makes, and rage. Steroids are just artificial testosterone. Nothing to mess with."

Brandon sat completely dumbfounded, staring down into his lap.

"What have I done? I didn't know anything bad would happen. I'm so sorry, Jaden. I'm so sorry, I'm so sorry." Brandon sat in despair, not looking up.

After listening to the doctor, her husband, and her son, Alice had keyed in on a word the doctor had used and had a question.

"Doctor, you mentioned rage. Brandon has been getting in trouble at school, fighting, and has been impossible at home. He was never that way before. Are you telling us that steroids could have caused that total change in behavior?"

"No doubt about it, Mrs. Hansen. If he has been taking them for some time now, and if his behavior is very different from before, then there's a good chance it's what is commonly called 'roid rage.' Finally becoming aware of it is the best thing that could have happened. It's the first step to resolution of the problem. I'll let you all talk together and will be back to check on Jaden later. I want to keep him at least another night for observation."

Still head down, realization of the consequences of his actions was hitting Brandon hard. A lot of things made sense now. He never really knew why he kept picking at people, egging them on, starting fights. He knew he didn't like Eric, but that was a different story. He had never picked a fight with a complete stranger. And look where it had gotten him, suspended from school, kicked out of baseball, beat up, and in the hospital. But the worse thing was he had almost killed his kid brother! Coming out of his reverie, he dragged himself up and out of the wheelchair, limping to Jaden's bedside.

"Jaden, buddy, please, please forgive me. I haven't been a good brother to you ever, but this is as low as a person can go. I promise I will never take any pills again, and I won't let anything happen to you, either. Why did you take them out of my backpack? I'm not mad about it, I'm just sick that they were there."

Donnie interrupted to say, "We need to get Jenny in here. The family is in crisis, and we all need to be together." He went out and returned with Jenny and Devon. Without a pause, Devon walked over to the opposite side of Jaden's bed.

He grasped Jaden's hand starting the beginning of their special hand-shake, and with tears in his eyes, and a raspy voice, said, "Jaden, you're my bro, my best friend. I'm so sorry I hurt you, saying what I did. I didn't mean it. I want us to be friends, like we were before. I don't care what all the other kids say."

Jaden slowly turned over to face Devon. He searched his face and hoped he was telling the truth. But when Devon bent over and hugged Jaden for a long minute, he knew it was the truth. He felt as if some of his burden had been lifted, and he tried a smile. With Brandon on one side of his bed, and Devon on the other, Jaden began to feel he really could face who he was and learn to deal with it. Feeling left out, Jenny eased to the head of Jaden's bed and laid her head on his pillow, her arm around her twin's shoulders. Donnie cleared his throat and began to talk.

Stumbling over his words, he said, "Jaden, I know that some of this is my fault." Pausing, then continuing, "No, that's not right. A lot of it is my fault. I haven't been fair to you, son. You don't do everything wrong at all, and I love you very much. I know I've been rough on you about your choices." Everyone could tell how painful this speech was for him. He stopped all together and looked long at Alice. "Your mother thinks I need counseling, and I'm going to give it a try. Maybe if I had done it before, none of this would have happened." He reached over and gave his younger son a kiss on the forehead.

Alice knew how hard it had been for her husband to get all that out, and her eyes shone with relief. She went to Donnie's side and put her arm through his. All the teens had been spellbound by Donnie's brief speech and sat thoughtfully, digesting it.

The charge nurse broke the quiet by stating, "Jaden is still in ICU, so it's time for all of you to leave and let him rest." There was a scurry of activity as everyone was hugging Jaden and telling him they would see him soon.

Jenny was the last to leave, and just before she moved away from the bed, she placed something under Jaden's pillow. Sleepily, he reached up and felt his phone. He was smiling as he drifted off, knowing he would text Trevor when he woke up. There might be a future for him, after all.

Epilogue

Miss Bonnie

*I*t took a little over three weeks, but my niece was finally strong enough to leave rehab and come back home to her family. My sister hadn't been well enough herself to shoulder the entire responsibility of taking care of her grandson, so I was glad I had gone to help. But I was so relieved when I got back home to my normal quiet life. I had become caught up in my sister's stress, and I was ready to relax.

Driving down my little street, I could see the flowers of summer starting to bloom. The robins were busy, and the mourning doves were calling. Everything was so peaceful and perfect as I drove into my driveway. As I was dragging my suitcase through the kitchen, I could see the light blinking on the answering machine. Absent-mindedly listening to the messages while making coffee, when I heard the fifth one, I was so startled that I inhaled sharply and dropped my cup, shattering it on the floor.

It was Devon saying Jaden was in the hospital because he had tried to commit suicide. Apparently, Devon had been to see him, and he was past the critical point, thank goodness! Ignoring the broken cup, I shakily sat down on a kitchen chair. My emotions were in turmoil. Should I have seen this coming? Was there something I could have done if I hadn't gone to my sister's house? Not being there for my young friend when he needed me made me feel I had failed him. No doubt his parents had unwittingly played a role in this tragedy, and I knew I had to speak to Donnie and Alice right away.

All children need loving support from their family and friends, but gay kids often isolate themselves for fear of ridicule and rejection, and Jaden had clearly felt both of these things from his father, his brother, and his classmates. I was raised in an era where to be outwardly gay was totally unacceptable, and because of my continuing to stay in the closet, I had missed a chance to be open with Jaden's parents in a way that might have been beneficial to him.

I've never been ashamed of who I am, but keeping quiet is no longer an option for me. It's hard to believe that some kids are still being made to believe that they are less worthy than other kids just because they are gay. Kids like Jaden need open support in the community and advocacy from their parents. Making changes has always *been hard for me, but if I am able to set a course of action that would result in even one less kid feeling unloved or ostracized, it would be worth any angst I might have about finally coming out.*

    I picked up the phone.